FOR BLOOD AND LOYALTY

A Novel By

Chris Kasparoza

KASPAROZA BOOKS

New York

Also by Chris Kasparoza

The Chapter

www.TheChapter.tv

FOR BLOOD AND LOYALTY

Copyright © 2013 by Chris Kasparoza. All Rights Reserved.

This book is a work of fiction. Names, characters, places, and incidents either are the product of the author's imagination or are used fictitiously. Any resemblance to actual persons, living or dead, events, or locales is entirely coincidental.

ISBN: 978-1492350675

www.ForBloodAndLoyalty.com

Published by Kasparoza Books
www.Kasparoza.com

For My Mother

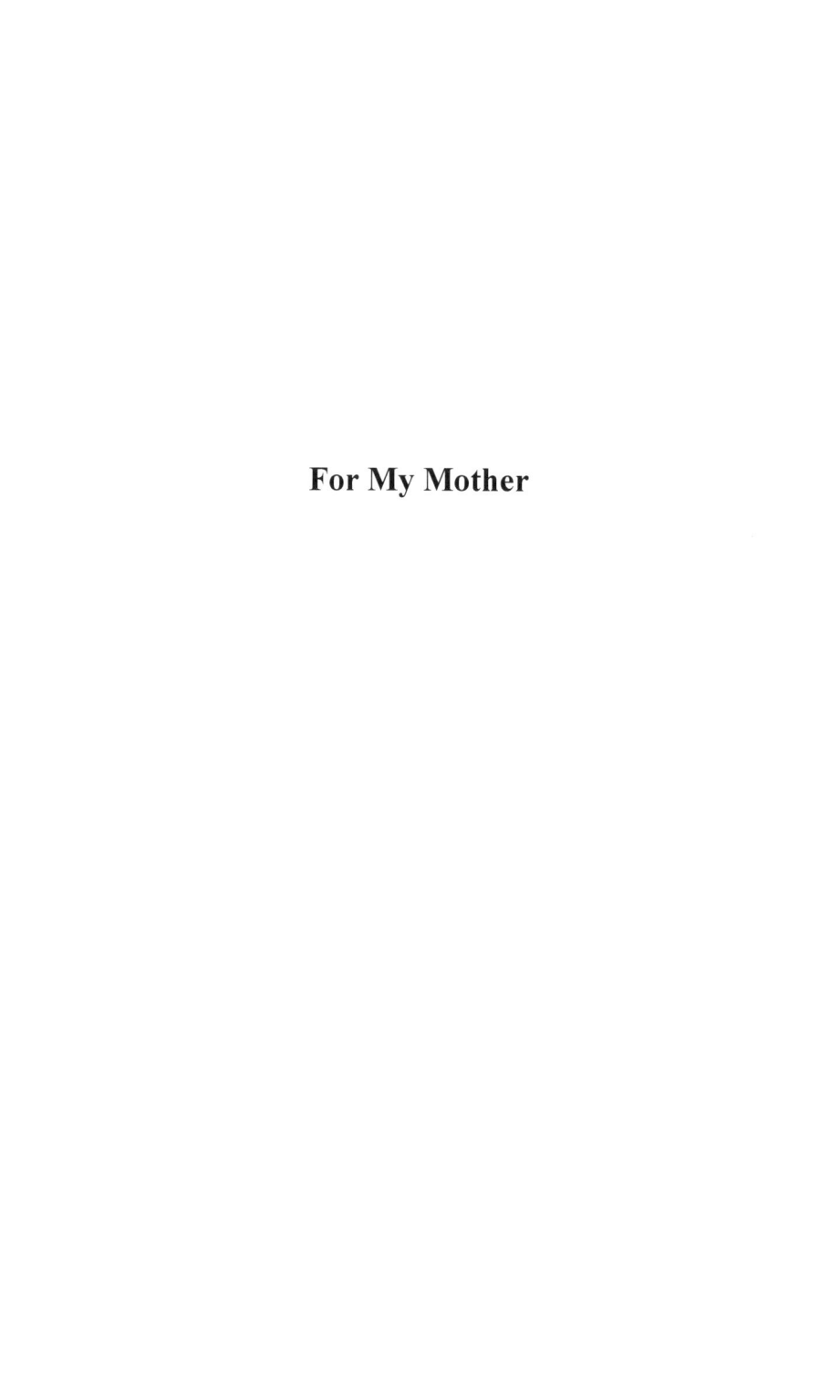

**and
For My Dogs**

FOR BLOOD
AND LOYALTY

ONE

TUESDAY, AUGUST 10th, 1999

"It's the little things that count. That's what Jackie always told me. The little things tell who a guy is. Where he comes from. Who raised him."

"Jackie also said the guy who doesn't wear a seat belt doesn't wear a condom. You should put one on," Bobby said.

But Victor could have cared less.

And there they were: two best friends.

But more importantly: two souls.

One of them lost, and the other just looking for a way out.

Why? Because he knew they were doomed.

However, regardless, they had someplace to go. And as they pulled up to the red light, Victor Saravano, angry, looked out. At the corner. At the kids standing on it. Three teenaged wannabes posing like thugs. And who knows? Maybe they were. But one of them was on a cell phone and all Victor could think was:

"My grandkids are gonna be the fuckin' Jetsons."

At the wheel though, Bobby Drakis had other responsibilities than just riding shotgun. So he looked at Victor: *What?*

"I used to walk three blocks to the pay-phone."

Bobby sighed. *Me too*, he thought. *Me too*.

And with that, as the light turned green, Bobby drove.

Other than the fact that they were dressed in all black, that they had just come from a funeral, it was a smooth ride. A nice black 1996 Nissan Pathfinder with nice black leather seats? Not bad for someone who just got out of the joint. But it was all over Bobby's face. He just wanted to get the fuck out of dodge.

He wasn't the type of guy to leave a friend behind, though. But at the same time, he wasn't prepared to die. Or go back Up North again, unlike Victor. So he drove carefully. He checked his mirrors all afternoon as they cruised through the neighborhoods of Northern Queens.

Bayside, Whitestone, parts of Flushing. Even Douglaston and Little Neck. Not every one of them was their stomping grounds but they were all a part of the hustle. And as they went down Francis Lewis Boulevard, past I.S. 25, their old junior high school, memories came back. They were both 26 but it wasn't too long before that everything was still in front of them.

Like another red light.

Everything moves slower when the world isn't turning in your direction. So Bobby checked the mirror again. The rearview. And he looked at his face. At the razor-made scar through the outside of his right eyebrow. It was a reminder of a past life. It was from a prison fight.

Shit happens.

And then he looked to his right. At Victor's face. The left side of it was all scratched and cut up. He was in a car a few days before when gun-shots shattered the window and he got hit with glass shards.

Shit definitely happens.

Overall though, they were good looking guys. They both had charisma with a dark side. And they shared some of the same qualities, too. Honor and Loyalty chief among them. The kind of Honor and Loyalty that you can only begin to understand when you've been testified against by someone who you thought was your fam.

But as they drove a few miles further up the boulevard, they saw their destination: an old Gulf gas station. The kind with no security cameras, just a couple of old pumps and a good place to launder money and run numbers. And as they pulled in, Victor looked out with curiosity. Maybe even a little envy, although he'd never admit it. If you had asked him that day he would have just told you that a few animals escaped from the zoo. So he lowered the tinted window halfway, just enough to get a clearer view: "Who the hell is raising these kids today?" he asked.

"Cam'ron and Wu-Tang," Bobby replied.

In front of the gas station store's door, not far from the dark green 4-door Honda Accord with black tinted windows idling at one of the pumps nearby, were two early 20s African American thugs in matching light blue jeans and black t-shirts and baseball hats. One of whom was tall enough to play basketball and broad enough to play football. While the other one was short and skinny enough to slip out of handcuffs.

But to Victor they were just moolies.

And to the black guys in front of the store, Bobby's car didn't need to be there. You could see it in the bigger one's eyes.

In Victor's eyes though, you just saw agitation. This was *his* turf. And they were on it.

However, while Bobby wasn't in the best mood either, he wasn't on a warpath. This was business. So he hopped out of the jeep. He walked towards the store. In dark slacks and a black dress shirt with the sleeves rolled up that fit his tall, dark and lean 6'2" Argentine New York frame, he nodded to the black guys as he went inside. Because he could have cared less if they were black.

Unlike Victor, who had Italy in his veins.

But not enough that he spoke the language.

Regardless, Victor stayed in the car, locking eyes with the basketball player as Bobby asked the Puerto Rican clerk behind the counter—well, he thought he was Puerto Rican, but all he knew was that he'd never seen him before—it was usually Hindus that ran this spot—"Yo, Shandeep here?"

But the cashier, a little nervous, a little off, just shook his head: *No.*

In the jeep though, Victor was just looking for a fight. And you wouldn't think it, either. Not the average stranger at least. Even though he was fit, at only 5'8", growing up, bigger guys who didn't know him often looked at him like a mark.

Always in the best clothes, the nicest jewelry and the worst parts of town, Victor just didn't give a fuck. He wanted people to challenge him. Because he loved cracking their heads after the fact. He was a boss in training, training himself.

But today was different.

His once warm heart was now ice cold.

Life can do that to you.

So, looking a little pale and skinnier than usual, he lowered the window even more, down to the bottom.

But the black guy, the bigger one, held his composure. However, the brother next to him kept looking at the Honda.

And inside, Bobby asked when Shandeep would be back.

"An hour," the cashier replied. "Maybe more."

Not something Bobby was happy to hear. But Bobby didn't let emotions get the best of him. Because 6 years in the joint, 1 of them in the hole will do that to you. They'll teach you how to control them. If anything, prison will teach you patience. So he took a few moments and skimmed through the newspapers on the rack in front of him.

As the cashier just stared at him with beads of sweat starting to drip down his forehead.

It was hot out that day.

A scorcher.

And as Bobby went for the 5 day forecast, inside the jeep, Victor had enough. However, he only knew one way to vent his anger. So he asked him: "You got staring problems?"

But the black dude just grinned. He wasn't a pussy. In fact, Victor amused him. *Who is this white-boy?*

Which enraged him—Victor.

So he hopped out of the jeep. He slammed the door behind him. He got right in the guy's face and stared upward into his eyes and said: "I asked you a fucking question."

However, inside the store, all Bobby was thinking about was what to drink. *Gatorade, Sprite, water—beer?* He was taking his time, appreciating it. It's not like you can just go digging through coolers when you're a guest of the government.

But outside, realizing this psycho was for real, the big black guy looked at the big picture of things. The big black guy eyed Victor up and down: black slacks, and a black short sleeved dress shirt—but more specifically, a 24 karat gold necklace, a 24 karat gold pinky ring, a 24 karat gold bracelet and a $25,000 gold Rolex watch—shit, he knew Victor didn't get all that working a 9 to 5. So he decided to smooth things over. So he asked him: "Man, where you from, dog?"

And Victor replied: BOOM!

He cracked him dead in his jaw, sending Kareem flying through the glass door behind him. Then Victor turned to the skinny one: "Get the fuck out of my neighborhood!"

Victor dropped him with a lightning quick 2-piece.

While Bobby, making sense of this, sees a half conscious Kareem getting up off the ground and pulling a Glock .40 pistol from his waist. He begins to set his sights on Victor. So Bobby reaches down, pulls the .38 special out from his ankle holster and smashes him over the head with it and returns him to the floor, his place.

"Tough guy, huh?" Victor doesn't give a fuck. Since he used to be a middleweight who loved fighting heavyweights dropping two guys with two moves was nothing new. So he goes inside to check on things and looks at Bobby pointing his gun at a rocked out Kareem on the floor as BOOM! BOOM! Two shots ring through the door and Victor takes one through the outside of his right arm and falls on the floor as Bobby blasts right back at the black driver on the other side of the

Honda, with another black hat on his head, and hits him right on the side of his head and sends the black hat flying into the air.

As the cashier screams.

And shoots at Bobby with another Glock.

Who ducks behind a rack as Victor, on the floor, pulls another .38 from his own ankle holster and blasts the cashier with 2 bullets to the chest.

Followed by one to the face.

Just another day in the neighborhood.

2

FOUR MONTHS EARLIER.

It was the moment Bobby Drakis had been waiting for. Looking forward to. Not knowing if it would ever really happen. But it did.

So he hugged his lawyer, loosened his tie and strolled through the old courthouse in the best shape of his life in a dark grey suit and a white shirt with a thick manila envelope in his hand. And a smile, a look of relief on his face.

He even flirted with a fat, unattractive female court officer on the way out. She was flattered. *What the hell*, Bobby thought. *Rhinos need love too.*

And he walked outside on that nice Spring afternoon down the long front steps of the Albany, New York courthouse past all the people wondering what he was so happy about and right up to his best, oldest, closest friend Victor Saravano who was illegally parked out front, leaning on his shiny, sparkling dark blue 1997 BMW 540 with black tinted windows and custom chrome rims in a white t-shirt, baggy grey sweatpants and white Jordan sneakers with a smile on his face bigger than Bobby's.

"You're gonna get a ticket," he told him.

"You're acting like I give a fuck," Victor replied.

And they hugged, embraced.

"I can't fucking believe it," Bobby said.

They hugged again.

"Believe it, Brother."

But Bobby just stared into his eyes. "Thank you," he replied.

And they took off. They were in drive.

"Oh my God I feel fucking great right now."

"You should."

"I do," Bobby said, as he finished up a burger, and fries, as they cruised down the freeway. "This is the best food of my life. This is the best day of my life."

"Yeah well hopefully tomorrow isn't. You're wakin' up with a hangover, Bro. You're goin' back to Queens a hero tonight."

"I don't care about none of that. Really, man, I'm just happy to be free." Which was all Bobby thought about as he breathed in the fresh, clean, Upstate New York air through the window. "But since you mention it, what's the plan for tonight?"

"Whatever you want, Brother. When we get back I'll show you the apartment I got set up for you. You could shower. I got some clothes for you over there. Take a nap if you want."

"I don't need a nap," Bobby smiled. "I slept great last night."

"Your bunkie tuck you in or something?"

"With lotion."

"Well then after you wash it off I'll take you around. Or do whatever you want, really. But later tonight we got a little something planned for you."

"It'll be nice to see everybody. What's up with this job though? I'm not trying to live off of charity."

"We'll talk about it. Why don't you just get settled first," Victor said, and he pulled over at the next rest stop.

They used the bathrooms, they washed up, and after walking outside Victor told Bobby what it was like. "First things first. I'm assuming you already know this, but in case you don't, never, ever, under any circumstances are you or anybody else to talk business in my car."

"I got you."

"Or my places of business. I'm not trying to be the guy that lets everybody down."

"I got you."

"I know. But yo, the lounge we're goin' to tonight, that's mine too. You're gonna love it."

"Just exactly how deep are you playing?"

"Deep enough."

"I hope not too deep."

"I'm not stupid. But things are good right now, real good. Which is why I wanted to ask you, again, right here and right now and not in some visiting room where anybody might be listening, are you sure you don't want to come in with me? I could use someone like you. Someone I could trust. And you'll be rewarded, *handsomely*."

"I appreciate all that, Victor. But after I save up some money man, I'm out, ghost."

"What're you gonna do?"

"I got no idea. But I got lost time to make up for. I got a lot of places I wanna see. And honestly, I kinda wanna live on a beach."

"There's always Howard Beach."

"Fuck those guidos. No offense."

"None taken. I don't really like it over there either."

"But I'm serious, man. These last few weeks I've really been thinking about it. I'm just trying to save up enough money so hopefully in the next two years, or at least before I'm 30, I can start someplace new. Maybe not forever but I got some living to do."

"Where were you thinking about?"

"Like I told you, someplace with a beach."

"Well listen, Bobby. I know you just got out. I know you want clean money. But I'm tellin' you, the entire crew's getting rich right now."

"Doing what?"

"Doing everything. Shy, sports, weed, whatever. And being with Jackie, we got access to it all. We got the whole area locked down."

"I appreciate the offer, Victor. But I ain't tryin' to go back. You did 1 year, I did 6. I'm tired."

"Which is why I thought this would rejuvenate you. You wanna put some money on the street, do collections, take bets, whatever, I'll back you up a hundred percent."

"I'm thankful. I am. I'm appreciative, Victor, but just hook me up with this clean job to get me started and I'll take it from there."

"Alright, man. But don't say I didn't offer."

"I won't. But tell me more about the job."

"What else is there to say? The apartment I got for you is right above the laundromat and next door is the gym, right there on Franny Lew. I own the property and you'll be the manager."

"In your name?"

"What?"

"You own the property, in your own name?"

"Not a hundred percent. But I own it. But really all I want you to do for me is just keep an eye on both places and more importantly keep your eyes open for *me*. You know what I'm sayin'? You gotta sweep that place."

"I got you."

"I know. I'll show you around when we get back. But then after you get acclimated, you want something else I'll help you find something. We got hooks everywhere."

"Anyplace interesting?"

"Well that depends on if you get your balls back."

"I'm being serious."

"So am I. We just got a new nightclub now, a titty bar, some restaurants, all kinds of stuff. Jackie's got juice, Jackie's got juice. Even vending machines."

"You talk about this guy like he's your hero."

"We go back, Bobby. And I'll tell ya, when my father got whacked, he was there for me. He practically raised me."

"Well whatever you do just make sure you're there for your Michael also. There's no need for him to grow up like we did."

"I know. He's getting older."

"I can't wait to meet him. How's he doin'?"

"He's 4, he's healthy. He's my *Little Pal*."

Bobby's face brightened. "That's a good song."

"I know. My old man used to sing it to me. But look, Jackie said he wants you to come by when you get settled, say hello. Couple a days. He'll be happy to see you."

"He was always good to me."

"More than you know. Without him I wouldn't be making this kind of money. I mean, I'd be okay regardless but you wouldn't have no apartment to come home to. You'd have a couch."

"Just don't get me sent back, Victor."

"Only you can do that yourself, Bobby."

"I know. But I gotta be honest with you."

"What?"

"I never really believed it would happen. I mean, I wanted it to, but I didn't wanna get my hopes up. I don't know how the fuck you pulled that off."

"I do."

"But still. I thought I was doin' the full 25."

"Well you're not. So shut the fuck up and get on with it," Victor said.

And they got back in the car.

3

To get to the old neighborhood in Queens coming from Upstate New York, the best way is to go through The Bronx and then take The Throgs Neck Bridge, which leaves you right there. As long as when you get off the bridge, you take the Clearview Expressway. If instead you merge onto the Cross Island Parkway, you get dropped off elsewhere. Victor checked in with someone on his cell while they were on the bridge and realized he had to take a detour. Something demanded his immediate attention.

"Right now?" Bobby asked. "I just got out. I thought we were gonna build."

"Bobby we've been building the whole way down."

"We're right here, though. Let's go to the old neighborhood. You don't wanna at least have a drink real quick?"

"Brother your lawyers didn't get paid for by sitting around and having drinks. I gotta work real quick," Victor said as he turned onto the Cross Island.

"What are you doing? Drop me off in the hood at least."

"I'll drop you at the apartment." It was a few miles away. "Don't you wanna relax for a second?"

"Relax? It's only 5. The sun's still out. You know the last time I was in the sun? When I wasn't in the yard?"

"Bobby I gotta do this, don't question it. You can see the sun on Francis Lewis."

"Fuck Francis Lewis. Drop me in the hood, I'll do some sightseeing."

"Sightseeing?"

"Sightseeing, people-seeing. I've been gone 6 years."

"Look, let me just drop you at the apartment, you gotta trust me. We'll meet up later on."

"Fuck later on," Bobby said as Victor got off on Northern Boulevard going west, the first exit.

"Let me do the driving, Bobby. You might like this route better. You've been gone a long time."

"I ain't been gone *that* long. To forget my roots?"

Victor smiled.

"You think it's funny?" Bobby asked. "You think this is funny?"

Victor did.

"Look, I don't care you got a prostitute over there or something, it's not funny."

"Bobby, you're roots haven't forgotten you either." He turned left off Northern Boulevard onto 215th Street and pulled up to the entrance of The Anchor Motor Inn, a nice, small, middle class hotel where 7 hoods, none of them Black or Asian were hanging out front. But to Bobby and Victor, they weren't just hoods. They were Family. Their second Family. What was left of the old O.S.N. crew.

"What the fuck?"

"Why go to the old neighborhood when you can bring the old neighborhood to you?"

Bobby smiled. "*Asshole.* You're an asshole."

Victor smiled as well. "I love you, man."

Bobby looked at him. "I love you too."

And they got out of the car, treated like royalty.

"Who's that, Bobby D?" Fat Mark asked. He was an Irish, obese, 28-year-old immature wannabe wiseguy. But, he was loyal, and he gave Bobby a hug.

"I fucking missed you guys, man."

"You think we didn't miss your crazy ass too?" Fat Mark replied.

"But you look healthy," Bell told Bobby.

"Thanks. I feel great. I've been working out every day for the last 6 years."

"Yeah I can tell. Look at those forearms," Bell joked.

And Bobby laughed. Bell, who got that nickname because he grew up in the bars a few blocks away on Bell Boulevard was the guy he counted on to make him laugh over the prison phone. At 27 he was a short, stubborn, nonchalant Italian-Puerto Rican whose only goal in life was to enjoy it. And there they were, standing there, laughing, the inner circle: a rowdy group of friends who grew up together.

"Don't worry," Victor told Bobby. "You'll see all the other degenerates at the lounge later on."

"I figured. So you bums wanna tell me what we're doin' here? We're a block away from a precinct if you didn't realize."

But even though the 111th was within walking distance, nobody cared. Instead Fat Mark just slipped him a room key.

Victor smiled. "Welcome home, Brother."

"Welcome home is right," Bobby said with an even bigger smile as the door to the suite opened and his dick stood up. He was greeted by two of the baddest strippers New York had ever seen, two dime-pieces in their early 20s who immediately threw him onto the bed and went to work.

One was Portuguese, the other was Colombian, and both of them were freaks.

Bobby spanked her ass. Then he spanked the other one's ass. He was loving it.

As Miss Portugal took off his belt and began slipping off his pants, Miss Colombia sat on his waist and breathed, moaned on his neck as she unbuttoned his shirt.

A few hours ago Bobby was in a jail cell.

Now he was lying on his back in nothing but boxers with two goddesses licking, electrifying his body all over the place.

"Freedom," he said.

Miss Colombia smiled. She started grinding, rotating her hips over his, and she just stared into his eyes with her fuck-me-face: "Freedom," she repeated. "*Freedom.*"

But, Bobby wasn't stupid. He wasn't a rocket scientist, but he wasn't stupid. It was the 90s and AIDS was raging. So he asked them if they had condoms. "I didn't think to bring one."

"No problem," Miss Portugal said. "Victor planned everything out." So as Miss Colombia began nibbling on his neck, Miss Portugal walked over to the coffee table and picked up the silver tray that had a big bottle of Grey Goose on it, some cranberry juice and two rolled blunts filled with Bayside's finest marijuana. Not to mention, a box of condoms. And she brought it over. The tray. To the bed.

But Bobby just looked at it: "*Asshole*," he said.

As Miss Colombia bit into his neck like a vampire. They all laughed.

The box was labeled *Snugger Fit*. You know, the ones for small penises only.

"That was a good one, I'll give you that," Bobby laughed to the guys.

"I had to," Victor smiled as they commiserated at his lounge, Covers, a comfortable little spot on Francis Lewis Boulevard with TVs, tinted windows out front and black leather couches and a bunch of small tables with 2 Joker Poker machines on the inside.

"We're gettin' too old to hang out in the park all day," he told Bobby. "Gotta grow up *eventually*. Plus, we needed a headquarters. Know what I'm sayin'? But you know what it is. Mi casa, our casa, su casa." It was Victor's version of a social club.

And Bobby was appreciative, very appreciative. Although, he missed hanging out in the park all day, without a care in the world.

Whatever, he thought. He was just happy to be free.

Aside from the bartender being hot though the thing that made Bobby feel happy and free the most was the early 90s hip-hop playing that he used to listen to before he got locked up. That and the endless stream of people who came through to say congratulations and pay their respects. After all, these were people he'd known for years. Some of them people he grew up with and knew as children. But more importantly, people who didn't look down on him because he blew trial and was convicted of murder. After all, he won on appeal.

"You're like a hero around here," Fat Mark told him.

"Word," Bell said. "You and Victor."

But Leto, another of the old O.S.N. heads who was at the motel earlier and a tall, skinny and smooth 28-year-old Albanian hustler who did a 3 year bid for dealing coke during the same time Bobby was away told him that "You know I wish we were together for some of that."

"I know," Bobby replied.

Victor chimed in: "What'd you guys, miss each other by 2 weeks I heard? In Coxsackie, right?"

Leto nodded. "Shit was wack."

"I know," Bobby said. "Shit was lonely."

"Well ain't no reason to be lonely no more," Victor told both of them, and for the rest of the night Bobby regaled them with his tales of prison-life while at the same time he was filled in on what he had missed while he was gone. The things they couldn't say over the phones.

"You don't understand," Fat Mark said. "Shit done changed."

"Change is good though, isn't it?"

"Change is always good," Victor mentioned. "But if you got a good thing going, stay with it."

"That ain't what I'm talkin' about, fam. This shit be depressin', Bobby." Even though Fat Mark was Irish he got along great with Black people. "You know what I'm sayin'? Every day you find out someone ain't down like he supposed to be. You know what I'm sayin'? You can't trust *nobody* no more."

"You're tellin' *me*," Bobby replied. But he didn't even want to think about it. Not right now at least. So when Jennifer came over, his hot, sexy, former high school fling, he squeezed her ass as she hugged him.

"Still the same old Bobby, huh?" She laughed. She wasn't much in the class department but she always loved Bobby even though Bobby never loved her.

"What are you, 23 now?" he asked.

"24. Did you get the letters I sent you?"

"I replied to them didn't I?"

"Not the ones I mailed last week."

"Well what did they say?"

She whispered, breathed in his ear: "That I was saving the care package for when you came home."

And later that night, she gave it to him. She finished him off. The third nut of the night was definitely a charm. But before they left, Victor snapped his fingers to get the bartender's attention, who poured out shots of Patrón for all the people there. And Victor Saravano, the macho guy that he was, turned off the music. He got emotional.

"You guys all know me here," he said. "Some better than others. Some longer than others. But one thing a wise man always told me, was to appreciate the good times. You never know when they're gonna end. But more importantly, appreciate the people around you. Because you never know when they're not gonna be there no more. You never know when you won't be lucky enough to have them in your life anymore. But—my Brother, Bobby D—we all missed you, friend."

The entire crowd reminded him of that.

"Thanks," Bobby told them. "I missed you guys too. You got no idea how I missed you guys."

Then Victor got back into it. He raised his glass. "To Bayside," he said. "To Kojo, God rest his soul. I know he's looking down on us right now. He's definitely looking down on us right now. But, for right now? For right now, this is to Bobby, you fucking maniac, you." Victor smiled. "We all love you, you know we do. Welcome home, Brother."

"*Welcome home*," everyone repeated.

And they all drank at once.

Bobby Drakis was back.

But not 100 percent. He had to catch his breath.

Forward motion, he told himself.

4

A little different than "Not tonight," which was what Lauren told Lenny.

She was just sitting on the couch, watching TV. In her pajamas, a little under the weather. But that didn't stop him, her new boyfriend, from trying to get in her pants. From trying to kiss up on her neck.

And who could blame him? Lauren Bassi was bad. Lauren Bassi was beautiful. The main reason he wifed her up to begin with. But there was more.

At 25, 5'4" and with a body to match her smooth Mediterranean skin, she was one brunette who looked unstoppable in anything she ever wore. But more importantly, she never acted like a whore. She was one of the good ones. The kind of girl you could take home to your mother.

However, her new boyfriend, Lenny Malco—he was an asshole.

"Stop," she told him. He kept trying to feel around, kiss up on her neck and put his hand between her thighs. "At least wait till the movie's over. You're acting like a teenager."

But Lenny, 28, didn't care. He was a scumbag. Not that anyone would say that to his face, though. He might have only been 5'7" but the steroids made him huge.

And since he was a DJ—and a drug dealer—which Lauren didn't know, he kept it on the low. She just thought he was "connected"—a lot of Italians were. He was paid. His apartment was dope. A 2-bedroom with flash, pizzazz.

But Lauren wasn't like the other girls. She was a prize. She didn't care about the extras. Besides, she was just trying to watch the movie. But not just because it was a love story. Because there was something missing from her life.

However, Lenny was ruining it for her. She was getting annoyed. He tried to kiss up on her neck again but Lauren pushed him off.

5

Two days later Bobby picked up where Victor had never left off. He was sitting at the front desk inside the middle class gym, skimming through a couple of magazines. So when Victor came in carrying a small black plastic bag, he asked him what he was doing.

"Just trying to figure out what the hell I'm gonna do with my life," he said. Bobby wasn't a brain surgeon but he was smart enough to know that he was approaching 30 and didn't have a dollar to his name. Or a skill on his resume.

"Well when you get your balls back gimme a call. I already told you."

"Likewise."

"Here, man." Victor pulled a sandwich and an orange juice out of the bag and gave them to him.

"Thanks."

"Don't mention it. I figure the less money you have to spend the quicker you can start payin' me rent."

Even though Victor was just being his usual old self Bobby didn't respond. It ain't easy being an ex-con. But he did tell him that "Lorenzo came by, looking for you."

Victor nodded. And walked through the half empty gym, across the main floor and went to his small office on the other side of it, in the back, behind the free weights. It didn't have much more than a desk, a Compaq computer, a file cabinet in the corner and a *Rocky III* poster next to the wall calendar. Plus some pictures of Victor from his boxing days, his teenage glory days. But he was there for something else. He locked the door behind him, and closed the shade. Then he moved the file cabinet to the side, and lifted up the carpet from the corner. He spun the knob on the hidden floor safe that faced the ceiling, put in the combination, then inserted the key, turned it and opened it.

Victor took out 20 thousand dollars in knots of 5. He put them in the sandwich bag and went back to the front desk.

"Yo, so you're gonna come by around 8, right?"

"Of course," Bobby replied.

"Good. Michelle's cooking," Victor said.

And he walked out the door.

6

Bobby knocked. He rang the doorbell too. And he waited in the hallway of the 5-story building. It had no doorman or elevator, but Victor only lived on the 3rd so for Fat Mark it wasn't that bad. Dude was obese. But still.

Even though the entire world had moved on without him—even though he felt like a visitor everywhere he went—Victor's home would always be Bobby's, and vice versa. So when Victor opened the door, after they hugged, he told Bobby he'd be right back as he went to the bedroom and Bobby just sat down on one of the fine black leather couches in the living room and looked around: The place was sick. Dope. Beautiful. But not nearly as beautiful as Victor's wife, Michelle. At 27, Puerto Rican and as sexy as ever, few women could compare.

Except one, Bobby thought.

As Victor walked into the bedroom, he slapped her on the ass as she walked out. When she did, Bobby stood up. They kissed on the cheek.

"How's this guy treating you?" he asked her.

"Like a housewife," Michelle replied. But their son, Michael, only 4 years old with long, cute curly hair stole her attention. "Did you say hello to your uncle Bobby?"

No response. He was too busy playing with his toys on the floor in front of them and the brand new 50 inch TV.

"Brat. Bobby the remote's over there, on the couch. Put on whatever you want, I got to finish up," she told him, and she went back to the kitchen.

As Bobby stared at the television. Not at Victor's old boxing gloves and championship belt that were hanging on the wall above it, but at what was on it: a show giving a tour of celebrity mansions. In fact, other than the assorted gangster stuff, this was Victor's favorite kind of program. He watched them all the time, thinking of the mansion he himself would one day own. Because getting money, stacking bread came natural to Victor and he knew that if he could just avoid doing another bid—or dying—it was only a matter of time.

But after six very long years in lock-up, surrounded by strangers, looking at other people's cribs didn't do the same things for Bobby. He couldn't help but to just stare around. Not at Michelle's plump ass or perky breasts but at the way she was working over the stove in the kitchen. At little Michael, playing with his toys on the floor in front of him. At the nice life Victor and his wife had built for themselves. At the Family atmosphere. And that's when it hit him, harder than it ever had before.

Fuck, Bobby thought.

He missed out.

7

The walls were old and wood paneled, the comfortable room wasn't huge but not exactly small, and while some people called it gambling, to the winners it was just hanging out. Although: in a room full of made men, it was a pastime. A joy. An escape from their wives. Except for Luigi, last name Carcaterra, 71 now and feeling his age, all of a sudden getting more conscious.

"You gotta get those walls checked out," he said. "Get an inspector in here."

"For what?" Jackie Iacone replied as he looked at the posters on the wall, one of James Cagney and another of Steve McQueen. "You don't think I don't personally sweep this place?"

"That's not what I'm talking about," Luigi told him.

But being that they, 5 of the 7 guys in the room were seated around a card table in the private back room/office of Ralph's Pizzeria, aka Jackie's headquarters, a few miles past Victor's gym down Francis Lewis Boulevard, Jackie was wondering if Luigi was just trying to distract him to pocket his poker money. So he asked him, "What then?"

"You don't understand. With all the grease in this place? Mold? It's all fucked up. You probably got cancer behind those walls."

"Well then you're welcome to lose your money at any of my many other fine dining establishments" Jackie replied as he laid out his hand and cleared the table.

Jackie loved winning. He loved taking. But he hated losing, a lot. He was a cheapskate at heart. But while Luigi was 5'11" and broad, Jackie was only 5'6", slight and balding with glasses. At 62, he looked harmless.

But regardless, he'd slit your throat in a second.

Jackie was as vicious as they came. However, he was more than a thug. He was cunning. He was an earner. Plus, for over 7 years now, since the boss got out he'd been an official capo with a crew of killers underneath him. Like Lorenzo Vissi, his favorite recruit, who was 34, well-liked, tall, lean and dangerous. Although right now he was just seated on the couch over in the corner, with Luigi's driver, reading a newspaper. Lorenzo was the kind of handsome, smooth operator you didn't see coming.

However, Luigi had his own crew out in Brooklyn. Like Jackie's, they too were hardcore. And bigger. Except while his had a knack for raping the unions, Jackie's team was after the simple things in life: gambling and extortion, shylocking and drugs. Although, they'd never admit the latter. After all, Jackie didn't consider weed a drug. He also never acknowledged that his guys shook down the local dealers. Drugs were a no-no. Which was kind of hypocritical since Jackie was arrested for selling heroin in the 80s.

But then again, almost the entire family was slinging that stuff back then including two of Jackie's closest comrades who were at the table with them. Two guys on his crew who he'd come up with and trusted his whole life: Nino Carbone, 55, a stocky bookmaker who looked like a shady accountant that would rob your grandmother, and Greg DePalma, 66, Jackie's husky, gruff, chief enforcer with catcher's mitt, cinderblock hands who'd spent 16 years in Attica for murder and another 4 in the Feds for assault.

Greg enjoyed the violence, and Jackie reaped the profits. But, Luigi was a cut above. He was on the family's administration, not just a captain anymore but also the acting consigliere while the official one was on house arrest getting ready to do time and Luigi had it in the back of his mind to make sure the crews were in line. Because even though he and Jackie, together, had done time, he always knew it was only a matter of time. One day in the future Luigi knew he'd be back in the pen again. After all, it was only 4 years ago that he wrapped up a 12 year sentence in Allenwood and only a few months since he got off supervised release. He got caught up in that whole Donnie Brasco bullshit.

But now, while he was free, and getting older he wanted to stack as much money for his loved ones as possible and stay out of jail for as long as possible in case the next time he didn't come back. So Luigi came out to Queens not to play Hold 'Em but to get the low down on what Jackie was up to. Especially since he'd been hearing people talk more and more about a young kid that Jackie had on his crew. However, he also heard that certain people wanted to see this kid wear a button, like his father had.

So he asked him, "How's your boy doin'?"
"Which one?" Jackie replied.

"The one who used to be a boxer. We went to his fights."

"Walter's kid?"

"Yeah, what's he up to? The concrete says he's your blue chip now."

But Jackie's soldiers looked to him to see what his answer would be, so he thought about it for a second, before responding. And then he said, simply, dismissively:

"He's young."

8

Victor walked into the gym the next morning but didn't find Bobby at the desk. Instead he was on the floor, doing pull-ups and push-ups, the jail workout.

"Trying to make a good impression?" Victor asked him.

"For you, always," Bobby replied.

But the truth was, Bobby, in a wife beater, he looked great. He was in the best shape of his life and those lion tattoos on his shoulders with the tribal bands underneath still hadn't faded. And neither had the letters O.S.N. that were written across his upper back. Victor, on the other hand, had slimmed down a little. Not to as skinny as he was before he started to fill out though, when he stopped boxing, when they went to jail. However, Bobby was confused. "I thought I was gonna meet you over there?"

"Plans changed. I gotta go see an old friend first. One of your old friends too. Take the ride with me."

"What are we doing down here?" Bobby asked as Victor pulled into the outdoor parking garage by the 109th precinct.

"Well we're not turning ourselves in," Victor replied.

But Bobby just looked around. "This fucking place hasn't changed at all."

"It's gotten worse," Victor told him. "Gooks, *everywhere*."

"Jesus Christ," Bobby said as they got out of the car, surrounded by Koreans.

"They're trying to take over Bayside too."

"A day I hope will never come."

"If I could run them out I would. Fucking parasites."

They were in Downtown Flushing, where all the shops were as well as where all the Asians in Queens congregated, by the bus depot and the 7 train. Most people called it Main Street and when they were younger it was an adventure taking the bus down there to buy clothes or take the subway into the city. But the thing was, since dozens of buses intersected down there on Main Street and all kinds of people passed through the neighborhood on a daily basis someone had to serve them food, which made Bobby happy as a motherfucker to see someone he'd forgotten about.

"Holy shit," he said as Victor smiled. "Jimmy, that you?"

"You weren't lying," Jimmy said to Victor as they walked towards his cart. "Let me see if I remember. If I remember your favorite," he told Bobby. "Shish kabob, on bread, with lemon, barbecue and hot sauce."

"You fucking asshole," Bobby smiled. "That was everyone's favorite."

As far as they were concerned Jimmy, a fat, gregarious, middle-aged Greek guy ran the best shish kabob stand in New York. So he asked Victor, "What can I get for you today?"

"The usual," Victor replied, as he slipped him $5. Because even though Victor was a drug dealer and an enforcer, he was also a growing loan shark and got 505 hundred dollars in cash back from Jimmy inside a brown paper bag that included two shish kabob sandwiches. There was no way he was charging him for it, but they still had to look good for the cameras.

It was nice to see a friendly face though, Bobby thought. And likewise, Jimmy was happy to see Bobby. He was always appreciative of the time Victor, Bobby, Bell and another of their friends named Dino, some wild Puerto Rican-Italian kid they grew up with kicked the shit out of a pair of black kids from the nearby Bland Housing Projects who stuck him up and gave him a black eye back in '89. One of them even ended up with a cracked skull because Dino went too far. It must have worked though because no one from those projects ever bothered Jimmy again. Especially when word got out that he was under Jackie's flag.

Needless to say, Jimmy hooked Bobby up with a nice box of shish kabobs to take also. And Bobby, upon seeing that Jimmy still had the same dog, a big, beautiful mutt that was half German Shepherd and half Boxer, pet it while it just sat there next to the cart waiting for the next plate of food to arrive.

Bobby always liked dogs. And so did someone else, he thought.

Forward motion, he told himself.

9

The big RALPH'S sign out front brought back memories and so did Little Jackie grabbing Bobby and giving him a hug after they walked through the front door into the nice, upper-middle-class pizza joint.

"So tell me, kid. How the fuck are ya?"

"Great, Jackie," Bobby said as he looked around at all the signed pictures of athletes and celebrities on the walls. "And I gotta say, again—thanks for all your help when I was inside, when we were on trial, for everything."

"What was I gonna do, let you boys rot? You delivered pies for me. You hit home runs for me. You're in the fucking picture over there for Christ's sake." And then Jackie paused. "I knew your fathers."

"Hey, man," Bobby said as he looked at him and Victor's old little league baseball picture, the one of the old Ralph's Pizza team. "I wish I'd known mine too."

"Well, what are you gonna do, huh? You're here now." And then Jackie said, with a smile: "*This*, is Family."

"I know. I feel fucking great. Incarceration sucks."

"You're telling *me*? C'mon, let's eat," Jackie said as he called out to the elderly little Sicilian behind the counter: "Pepe, have the kid bring Bobby a menu." And then he asked Bobby, "You like chicken parm? You want some veal? What do you like?"

"Victor tells me the pork chops and vinegar peppers here are to get whacked for."

Jackie found it funny. "Got that right, Mr. Drakis."

It wasn't just the three of them, though. They had gone past the booths in the front to the tables in the back dining room where they were joined by Bert Ragsdale, another goon on Jackie's crew. Who was 45, German-Irish, and an asshole. But, since he was also tough, tall and husky, he was a valued member of Jackie's mob squad. Plus, he had a shiny bald head and did 10 months with Bobby in Elmira.

So, as they feasted, Bobby said, "That place was wild, man."

Bert sighed. "I remember when you got that beauty mark." The scar through Bobby's eyebrow.

"Yeah, how did you get that?" Jackie asked.

"I was sitting in the barber chair, the prison salon. Then out of nowhere some wack-job comes after me with a razor."

"Jesus," Jackie said.

"Fucking gladiator school," Bert threw in.

"I got sent to the hole for that. I ended up spending 14 months there."

"For getting cut?" Jackie asked. He instinctively had to wonder if Bobby checked himself into protective custody.

"Nah. 'Cause I stomped his head in after."

Bert laughed. "I walk in and he's kicking him in his face."

"I lost it," Bobby said. "Doing 25 to life for some bullshit? I lost it. I blacked the fuck out on this asshole."

Jackie could see that just thinking about it was causing Bobby stress. So he told him, "Well, you're back now, where you belong. That's all that matters."

"Still," Bobby said. "What a fucking waste. I don't care if I gotta do time but at least let it be for a good reason."

"It couldn't have been easy for you," Bert chimed in. "Comin' from a college and all."

"It wasn't. I was tryin' to do the right thing, go to school. I had my baseball scholarship. Then they pinch me while I'm in class with my girlfriend. She freaked out, started screamin' and cryin'."

"You still speak to her?" Jackie wondered.

"We lost contact," Bobby said.

"Well listen," Jackie told him. "You were a man. You stood up. You could have been like your friend there, that fuck, Dano, Dino or whatever. But you weren't. You were a fucking man and no one can ever take that away from you, you understand?"

"Especially nowadays," Victor said.

Bert offered his opinion too: "Fucking stool pigeons, *everywhere*."

But Jackie got back to the point. "You were a man. Be proud of yourself. Buck the fuck up."

"Nah I know, I'm fine," Bobby said. "But still, if they didn't put me in the solitary I would a killed somebody in there."

"Or got killed yourself," Bert said. "Max ain't no place for scholarships."

"What the hell is wrong with you?" Jackie asked. Bert had a habit of saying asshole things. So he turned back to Bobby. "Listen. I want you to come by the club. We got a nightclub now, a new one."

"Where is it?" Bobby asked.

"Oceanside," Jackie said. "They're doin' renovations right now, get it ready for summer. But when it opens again, couple a weeks? You come by. You gonna like this place. Tell him, Victor."

"What can I say? We were there the other day, it's beautiful."

"You bring your friends," Jackie said. "You boys will be V.I.P. And for the two a you, bottles on me."

"Or on the previous owner," Bert cracked.

Jackie majored in extortion.

10

Extorting anyone was the last thing Bobby was doing, though. It was 6 weeks later and there he was, back at the gym, working his underachieving day job.

He wasn't resentful of Victor or anyone's success, but some nights when they went out to party, on Victor's dime, he had to try not to be. Everywhere they went Victor would grab the check. Then they'd go to the mall, and Victor would buy Bobby clothes. Victor was living like a king.

But that was *his life, not mine*, Bobby thought. *Gotta stay loyal*. Victor was by far the best friend he ever had. And while he sat there at the front desk, combing through the Yellow Pages there was only one thing on his mind. However, when the boss walked in Bobby folded the page he was reading and closed up the phone book.

Curious though, Victor picked it up off the desk. He looked at it. "20 bucks says it's the G-section."

Bobby didn't say anything. Instead he smiled when Victor opened it up to the D-section. Specifically, the dog section.

"So you wanna be a professional dog walker now?" Victor asked.

"What?"

"If you don't like it here just tell me," Victor said.

"Don't flatter yourself," Bobby told him.

Victor put the book down. He pulled out a knot of at least $2,500 and gave Bobby a 20 from it.

"If you insist."

Victor smiled. "You got plans for tonight?"

"Jennifer called me. She wanted to hang out again."

"Are you going to?" Victor asked.

"Not if you got something better goin' on. What's up?"

"Let's go to Snap."

"We were just there."

"Well let's go back. There's somebody there tonight I wanna introduce you to."

The old crew, back together again. Or at least part of it, Bobby thought, as they passed a blunt around while cruising down the Long Island Expressway that night. Riding in Victor's Beamer, Fat Mark and Bell in the back with Bobby up in shotgun and The Lox's *Money, Power & Respect* playing on the radio. The track featured DMX and Lil' Kim on it, too.

But Fat Mark had to ask him, "You smell this shit, Bobby D? Now I know they didn't have nothin' like *this* in the joint." He was talking about the high quality of the insane bud they were smoking.

"My man," Bobby replied. "They didn't have nothing like this *before* I was in the joint." He coughed. "Jesus Christ. Where'd you get this from?" he asked Victor.

But Victor didn't respond. He just gave Bobby a look.

"Bobby D you know the best weed in New York was always in the neighborhood," Fat Mark told him.

"It was funny actually," Bobby said. "When I was Up North? There was a blurb about the weed in Bayside in *High Times*."

And Victor was amused by it. "I saw that. I'm the one who showed it to you. It was when we were in jail, in Albany, waiting for trial."

"That's right," Bobby said. "I remember you being proud of it."

"An escape, I guess," Victor told him.

"Yo Mark the weed they had in there was horrible. Straight dirt, chocolate shit."

But Mark said, "Mad niggas in the city be thinking the best weed is from The Dominicans, *Uptown*."

"I remember," Bobby replied. "We used to troop it up there in high school."

"Word," Mark said. "But they don't know, the best strands be in Queens."

Before they knew it, though, they were out in Long Island, pulling into a parking lot near a warehouse by the water in the middle of nowhere.

And Bobby, a little dazed, a little faded from the weed, was woken up when he saw the logo for Snap Nightclub in bright lights with a long line of people underneath. Guys looking impressive and girls looking sexy. It was trendy.

But after driving past the valet and parking the car themselves in the lot, right next to Leto who was parking his maroon, 2-door Mercury Cougar with 2 other O.S.N. members inside it, the whole group of them just walked past everyone, following Victor, who said "What up" to the bouncers and walked around the metal detectors like a boss.

The good life, Bobby thought, as they sat there in one of the V.I.P. sections on the side of the club, in the cut. Being treated like royalty as the dark lights flashed, bodies grinded and House of Pain's *Jump Around* blasted off the speakers. A few more of the hoods from Bobby's coming home party were there too, popping bottles and flirting with the waitresses, pulling girls off the dance floor past the velvet rope. But the truth was that they—all of them—O.S.N. included—had that pull there because of Victor.

Sure, some of their crowd made money, some of the guys had some juice. But Victor was in charge. He was the heart of that neighborhood, the heart of that crew. Maybe not Jackie's crew that he worked for, but the crew that he grew up with at least. In fact, that was his crew. He was the de facto leader of the O.S.N. He was their Jackie, and everyone wanted to be nice to him. If anything, they were scared of him. Victor was the only real gangster in that bunch, everyone else was just a hood or a hustler.

But to Jackie, O.S.N. was an unofficial farm team, extra muscle via Victor whenever he needed it. They controlled one of the most profitable neighborhoods in the city for him and then some. However, out of everyone in that neighborhood and the surrounding area where they dealt drugs and shook down a variety of other crooks on Jackie's behalf, Victor was the only one who he saw enough balls, potential and Italian blood in to possibly move up to the majors one day. Out of everyone in that district, Victor was the only one officially on record with Jackie and his crew, the only one officially on record with the Bonanno mob. Everyone else was just on record with Victor, and that's exactly how Jackie and Victor liked it.

Although, as far as Victor and Bobby went, they had a different bond. Neighborhood ties ran deep, yeah, but it's not every day you go on trial for murder with someone. They were best friends. And while everyone else was out there having a good time, being fools, trying to stunt and get laid, Bobby and Victor just chilled on the side. Sitting down and having a drink, enjoying their freedom.

"The first night I was back," Bobby said, "I woke up like 2 or 3 hours after I went to sleep. I didn't know where I was. I thought I was still in jail for a second."

"Same thing happened to me. I think that happens to just about everyone. I know it happened to Leto."

"Yeah. This place is nice, though."

"It is."

"I know. Reminds me of this guy in Dannemora I was friendly with, some old school black dude doing life. He was an artist, though. He used to paint all these pictures, paintings, whatever. Of houses, mansions, nature, nightclubs too sometimes."

"That's depressing, isn't it?"

"What do you mean?"

"Drawing pictures? Doing life? Of somebody else's life? It's hopeless."

"Yes and no. I'm about to write that guy a letter though, send him some commissary and tell him to mail me somethin'."

"He'd like that."

"Yeah, voice to the outside."

"This is true. Gives him a purpose, I guess."

"That's what he told me, shit was like therapy for him. But now, you know since the other day when we were here this place has me thinkin', let's give one to Jackie or somethin'. He might like it."

"If it's nice, sure. That guy loves free stuff more than anything."

"Who doesn't?"

"You know what?" A light went off in Victor's head. "Fuck it. Tell your guy to send us whatever he's got. We can probably sell it."

"That's not a bad idea. I'm fucking broke right now."

"I told you, Bobby. The offer's there. Matter of fact, it's there more than it was before. I gotta find somebody to put in charge of my collections. Petey's goin' to the Marines in a few weeks."

"So put Mark in there."

"Mark's good for certain things, Bobby." Victor paused. "But for this kind of work? I need someone who scares people."

However, at that moment the waitress, a cute, skinny brunette in black spandex pants and a tight black t-shirt that said *SNAP* written in rhinestones over her c-cups brought two bottles of Grey Goose and some cranberry over to Victor. She smiled. "These are from management." And a nice smile she had. She was pretty, Italian pretty.

So Victor introduced her. "This is Toni-Ann," he said. "Toni-Ann this is my best, oldest, closest friend Bobby. And I think you two should get to know each other."

"Why?" Bobby asked him. "She one of the good ones?"

"No," Victor replied, "because you have a very small penis."

They all laughed. "I have to get back to work," Toni-Ann said.

"You can hang out for a few minutes. I was bein' serious, you two might like each other."

"Putting me on the spot, huh?" Bobby said.

"What do you think I brought you here for?"

"Bobby, your friend's a clown. I have to get back to the kitchen."

"See what I'm talkin' about, Bobby? She knows her place."

"Shut up," Toni-Ann said, harmlessly. "It was very nice to meet you, Bobby. Make sure I see you around."

They exchanged smiles. "I will," Bobby told her. "It was nice meeting you too." As he watched Victor pull out a knot in a rubber band of at least $3,500 and slip her a 20 from it as she left the V.I.P. section.

"I was being for real. You guys might hit it off."

"You never know," Bobby said. "Right now though I'm just trying to figure out what the hell I'm gonna do with my life."

"You already know the answer to that."

Bobby thought about it a second. "You never told me."

"I've told you repeatedly."

"No, I mean you never told me how that guy got this place. I don't think I'd mind spending more time around girls like that."

"What, do you want to be a bartender?"

"What?"

"Either that or a bouncer."

"Not really what I was thinking."

"Then what were you thinking?"

"Something that pays money."

"You could be a bartender. I'll make sure Mark tips you."

"That fat bum never tipped anyone. Seriously though, I don't mean to be nosy or anything, but—"

"Speak your mind."

"How did Ja—how did that guy get this place?"

"Between me and you—and only me and you."

"Of course," Bobby told him.

And the truth was, Victor was happy to confide in him. Other than Jackie, he was the only guy in the world that he was positive would never rat him out. So he told Bobby, "Between me and you, I'm not really sure. But the way I heard it? You remember the Omega Diner?"

"I was actually gonna tell you that we should go by there one of these days. That place was great."

"Fuck that, now it sucks. But between me and you, the way I heard it he was in there one day with some heavy hitter from Brooklyn, this guy Luigi. He's the new Number 3 now. They were in there one day having breakfast and some guy got into an argument with them, over nothing. But he must've done something real disrespectful 'cause Jackie tells Lorenzo who's outside in the car to follow him and see where he lives. Then it turns out the guy just opened a nightclub. So, after Lorenzo gives him the ass kicking of his life and works him over with a baseball bat they take control of this place."

"So, what's the moral of the story?"

"Don't be an asshole. I mean, shit, Jackie didn't even want to repeat whatever he said to Luigi. Told me that old man never heard something so disrespectful in his life. But then they did some digging and found some dirt on this guy and they've owned him ever since."

"Sucks to be him."

"I guess. I mean, I've never seen the numbers but I know this place was making major coin. Not that he's seeing any of it, though. I don't ask too many questions I just show up and drink. Listen to the music."

Which made Bobby think that "It's probably fun to be a DJ. That's gotta be a good job."

"Definitely. Party all night, whores everywhere."

"Just what I was thinking."

"Actually, the guy that's here tonight…"

"What about him?"

"He works for us. Well, for Lorenzo, kind of. But in a way he's with us too."

"Yeah, he's your DJ."

"No, I mean—I don't know, he does some shit with Lorenzo."

"He's good people?"

"He's a fucking asshole."

"Where's he from?"

"Whitestone."

"Typical."

"Yeah, he's a jerk off. It was funny though, me and Jackie ran into him spinning records at a wedding in Philly a few months ago."

"I'm sorry to hear that."

"Why? You had family out there, didn't you?"

"Years ago," Bobby replied. "Haven't really spoken to them since I got convicted, though. *You know.*" And Victor did. He just needed a reminder. It was a sore subject.

So, to quickly change it, he looked at the DJ, and asked Bobby, "Check it out though, you ever meet this guy? I don't really fuck with him like that but from what I'm told he's an earner, big time."

"Working clubs?"

"Working all kinds a shit."

So, Bobby took a look too. Then he told Victor, "Nah," as he watched him spin records in the DJ booth with a group of friends by his side, 15 feet above the crowd. "I never did. I never met him." But, Bobby was enamored, in a way. This guy up there, king of the mountain, living the good life with his crew around him making tons of cash.

And here Bobby was, *some schmuck*, he thought, living off of Victor's charity.

However, when the DJ, Lenny Malco looked towards Victor's section he made eye contact with Bobby and never let go. He was ice-grilling him and Bobby had no idea why. "Yo, Victor, you see this right here?"

"See what?" he asked Bobby. He was distracted by one of the waitresses. So Bobby backhanded his shoulder. He motioned to the DJ booth.

Only to see Lauren Bassi, in a tight black dress, step out from behind Lenny. Followed by Lenny planting a huge, wet kiss on her mouth while staring into Bobby's eyes. Rubbing it in his face.

As his heart sunk into his stomach. His whole world stopped. His ears went deaf.

And then Lauren saw Bobby, and hers did too.

"I gotta go smoke a cigarette," Bobby said to Victor. He just got up and left the V.I.P. section, uneasy.

But Victor knew Bobby better than that. *Bobby doesn't smoke*, he thought. Something wasn't right. He watched him walk towards the exit.

Outside the club though, in the parking lot, Bobby got a Newport from a valet. He lit it up for him. Bobby smoked them in prison when he got stressed.

But inside the club, Lauren tried to stop Lenny from going in Bobby's direction. She got in front of him. So he moved her aside. He could have given a shit.

And outside, as Bobby just stood there, staring into the distance and thinking to himself, reminding himself how much he had fucked up his life, he heard someone ask him, from behind, "What's up, pal? What's goin' on?"

It was Lenny, with two big, tall, mean and white juiceheads behind him. They were steroid freaks. But, Bobby wasn't scared. However, he wasn't trying to beef, either. So he just said, "Can I help you with something?"

"The fuck you doin' over here?" Lenny asked him. "You want somethin'?"

Bobby just looked at him, though. It was almost like he knew just who Bobby was. Like someone else had told him about him.

Again though, Bobby wasn't trying to beef, and as Victor came out of the club to check on things he came up not too far behind Lenny and his goons and watched Bobby say to him, politely, "Just go back to the DJ booth, okay?"

"Pussy."

"*Right*."

But while Bobby was in no mood for this, Victor always was. If you insulted one of his, you insulted him. So, he asked, sternly: "Is there a problem here?"

"The Xanax king himself," Detective Springer said.

"Lenny motherfucking Malco," Giardino replied.

There they were, two Caucasian detectives, 37 and 45 years old, feeling hard because they were allowed to carry guns, sitting in the back of a dark blue undercover Dodge van in the parking lot sipping coffee staking out the club. But now they were watching a show unfold. They were videotaping it.

"Don't you just love it when this happens?" Raymond Springer asked.

"Absolutely," Michael Giardino replied.

Victor wasn't as amused. "'Cause let me tell you something, Lenny. If you've got a problem with *him*, then you've got a problem with *me*. And you don't want that."

As Lauren, standing at the front entrance to the club, didn't want that either, or any of this. She didn't ask for it. So upset, she went back inside.

And so did Lenny. "I'm goin' back to work," he said. He knew better than to screw with one of Jackie's guys. But in a way, he was one of them, too, as far as he knew. However, he heard stories about Victor on the streets. His viciousness spoke volumes. So, he just looked at Bobby, right in the eye, and told him, "You. I'll see you later, *my friend*."

"Then don't think I won't see you too you fucking cocksucker" Victor shot back. "Go stick another fucking needle in your ass."

Lenny gave both of them a dirty look and Victor returned it as he went back inside with his guys. After a moment though, Victor just asked Bobby: "You good?"

Bobby nodded his head.

But Victor had no idea what just happened. So he asked him, not seriously, "What, were you gonna slash this guy's tires?"

"What?" He threw Bobby off with that one.

Victor motioned to the big, brand new, shiny white Cadillac Escalade that was right by them, with the 22 inch chrome rims. "That's him over there."

"That's *his*?" Bobby asked.

"If I remember correctly. Why?"

"How do you know him?"

"I told you."

"No, I mean like what's his deal? He's with you guys?"

"Not really. He's friends with Bert. He pays points, though. He sells work under Lorenzo."

"What kind?"

"Pills, coke. What do you care so much for?"

"Did you see the girl he was with in there? In the DJ booth?"

"I guess. I don't know."

"You didn't recognize her?"

"No. Why?"

"That was Lauren."

"Who the fuck is Lauren?"

"My ex."

"Your ex?"

Bobby nodded.

"Oh, shit. Yeah, I see it now. Talk about a throwback. I thought she looked familiar. I didn't even know. What're they, goin' out?"

"You tell me. How the fuck should I know?"

"Take it easy. The last time I saw her was like over 4 years ago."

Fuck, Bobby thought. "Who the fuck is this guy? Tell me more about him."

"I told you, I don't know him like that."

"Fuck."

Fuck is right. Bobby put a seed in that girl. He loved her. So he asked him, "What do you wanna do here?"

Bobby thought about it for a second. "Forget about it," he said. "That's an old chapter in my life."

And Victor knew it was a lie.

Inside one of the stalls, though, in the ladies bathroom, inside the club—it was a different scene. Lauren was on a toilet, but she wasn't using it. She just sat there. Her head and tissue were in her hands.

And as they drove back to Bayside that night, Bobby just stared out the window. The four of them passed another blunt around, too, but there wasn't much dialogue. Just Bobby staring out into the abyss.

So as they got closer to the neighborhood Fat Mark asked if they wanted to hit up an after-hours spot. But Bell just said to take him home. "It's startin' to rain."

"You're acting like that matters," Mark replied.

"It's goin' on 4 in the morning," Bell said.

"You're acting like you got a job."

"And you're acting like I give a fuck." Bell could be the happiest guy in the world or the worst. When he got tired he got miserable.

But Victor had shit to do too. "I gotta wake up tomorrow," he said.

Already knowing that he was dropping Bobby off last, and a little later, parked outside the gym, he asked him, "You alright?"

"What're you gonna do?" Bobby said.

"I mean, I'll just be honest with you, Brother. You wanna smack this guy then I wanna smack this guy. But from what I understand this guy makes that guy a lot of fucking money. *A lot*. So I can't be causing trouble like that, not if he's with him. Know what I'm sayin'?"

Bobby did.

"But I know this is about more than that."

"Forget it," Bobby said.

"C'mon, all we been through? You don't gotta lie to me, man." Besides, Victor always wanted to know everything about anything that was ever going on. The streets were his livelihood. They were his whole, entire existence.

"That's not what I'm talkin' about," Bobby said.

"Then what are you talkin' about?"

"Your offer. Forget about it. I'm in."

"For work?"

"Yeah. I'm in."

"You sure? Never make a business decision off emotions, Bobby."

"Fuck you. I'm in, all the way," Bobby said as he just looked forward, staring out the front window, with the rain starting to pour over a desolate stretch of Francis Lewis Boulevard.

"If you don't mind me asking, why? Why now?"

"Why not? I'm 26 and I ain't got shit. I'm broke."

"I'm putting money in your pocket though."

"My man? Since I got out? What has it been, six weeks? What am I, gonna sit here and just live off your charity?"

"I don't look at it like that."

"I feel like a fucking loser."

"You're not."

"Victor I'm 26 years old and I've got nothing to my name but a felony."

Victor sighed. "Alright, then. But, look, I'll swing by the gym tomorrow. Well actually I got somethin' to do tomorrow, but let's talk about it in a couple a days. And if you still want to, if you're *sure*—I mean, we'll find something for you."

"No doubt. Thanks."

"No problem. But, uh, look. You're still gonna look after the property for me, right?"

"I wouldn't leave you hangin'. I would *never* leave you hangin'."

"I know," Victor said. And he watched Bobby get out of the car.

11

The rain was coming down harder now than it was before, a few minutes earlier when Bobby got out of Victor's car. But this wasn't Victor's car and the rain was perfect for these kinds of clandestine meetings.

Because this was a cop car.

Unmarked. A Crown Victoria. And in the front seat, the Caucasian detective asked the snitch in the back, "Anything on the street about Lattimer?"

"The home invasion?" Bert replied.

"Yeah."

"Not much. Nothing I know 100 percent at least."

"So then what do you know that's not 100 percent?"

"Someone told me maybe some kids from Springfield had something to do with that."

"Springfield Boulevard?"

"Yeah. Maybe some of them kids who hang out at that park up there by 73rd, off a Bell. Teenagers, maybe a little older, some graffiti crew. I don't really know though."

The cop marked it down in his notepad.

"Why? What'd *you* hear about it?" Bert asked.

"That it might be connected to those gas station robberies. You hear anything about *those*?"

"With the moolies?"

"Who else?"

"There's always the Puerto Ricans."

12

"So how was your evening?" Michelle asked Victor. She was in a t-shirt and pajama pants.

"I couldn't wait to get home," he replied. In basketball shorts and an undershirt that revealed the tattoos on his shoulders and the O.S.N. letters across his upper back like Bobby's.

The two of them were on the couch, in the dark, her resting her head on his chest with his arm around her as Victor watched TV and Michelle just looked at their son who was fast asleep on the other couch next to them. It was still pouring outside.

"Was he good tonight?" he asked.

"He's an angel. We're so fortunate, Victor."

Victor just looked at her. Then back at the TV.

"He really loves you, you know?"

"Good," Victor said.

"And I love you. I love you, too." She gave him a kiss. Then she went back to cuddling.

13

At the apartment where Lauren was staying though, in her bedroom, still in her dress, it wasn't the same. But it was neat. No children's toys, just white walls and a queen size bed with white sheets and a flower pattern. However, sleep wasn't on her mind.

The closet was. She opened the door to it and reached up to the top shelf where she kept her shoes. There were a lot of them, all stacked in shoeboxes. But she pulled one of them down off the top and lied on her bed with it.

And she opened it.

And she just smiled.

It was full of letters and pictures of her and Bobby.

Some memories never die.

14

Not to mention, some minds never stop scheming.

Greed, jealously, those things will destroy you. Now, if you're lucky blood and loyalty might save you, but the darkness within will tear someone or something apart. Not that Bert cared, though. He needed money, and revenge, more than he thought.

So, he sat there. In his car. An old, dark blue, early 90s Jaguar 4-door. Parked on a small, narrow side street in Whitestone, waiting for someone to show up. Hoping he'd get there before the sun came up.

Then, after about 20 minutes, Lenny pulled up from the opposite direction in his Escalade. He lowered his window.

After which Bert reached out of his own and passed him a small, folded piece of paper through it.

Lenny opened it up and looked at it:

Green Rock Motel – Friday – 7:30.

"You see the time on there?" Bert asked him.

Lenny nodded.

"Then don't be late." And Bert drove off.

15

"It all depends," Victor said as they walked up the street. They being him and Bobby, walking up Bell Boulevard just above 36th Avenue on a sunny Tuesday morning. "It depends on what you wanna do."

"I mean, I think I'm entitled to a little somethin'. To an opportunity to earn, know what I'm sayin'?"

"Absolutely."

"Me and you, we stood up for the entire crew, for the entire neighborhood, really. O.S.N. and all."

"Got that right. But since you're gonna to be with me, whatever you do, it's all gotta get cleared with Jackie first, anything big at least. We gotta keep it organized."

"Like what?"

"Like it depends. You wanna sell weed or anything like that I don't give a fuck. That's on you. But you gotta get the product from us."

"Who specifically?"

"From me, directly. I mean, if you were anybody else I'd send you to one of my guys, know what I'm sayin'? I'd send you to Mark, he's in charge of that. But you, you can do whatever you want. Sell coke for all I care. And you wanna do that, then I'll put you with Leto. Bayside's a fucking goldmine, all the fiends around here."

"I'm good on that."

"I figured. You know, I just make sure that any distributors around here, anybody doing anything illegal around here, they wanna stay in business, then they gotta buy it from us or give a piece to us, directly or indirectly. But with you, it's different," Victor said, as they stopped at the street corner on 37th. "Look, I already spoke to Jackie. Matter of fact he spoke to me, and the thing is, if you're motivated, if you're ready, and if you really want—he'll put you on record with the crew, full time. His crew, not mine."

"He'd do that for me? I figured I'd just be with you."

"I mean, we did both work for him as teenagers."

"I wasn't sure that delivering pies counted."

"Well it wasn't just that. There was collection and gambling money being delivered also."

"Yeah, but still. You dropped out after the 9th grade. It was different for you. To me it was just a way to make some pocket change."

"Look, all I'm sayin' is that Jackie likes you. I mean, you had the balls to eat a murder charge. And that means somethin'. At 20 years old? It says somethin'. It impressed him. And forget that Halloween bullshit."

"He did do time with both our fathers."

"Exactly. You know how much dope they were movin' back in the day?"

"Not like we got anything to show for it."

"Yeah, no shit. We should be on a fucking island somewhere."

"Tell me about it."

"Whatever. Can't get stuck in the past. But regardless of all that, back to my point to begin with. You're not just another hooligan from the neighborhood to him, Bobby. Not to mention with Nicky and Charlie White in the Feds the dugout's feeling a little empty right now anyway."

"I just don't wanna catch a RICO charge, you feel me?"

"Well that's part of the game, man. But if you're quiet, just trying to make a little money, do collections, you should stay off the radar."

"I told you, Victor, I'm just tryin' to stack enough cash to start a new life."

"I know. So maybe then just stay with me and let me deal with Jackie."

"I figured."

"Me too. But sometimes, shit happens. Matter of fact shit always happens. So it all comes down to how deep do you wanna play it?"

"What are my options?"

"How much time are you willing to do?"

"What kind of question is that?"

"A good one, 'cause if you wanna take bets, or run shy, or card games, install some poker machines, whatever, you could start making some good money real quick if you're smart. Gambling is big business, Bobby. That's Jackie's business. You know that. He's got it on smash. But chances are if you start making money you might have to do another bid. But then again, if you got that cash waiting for you when you get out? Not such a bad idea."

"As long as that cash doesn't get swallowed up by the lawyers so they can *get* me out."

"It could be worse."

"Then what are my other options?"

"Sell cars. We got a hook at a dealership."

"That how you got the 540?"

"I would've had the 540 regardless. But now that I'm making more money on paper I'm thinking of getting maybe a Benz next time. It's more my style."

Bobby thought about it. "What the fuck am I gonna do selling cars? Give me somethin' else."

"Somethin' that requires you to work a 9 to 5?"

"I already got a 9 to 5. I work at a gym."

"Bobby, you read a magazine at a front desk from 12 to 6."

"Just let me have my moment, alright?"

"Look, we're simple guys, Bobby. Jackie doesn't want anything crazy goin' on, nothing that's gonna attract any attention, not around here at least."

"I hear that."

"But you wanna come in with me, my suggestion, just pick one of the basics and focus. Gambling, shy or pot. Treat it like a business."

"I got you."

"I know. But get this. If you find anybody that's not paying points that should be paying points?"

"Extort him?"

"Fuck yeah, extort him," Victor cracked. "Extort his guts out. But honestly until you get enough doe to put it into something legit, you can make so much cash from those things alone there's no need to do anything else. Ever since those Irish assholes got knocked a few years ago we've had everything on lock."

"Hence why Jackie wants to keep it quiet around here?"

"Exactly. This isn't Bensonhurst, it's Bayside."

"And the surrounding areas."

"Yeah, but down here, Bayside, at the headquarters, his and mine, there's no need to make it loud. I mean, it does get loud sometimes, but let the other assholes make it loud while we stack paper. This place is a goldmine, it's been like that for years."

"Especially with all the fucking Jews around here."

"Exactly, these people gamble their lives away. But if you wanna do your own thing someplace else go for it, same as if you wanna do something legit. I'll help you out however I can. You know that. But the thing is though, you wanna make street money? You wanna stack some samoleens? Then you're gonna need someone watching your back, and that's where we come in. So fuck it. You wanna deal ecstasy? Coke? Vicodin? I don't give a fuck. I mean, dope's not an option anymore ever since that Blue Thunder bust, but other than that? I don't give a fuck. Just make sure that whatever you do, whatever you do, you just treat it like a business. Pimp hoes for all I care. But you start making street money you're gonna need to pay someone and it wouldn't be good for you if it wasn't us."

"All I need is one big score."

"So put a crew together. Rob a bank. Maybe you'll get real rich real quick. But that cowboy shit though, Jackie's trying to stay out of jail and so am I so don't take any scores in this zip code. And that includes burglaries and all that, Jackie's orders. We figure the neighbors stay safe, they keep us safe. One hand washes the other. You feel me?"

"I do. But what if I had a line on something really good?"

"Well I never say never but you start taking scores eventually something's gonna go wrong, so it better be really, really good."

"Well it's not. So tell me more about the pot."

"What about it?"

"You guys growin' it?"

"Nah, we just middle it. But we get political contributions from several people who are."

"Anybody I know?"

"You remember them T.M.R. niggas?"

"Those psychos? How could I forget? I told you I bidded with Smiley in Dannemora, right?"

Victor nodded.

"He used to pass the time by designing customized shanks."

Smiley, Victor thought to himself. "That guy was a nut. I believe it. But a few of those guys who are still around and not dead or in jail for life, the real ones, not the fake ones, they got somethin' goin' on, big time."

"And they're paying you guys?"

"Not exactly, but we've got an arrangement," Victor said as they stopped outside the door to an old dive bar, Winnie's, just past 39th Avenue.

"They're the last people I thought would need protection."

"Well I wouldn't call it that. With them protection is the last thing I would call it. Those guys are nuts, lunatics. I'd never cross them and neither would Jackie or anyone else with a brain. But believe me, they're not the only psychos in this city."

"I hear that," Bobby said. "So where you gettin' your product from?"

Victor paused. "The Bronx."

Bobby smirked. "The Bronx? Why The Bronx? Fucking no-man's-land up there."

"Not even. But you keep this between me and you."

"Of course."

"I'm being serious. Seriously serious."

"I got you."

"Our guys up there, in The Bronx. They're bringin' it down from our guys up in Montreal, Canada. They got that whole city on smash."

"You guys are doin' it like *that*?"

"We're strongest family around right now, Brother. Except for The West Side people, everyone else is in disarray, and various states of it."

"That's what I heard in the joint. I heard a lot in the joint."

"Well let's talk more about that later then."

"Alright," Bobby said. He looked at the door. "This it?"

Victor smiled. "This is it." He held the door open and told him, "After me, my friend." Then walked inside where a handful of degenerates were drinking on that beautiful Tuesday morning.

But one of them, a 31-year-old Jewish asshole named Noah who was sitting on a stool saw Victor and froze. *In fear.*

As Victor smiled. "How you doin', buddy?"

Noah ran for his life towards the back door but Bobby chased him down and threw him onto the floor. Then he grabbed him. They dragged him into the bathroom.

"You think we wouldn't find you?!" Victor screamed. "You don't think I got spies everywhere!?"

"I'm sorry!"

Victor wasn't trying to hear it. He kicked him in his stomach. "The fuck do you think this is!?"

"I'm sorry, Victor. I'll get your money."

"Shut your fucking mouth."

"I'm sorry."

Bobby kicked him too. "He told you to shut your fucking mouth."

And Victor, impressed and surprised, kicked him one, two, three, four more times. He looked at Bobby. "Get him up."

Bobby lifted him off the ground and held him against the wall.

Victor looked at him. "You come back to town, you don't even call first to say hello?"

"I'm sorry, Victor." Noah started crying. "My mother, she's sick. I had to—"

Victor cracked him in his jaw and dropped him. "You think I give a fuck? Get him up."

Bobby pressed him back up against the wall.

"You think I wanna be here? Doing this to *you*?" But the truth was Victor loved it. He loved the power. He was a sick fuck. But all he told him was "This is a disgrace to me. You come back around here, when people know you owe me money, when people know you skipped town, and you don't even call first? How the fuck does that make me look?"

"Bad," Noah cried.

Bobby dropped him with a right hand. "Did he tell you to speak? He told you to shut the fuck up!"

Victor squatted down. "Listen, Noah. My desire in life is not to be here spending it with degenerates like you."

"I'm sorry," Noah cried to him. "I'm sorry."

"Noah, where are you staying right now? Whose couch are you on?"

"I'm at Flappy's," Noah cried.

But Victor already knew that, the bartender who also owed him money called him and told him an hour before. He just wanted to see if Noah would lie to him. "Listen, Noah, you took off with 5 grand of my money. So with interest…" Victor thought about it. Victor stood up. "With interest, and don't get it twisted, I'm just sayin' this 'cause I'm a nice guy, and we're from the same neighborhood and we've known each other a long time and all. We practically grew up together. So with interest, let's call it 7. But with disrespect, let's call it 10."

Victor gave him a swift kick to the gut.

The next few weeks were great. As long as you weren't an asshole or behind on your payments. But Bobby, finally feeling alive again, was having the time of his life. He felt accepted. He felt respect. Or at least, some twisted version of it.

"The thing is," Victor told him, "when you're out there running around out there, you never really know who your friends are."

"You know, most people would think that everyone wanting to be nice to them is a good thing," Bobby replied. "I got a bounce in my step."

Victor agreed. "It's true, most of the time you don't even have to hurt people. I tell ya, sometimes the free shit you get, the treatment, the action, the girls, sometimes it's even better than the money. I love my life."

And love it he did as over the next few weeks he used his connections to hook Bobby up. "If you're gonna be my wingman, if you're gonna be in charge of my collections? If you're gonna be my number 2 you gotta go out there looking decent. You represent me."

"Give me a fucking break," Bobby said.

Sometimes Victor even amused himself. They were at the used car dealership in Great Neck, Long Island. Victor was leasing a black 1996 Pathfinder registered to the gym, *for business purposes*—for Bobby. But Victor told him, as he gave him a brand new pager also, "Listen, while you're out there running around, meeting with custees, whatever—keep your eyes open, for any new opportunities. Somebody needs restaurant linens, business cards, menus, whatever, most likely if I don't got the connect for it Jackie does, or somebody on the crew. So we might as well make a few bucks in the middle too, you feel me?"

Bobby did. Victor was a hustler, straight up. And for Jackie he was a fucking cash machine, he made money everywhere he went. Plus: he was muscle. A shooter *and* an earner. His businesses were booming. But to Bobby, he was a friend. He was a Brother. He was a lifesaver. And after he went with Victor and Lorenzo to a fence in College Point to see some vintage Omega gold watches they went up to Vito's in The Bronx where they got some new suits and wore them out a few nights later to a restaurant in The City. Manhattan.

They went to Da Nico, an upscale Bonanno hangout in Little Italy. After a Broadway show with some former college cheerleaders from Syracuse University Victor knew from when he went up there to sell a few pounds of weed one time. But, the talk, over dinner, of how they met, of how Victor kicked game to one of them from courtside, made Bobby think about Lauren again. However, he was a little more optimistic now because he had some money in his pocket. Not like he was instantly rich or anything, but enough that he could afford to drink a bunch of nice red wine.

When he went to the bathroom to piss it out though, standing there facing the urinal, someone walked in, and then after a moment, said to him from behind, "Bobby?"

Bobby turned his head to look. "Oh, shit." He zipped up and flushed. "What's up, man?" They were about to hug but they didn't because he just had his dick in his hand.

"They let you out?"
"You didn't hear?"
"Nah, what happened?"
"I came around on appeal. They dropped my murder to a manslaughter and gave me time served. That whole case was bullshit."

"Actually, you know what, I think I did hear something about that," J.C. said. He was an old college buddy of Bobby's. "Truth is man I think I fried my brain a little from all the weed I smoked out there. I'm still recovering."

"I hear ya," Bobby said. J.C. was an Irishman from The Bronx and an all-around good guy. But Bobby also remembered selling him weed via Victor that J.C. then resold to various students all over their campus, so he asked him, "What're you up to these days?"

"You know. A little of this, a little of that." J.C. smiled.

"You still pumpin'?"

"I'm paying the bills," J.C. said.

Which got Bobby intrigued.

"But, yo," J.C. asked, "you were from Bayside, right?"

"Still am."

"Nice. I've actually got a place in Little Neck now. I'm by Bayside all the time."

"No shit."

"Yeah."

But Bobby had to ask, "How'd you go from The Bronx to Little Neck?"

"Just wanted a change of pace, I guess."

"I hear that."

Little Neck was another area, a nice one a short trip from Bayside up Northern Boulevard, so Bobby told him, "Well, look, brother. I gotta get back to the table but give me your number, let's link up one of these days. Maybe I could help you out. Maybe we could help each other out. And regardless, let's grab a drink. It's been too long."

"Definitely," J.C. said.

Bobby returned to the table with a smile on his face. Some pep in his step.

But, Victor had to wonder why. "What, did the waiter blow you in the bathroom or something?"

Bobby brushed him off. "The fuck are you talking about?"

"You look happy."

"I am," Bobby said.

As Lorenzo took a bite of his veal. "Why?"

"I think I just spotted an opportunity."

Victor took a sip of his red wine. He found it funny. "So he did blow you."

16

They were in the back room of Ralph's Pizzeria. Jackie was at his desk, Victor was on the other side of it. And Lorenzo, in the cut, on the couch, reading his newspaper looked on as Jackie leaned back in his swivel chair. He told Victor to get him up to date.

Victor smiled. He gave him a thick white envelope.

Jackie peaked at the stack of cash inside of it. Jackie was pleased.

"Everything's going great," Victor said. "I can't complain. Financially, we're killin' 'em."

"I can see that."

"So can my crooked accountant."

Jackie nodded. "Which is why I have another question."

"Anything."

"Your boy, the homecoming king. I can assume everything's going good over there?"

"For me, personally? Having him back is great."

"Business-wise, though. How's he performing?"

"Fine as far as I can see. I gave him a shot and he's running with it, plus people are scared of him. I mean he's a nice guy and all but since he's got that murder charge on him? It works out great."

"Look, you got to be careful, Victor." Jackie looked at Lorenzo, who was looking right back. Then Jackie returned his attention to his rising star. "Look, you gotta know. You're smart, so you gotta know, you gotta realize. These kids that are mixed? These mutts? Sometimes—most of the time—they got no country. You understand?"

"I'm his country. He's my Brother."

"So you trust him then? 100 percent?"

"Yeah, don't you?"

"I'm the one asking the questions here."

Victor nodded. He knew it.

"Thing is though, that's not the reason I wanted you in."

Victor got curious. He looked at him: *What's up?*

"He had an issue with that DJ there, at the club that time, right?"

"I saw the whole thing. Bobby didn't do shit, it was all that other prick." Victor looked at Lorenzo: "No offense."

Lorenzo shrugged his shoulders. "None taken."

"That asshole started with him over nothing," Victor said.

"He's dating his girlfriend, Lorenzo tells me. His ex-girlfriend?"

"From what I heard, yeah," Victor said.

"Well then let's just say that your boy there, he's lucky. *Very lucky.*"

"How so?"

"I'm gonna let Renzo fill you in on the details."

Victor looked at him: *Okay*.

"But just remember *this*," Jackie said. "You're one step away from taking a step up. You understand?"

Victor did. He was close to getting made.

"So be smart," Jackie told him. "Keep up the great work, keep up the earn, and keep your fucking nose clean. But whatever you do, like I've always told you, since you were a God-damned baby boy, you be careful who you associate with. You've been like a son to me, Victor, you know that more than anyone. You know that. And your father? He was a brother to me. We came up together, we did time together, we thrived together. We got made together. He was my best friend, my closest comrade. You know that. But you be careful who you associate with, Victor, 'cause if you don't, it won't matter, none of it will. Don't ruin anything for yourself."

"I won't."

"I hope not. It would be a major disappointment."

"I know."

"I hope so. But whatever you do, Victor. You make sure. You make sure that when you see this asshole? You make sure that you give this prick a memory that he *never* fucking forgets."

17

Bobby and J.C. sat at the end of a dive bar on Northern Boulevard. 2 Coronas were in front of them. There were a few people there, but the-have-a-drink-after-work-rush hadn't kicked in yet. It was only 4:00. However, although the bar was a wreck, the surrounding neighborhood, Little Neck, on the edge of Queens near Long Island was a nice area. There were a lot of white people, plenty of Irish. But J.C. assured Bobby that wasn't why he moved there.

"I was just thinking about it, man. Been thinking about it for a while now. We're not getting any younger, you know what I mean? I want to have kids one day. But do I really want to raise them out in The Bronx? Surrounded by madness? I wanted to try something different."

"Do you like it here though?"

"For me, it's alright. I could rock with it. Plus for my girl, her mother lives here too, so it makes her happy that I'm around if she needs someone to help her out."

Shit, Bobby thought. *It must be nice to have a mother.*

He had to stay focused, though. He was trying to finance a new life away from all this, from all the pain and regret. So he figured he'd try to make J.C. happy. "Well this is how I can help *you* out," Bobby said. He opened the small black shopping bag he was carrying that had 8 glass jars in it, each with a gram of a different kind of weed in them.

J.C. carefully inspected and smelled each one. He was impressed. "You know, I'm happy we ran into each other."

"Me too," Bobby said.

"I've been trying to find a new connect."

"And now you're connected."

"I hope so. But that all depends on the price."

"And that all depends on the weight."

"Well, tell me then. Just how much weight can you handle?"

Bobby smiled. He took a sip of his beer. "I can handle whatever weight you need. No homo."

On Cloud 9, *temporarily at least*, Bobby thought, as he left the bar, 3 drinks later. Happy about the way things went. If he could hook a fish like J.C. to start copping pounds from him he would be well on his way.

So, enjoying the early evening breeze, he took a stroll down Northern through the nice neighborhood he was in. He was about to check out an art gallery, he had never been in one before. But next door, was a pet shop. A medium sized one. It caught his eye.

He walked inside, started checking out the fish and the turtle tanks. They even had some snakes, but he didn't really like snakes. Who really does? Then he walked up and down the aisles, checking out the latest gadgets and toys for dogs. *Shit*, he thought. They had more stuff for them than they did for guys like him, when he was in prison.

However, the thing that caught his eye the most wasn't the latest doggie treat. It was the angel in his sights. He couldn't believe it. He looked up to the front of the store and saw Lauren walk in and go right to the cashier. She was in blue scrubs, the kind they wear in hospitals. They had two stuffed shopping bags there waiting for her.

She paid, and thanked the girl at the register. Then she turned around.

Only to find Bobby right there in front of her.

"Hey," he said.

"Hi."

"Long time. How are you?"

"*What are you doing here?*"

"Nothing, I'm just. I wasn't, I wasn't following you."

"Then what? What are you doing here?"

"Relax. I was in the area. I was in the store before you were."

"I have to go, Bobby." She started to walk away.

He got in front of her. "Wait. Give me a minute."

"For what? I have to go."

"Don't."

"I have to."

"Well do you have a phone number at least?"

"No. I don't know. I already told you, I have to go."

"Lauren. It's *me*."

"Then don't make it difficult."

"Please."

"I'm sorry." She turned to the cashier and told her, "Take care, Susan." Then she walked out the door, and left Bobby standing there. Feeling like shit again.

18

Not that her life was any happier, though. She might have been dressed up, in a tight black dress, having dinner at a fancy Italian restaurant with her boyfriend seated across from her and a bottle of Chardonnay seated in between them, but things weren't going as planned.

"I was just trying to be honest with you. I don't even know why I brought it up."

"I do," Lenny said. "'Cause your ex-boyfriend's an asshole."

"Do we have to talk about this?"

"And what the hell was he doing hanging out in a pet shop anyhow? He must miss those black animals from Upstate."

"Jesus Christ, Lenny."

"Jesus Christ my ass."

"You're drunk."

"Fuck you, I'm drunk."

"Nice way to talk to your girlfriend. *Real nice.*"

"Look at you," he said. "Look how upset you're getting over this piece of shit. This fucking piece of fucking dirt that just abandoned you, pregnant with a baby on the way. Left you crying for years on end."

"You don't even know him."

"I know plenty. More than you, believe me."

"And why should I do that? Why should I believe you?"

"'Cause I'm gonna crack his head. I'll put him in a fucking vice."

"Look around. We're in a nice place. Are we really having this conversation?"

"Oh, we definitely are. 'Cause I got news for you."
"What?"
"How do you think he got out of jail? How do you think he got out of jail so early? He started ratting on people and don't you think otherwise."
"I don't even know why I'm with you anymore."
"Then maybe you should go back to the way it was. Go back to that packrat and see how it turns out."
Lauren shook her head. *I can't believe I'm hearing this.* "I don't even know why I got with you to begin with."
"You think your ex was some hero? He was a piece of dirt. Watch what happens when his karma comes around."
But Lauren didn't even want to hear it. Or say it. She just got up, and told him, "Goodbye, Lenny." She put her napkin down on the table, and walked away. Upset.
Whore. Lenny took another sip of his drink.

19

It was scorching outside. The next afternoon Bobby was playing handball at O.S.N. Park, aka the park at P.S. 169 in Bay Terrace, the neighborhood in Bayside where he grew up with Victor.

A couple of guys were on the court, a boom box was playing Wu-tang on the side and Fat Mark, Bell and Leto were sitting next to it enjoying the show as a bunch of younger kids rode around on bicycles and some teenagers played full-court basketball. It was nice. Especially the two 12-year-olds slap-boxing in the corner, they were going at it. In a friendly way, though.

"Growing up? It's a beautiful thing," Bobby said. All sweaty in jean shorts and no shirt, he looked good glistening in the sun. And so did Victor's freshly washed, sparkling BMW when it rolled up outside and parked in between a Lincoln Navigator and a Lexus bubble. The hustlers were there that day. But, all Victor had to do was snap his fingers and they were all out of business.

So, Bobby picked up his undershirt and wiped off his face with it. Rubbed down some of the sweat off his chest too and walked over to Victor who was getting out of the 540.

"Yo, let me holla at you," he told Bobby.

"What's up?" he answered as they walked a few steps down the block.

"Why aren't you smiling? You should be smiling right now."

"Okay." Bobby smiled. "What's up?"

"Get ready to be happy."

"Get ready to get to the point. What do you want?"

"Well, before we get into that, how did that thing go? With your guy?"

"Great. He wants 4 pounds to start off. 2 of the Exotics and 2 of the Lights."

"You trust him?"

"I don't trust anyone."

"I hear *that*."

"Except you."

"I wish I could say the same."

"Asshole. The thing is though, if he's on the money this could be good. He said if things go smooth, at these prices? Next time he might take a lot more."

"*If* he's on the money."

"Obviously. So what were you sayin' before?"

"About what?"

"About me being happy."

"Oh, yeah. Jackie put a green light on somebody."

"He need me to do something for him?"

"Nah, he wants me to handle this one."

"So then I should care *why*?"

"'Cause it's your friend."

"Who?"

"Your *friend*."

"Nigga, tell me who."

"The DJ."

"*What?*"

"Yeah, he fucked up."

"And he wants him dead?"

"No. You crazy? He just wants an example set. At least until we get the money back, figure out what happened."

"What happened?"

"A few things. One—we think he might've took part in Lorenzo's card game getting robbed. We found out yesterday."

Seven guys were around a poker table, all of them white, middle-aged and older. A few others were on the side too, on a couch, next to some trays of food laid out on a dresser inside the fancy, old school motel suite. It was at The Green Rock Motel on Long Island.

The pretty 27-year-old girl behind the bar mixed a few drinks as Lorenzo, hosting the event, looking casual yet dapper came over and asked her, "So how you doin'?"

"Much better than minimum wage," the redhead Rebecca smiled. Lorenzo smiled too. He was trying to bang her. So he pulled a knot out of his pocket and began to peel off a $100 bill for her when:

The front door was kicked open. Three guys in ski masks with guns drawn rushed in and threw the beefy, bloodied kid who was doing security outside onto the carpet.

"Everyone! On the ground!" the ringleader screamed.

As his backup just looked at Lorenzo, who was stunned. But not scared.

They took the knot out of his hand.

"Moron," Bobby said. "He was one of the robbers?"

"Nah. We think he knew about it but didn't stop it. We're pretty positive. We're not sure. Jackie told me to find out for sure."

"Asshole. What an asshole."

"I told you he was from Whitestone, didn't I?"

Bobby smirked. "Friends with Bert too, right?"

Victor smirked also.

"I mean, of all the games to not stop from getting robbed?" Bobby asked.

"I can't lie, the scumbag's got balls. He's not that bright, but he's got balls."

"We'll see about that."

"Yeah. But that's minor, it's not even why I'm here. It's not even really why it's goin' down, not to me at least."

Bobby sighed. "What then?"

"Get this. The day before that?"

"What?"

"He went to someone. He tried to put out a contract to have you worked over with a baseball bat."

"Are you fucking kidding me?"

"Not at all. He went to Jimmy Mackie, Jimmy brought it to Lorenzo and Lorenzo brought it to Jackie and Jackie brought it to me."

"When are we seeing him?"

"The DJ?"

"Yeah."

"There is no we, it's just me. I'm going over there in an hour, to his office."

"I'm not invited?"

"Nah, I already talked to Jackie, he wants you to stay out of it."

"But I'm already part of it."

"Doesn't matter, he wants it to be business not personal. Don't worry about it though, I'll handle it real good."

"You sure?"

"Yeah, but to be honest I don't want you going either."

"What? Why?"

"Why do you think? God forbid the cops got that place surveilled, you just got out, Brother. Don't get caught up in any shit."

"Kind of hypocritical, isn't it?"

"So what? I told you, treat it like a business."

"Whatever."

"Don't worry, I got you. I'll give you a shout out."

"You're crazy."

"And?" Victor asked.

"Whatever."

"Yeah," he said, as he noticed the kids slap-boxing near the handball court. "Check *this* out. Young bucks." Victor went over to them, and told the shorter one, "Kid, come here. Let me show you somethin'. Drop your left a little."

"Fuck you," the brat responded.

Victor smiled. Then he smacked him upside his head. Put him on his ass. "Respect your elders," he told him.

Fat Mark shook his head. "It's a shame," he said to Bell and Leto, sitting on the side.

"What's a shame?" Bell asked, as he watched Victor help the kid up, showed him a proper boxing stance.

"He was gonna be a legend."

"He already is a legend," Leto replied.

20

"Yeah, yeah, yeah, go fuck yaself, alright?" Lenny said into the telephone. "No, fuck that. No. What is it, still 3 to 1 on Cleveland?" He was sitting at his desk, in his small office. The door was open. "What's the line on Philly?" he asked as his intern, Roger Boscowitz, a frail, pimple faced Jewish college kid walked in with his food. A sandwich and a protein shake in a shopping bag from the deli. "You made sure it's Muenster, right?"

"Yes sir, Mr. Malco."

"You checked?"

"Of course."

"Don't let me find out," he said, "'cause I'll smack you just like I did last time."

Roger wasn't happy being bullied.

"Now sit down," Lenny told him. "Go get some plates."

Roger went to the small kitchen for a second, and then came back. He laid them out with some napkins and juice and plastic cups on Lenny's desk, next to a picture of him and Lauren and a set of keys for his Cadillac truck.

"Okay, here's what I want," Lenny said, into the phone again. "Give me, no, I don't care. Give me 2,500 on Philly and 3 on Cleveland. Yeah, 3 thousand."

Then Lenny heard the bell chime. The front door opened. He looked up and saw Victor standing there, in the small reception area, in front of the sign that said *Sharper Soundz*.

"John, I'll call you back," Lenny said. He hung up.

As Victor swaggered right into Lenny's office.

"Can I help you with something?" Lenny asked.

"No," Victor replied. He pulled a nigger beater out of his back pocket, whipped it open and smacked him across the face with it, knocking him out of his seat onto the floor.

"So you don't like to look out for your people, huh?"

"What?" Lenny cowered.

"And you like to give orders too. Fucking boss, huh?"

Boom! Pop! Crack!

Victor laced him one, two, three more times in the face and head with the extendable baton as Lenny started gushing blood. Then he looked at Roger: "You. Go to the bathroom."

Roger did, real quick.

Victor squatted down. He grabbed Lenny by his hair: "Let me tell you something you fuck. I ever hear you steal from us again? Next time I'll put a fucking hole in you." Victor paused. He stood up. "And if I ever hear again that you want to hurt my friend? Then the next time I'll fucking kill you."

Boom! Victor smacked him across the head again with the baton and then kicked in his stomach, then stomped on his leg, then stomped on it again, and then stomped on it again, and then kicked him in his chest, and then kicked him in the stomach, and then stomped on his head, and told him, as blood gushed out of it and Lenny cried in pain, "What's that, do I hear a little girl crying? Is that a little girl? What happened to the tough guy from the parking lot?"

Boom! Whap! Victor smacked him across the face again with the nigger beater and then smacked him a second time with it, and then stomped on his left hand, and then stomped on his arm, and then like a professional NFL field goal kicker, he backed up for a second, braced himself, and then—

Paused. He caught his breath. Victor took a moment to reflect.

He stood there over his prey, blood splattered all over the place. Lenny was in another decade. Victor though, he had the rage of a lion in his eyes.

Until they moved to the car keys on Lenny's desk, then panned to the picture of Lenny and Lauren next to them.

Victor picked up the keys, dangled them in his hand for a second. He looked at them. Then he dangled them some more, and put them in his pocket. Then he looked at the picture again. He turned it down on its face.

"Don't ever fuck with my Family again," Victor said.

As Lenny moaned in pain, in the fetal position. He tried to cover his face, but couldn't.

So Victor smiled. Then he kicked him in his balls.

21

"Here you go, pal," J.C. told Bobby, handing him an envelope stuffed with cash.

They were in a parking garage, sitting in an old, beat up Mazda from 1985. It was a hoopty. The thing was though, Bobby, sitting in the driver's seat, wanted to take the Escalade the guys took from Lenny, punishment for not stopping the card game robbery. Because you know, Bobby wanted to make a good impression and all.

But Victor wouldn't let it happen. "What are you, stupid?"

"What?"

"What do you mean *what*? You'll make a retarded fucking impression. You're gonna get popped by the Feds."

"Whatever," Bobby said, acting more nonchalant than he really was.

But Victor had told him, "No matter what, never have the money and the bud in the same place."

So after Bobby counted it, he radioed Fat Mark on a walkie-talkie and Fat Mark drove from the other side of the parking garage, on a separate floor, in another hoopty, a blue 1984 Buick 4-door. He pulled up next to a guy just standing around who hopped in, picked up the book bag in the front seat with the pounds in it and got dropped off by Mark on a floor below.

Before he got out of the car though, J.C. told Bobby that "You know what; you know who I saw the other day, after I left the bar?"

"Who?" Bobby asked.

"Your chick. What was her name?"

"Who?"

"Your girlfriend. Ex-girlfriend, whatever, from college."

"You talking about Lauren?"

"Yeah, that was her name. How's she doing?"

"You tell me. Where'd you see her?"

"At the vet."

"At the what?"

"The veterinarian, at Bell and Northern."

"What'd you go *there* for?"

"I didn't, I stopped at the Blockbuster next door. I think I seen her through the window though when I was leaving. I'm pretty sure it was her."

"What was she wearing?"

"Scrubs. You know like they wear at the hospital, animal hospitals, and all that. You still talk to her?"

"Here and there."

"It looked like she worked there. She was carrying in shopping bags or something."

Interesting, Bobby thought.

22

It felt good having a couple of dollars in his pocket. It always felt good, even if it wasn't his. It was a couple of days later and Bobby was walking down the street in Flushing to go see Jimmy, on a sunny afternoon.

"Bobby, my friend," he told him as they shook hands. "What can I get you?"

"The usual."

"Coming right up," Jimmy said, as he put two shish kabob sandwiches into a brown paper bag that already had $500 in cash in it. "You want something to drink with that? Some water? Soda maybe?"

"I'm alright."

"You sure? You don't want something?"

"I'm alright," Bobby said as he pet his German Shepherd/Boxer dog, just stared at it for a second. "But let me ask you a question, though."

"Of course, anything."

"Where do you find a dog like this? Where can I get one?"

"Ah, Bobby," Jimmy said, with a proud smile. "My friend has them. He's Greek."

23

Detectives Springer and Giardino walked into the hospital room. It was early in the morning when they found him there, watching TV in his bed, all patched up. His right leg elevated, his left arm still in a sling with his left hand in a brace and his head and ribs wrapped in bandages. His face the right amount of black and blue.

"So what are you gonna spin today, DJ?" Springer asked him.

But Lenny didn't respond. He just looked at them, without moving his neck, which was in a cervical collar.

So Giardino let him know how he felt: "It seems like you're making all the right moves, Malco."

Then Springer chimed back in: "Don't let this be your last move."

24

This feels strange, Bobby thought to himself. *But in a good way.* He was a little nervous but had no intention not to go through with it. He had come way too far, been through way too much.

So, he looked into the rearview, and he told Benny, the 2-year-old in the back, lying on a pile of towels with the back seat folded down, "Don't fuck this up for me." But the dog just stared at him as they cruised down Northern Blvd.

And when he pulled into the parking lot, Bobby stopped, parked, and turned his head to the back and stared at the dog also. He rubbed its head. He rubbed its face. Bobby had to catch his breath.

When he finally did, he walked into the reception area with the well-behaved dog on a leash. Meaning that Benny didn't go crazy when he saw all the animals in there. Instead he just loyally accompanied Bobby as he went right up to the cute redhead behind the counter, and asked her, "How's it going?"

"Not bad." She smiled. She found him handsome. "And how's it going with you?"

"Ah, I'd complain," Bobby said. "But only my dog would listen."

It made her smile again. Now she found him funny on top of it. Bobby looked nice that day in khaki slacks and a short sleeved blue polo shirt. Nice brown shoes and belt wearing his vintage gold Omega, dressed for success.

"What can I do for you?"

"Well, I've got this dog here," he said.

Just as Lauren, in her light blue scrubs walked out of the back with a stack of papers in her hands, looking down at them. But then she looked up. And she had no idea what to think. They just made eye contact.

But then she looked down, at the cute dog.

It totally threw her off.

"So what have you been up to?" Bobby asked.

He was sitting with Lauren at one of the outdoor tables at the Raza Café, a few blocks from the animal hospital. They were having lunch, and so was Benny, sitting next to the table eating some plain chicken and rice the waitress got together for him.

"Just working, really," Lauren responded. "I came back to Queens the end of last year. Right before the holidays."

"From Europe?"

"Yeah, Florence."

"How was it?"

"Florence?"

"Yeah."

"It was beautiful. You've gotta go sometime. It was beautiful."

"Maybe one day."

"No, really, you've really gotta go. I mean that. I can't express it enough."

"Well, show me the pictures sometime."

Lauren smirked.

"So where are you now?" Bobby asked. "Back over there in Fresh Meadows?" It was another neighborhood not too far from them, the one where Lauren grew up.

She nodded. "With my sister."

"Lisa? How is she?"

"She's good. She's letting me stay at her place till I get on my feet. Europe was expensive."

"That's what they tell me."

"Yup." Lauren sighed.

"But, so, what then? Are you still going to vet school?"

"It doesn't look like it. I still want to do something with animals, though."

"Like what?"

"I'm not sure. But my friend and I, we were talking about maybe opening up a shelter for dogs or something, a non-profit. You know, like a dog adoption agency or something. We're not sure yet."

"Well, that's good. It is."

"Thank you."

"I mean it. I mean I'm happy to see that you're pursuing what you always wanted to do. Doing something good in the world," Bobby said as he scratched Benny's back.

But Lauren just paused. "I don't believe you."

"What are you talking about?"

"I don't believe *this*."

"What?"

"Why did you buy a dog?"

"I didn't. It was a gift."

"For all that time that I knew you, all you did was remind me of your allergies."

"I took some pills."

"I bet you did," she said as she drank a glass of water.

"In all honesty, Lauren. There's nothing better to desensitize you than six years of smelling the sweat drip off your roommate's balls."

Lauren laughed, hard. The water came out of her nose. "That's disgusting."

Bobby smiled. "You just pictured it in your mind, didn't you?"

"No, but now I just did. Thanks for that."

And then Bobby just looked at her: "That was nice."

"What was nice?"

"Seeing you smile again."

Lauren wasn't sure what to say. She just looked at him cynically. "So, what's up? What are you doing now that you're out?"

"In regards to what?"

"Job-wise. What are you doing with yourself?"

"I'm working at a gym."

"I heard."

"What'd you hear?"

"You're working at that place on Francis Lewis, right?"

"Yeah."

"And that's Victor's place, right?"

"What are you getting at?"

About to say something, she stopped herself. She just looked away. As a teenaged couple walked by them, holding hands, smiling and laughing. Smitten. *Clearly in love.*

"Why didn't you call me?" she asked. "Why didn't you talk to me? I never heard a word from you and now you just show up out of nowhere."

"Whatever you have to say Lauren, just let it out."

"*Whatever I have to say?* I wrote you letters, for years. Did you even read them?"

"Honestly—I couldn't."

"Well forget it then. I can't do this, Bobby. Have a nice life." She got up to leave.

But Bobby did also, and so did Benny, wagging his tail, sniffing her leg.

"Don't go," he told her.

"I have to get back to work."

"Give me another chance. Let me explain."

She thought about it. She looked at the dog, who looked right back at her, the way all puppies do. So reluctantly, she sat back down.

And he followed.

"You killed me, Bobby."

"Lauren."

"Inside. You killed me *inside*, Bobby. Every night I died wondering what was happening to you. Wondering how *you* were. Wondering if you were even still alive."

"You don't understand."

"Then make me." Her eyes got watery. "Because you dropped me like I was never anything to you."

"I had to survive."

"And you think I didn't? I felt like shit for so long, Bobby. And just when I'm over it, here you are showing up like everything's perfect."

"Then maybe you never really were over it."

"So, what then? Why are you coming around? To rub it in my face? You made me feel like such a loser. All my friends looked at me like I was such a loser. I felt like I wasted years of my life with you. Like I wasted—like I wasted *my future* on you. Jesus Christ, *the baby, Bobby.*"

"I'm so sorry, Lauren. I hate seeing you like this. I'm so sorry for ever hurting you. I'm so sorry, Lauren."

"I'm sorry too."

"But I have to be honest with you. What the fuck was I supposed to do? Every fucking day, every day, Lauren. When you were going to the dining hall, I was standing on a prison lunch line. When you were going to the gym, I was doing push-ups in a cell with cockroaches in it. Every day I was wondering if the guy next to me was gonna stick a knife in me and every night I'm wondering if I should sleep with an eye open. I had to survive, Lauren. And maybe I didn't know how to do that."

"Bobby."

"What am I supposed to say? What am I supposed to tell you? My father got bodied when I was six? I had to go to my mother's funeral in handcuffs on a furlough? My whole family turning their back on me, ashamed of me? Those fucking hypocrites? Lauren the whole time you're out there in freedom on a beach somewhere I'm adjusting to life in a cage."

"Bobby."

"Lauren. I'm so sorry that I hurt you. I'm so unbelievably sorry, you have no idea. I wish I could turn back the clock and absorb every ounce of pain you ever felt in your life. But what was I supposed to do? I'm so sorry if I hurt you, Lauren. If I made the wrong decisions. If I didn't handle things the right way. If I let you down. But, when people found out I was in college, and now I'm Upstate in maximum security? Surrounded by murderers and rapists? I was done. I was through. Every day somebody was trying me. Every day I had to prove I wasn't a pussy just to stay alive. I was a target. I'm sorry, Lauren. I'm sorry I shut you out. But I was a kid. I didn't know any better. I was just trying to survive. And trying to think about you at the same time was destroying me."

A tear came down her face. She sniffled. "I'm sorry."

"No, don't be. I was young, and I was young, I was stupid, Lauren. I didn't know what to do. I thought cutting you off, cutting you out was the right thing. For you, not for me. For both of us, really. I thought I was done and I wanted you to enjoy your life instead of spending it worrying about me. But you don't know how much I regret it now, seeing you like this. Knowing I did you wrong."

"I just wanted to hear your voice, to know that you were okay. You were my rock."

Bobby paused. "When you go away, Lauren—when they put you on that bus? You look around, and you realize, there's nobody you can call. There's nobody you can trust. There's nobody that's gonna come help you if you're in trouble. You're on your own. You're alone in there, in the pits of society surrounded by the worst in society. It's scary. Snakes, murderers, rapists. I just want to forget it, Lauren. I want to forget that part of my life ever existed."

"So, what then? Where do we go from here?"

"Honestly, I don't know. It's just, it's just that ever since I got my appeal—I don't know. Things have changed. But this isn't the place for this conversation. I know you got your job and you can't go back there to work there looking like this."

She wiped a tear from her eyes. She sniffled again.

So Bobby tried to make her feel better. "Come by my place one night this week," he said. "I'll cook."

"*Cook?*"

25

"Whatever you want, I got it," Rucker said. With no neck, a short stocky body and a thick Brooklyn accent. "And if you don't see it here, I'll find it."

He escorted Lenny, on crutches, looking very fucked up through a shady, filthy junkyard with rows of useless cars stacked everywhere. Shit-boxes with just a few more miles on each of them left for dead all around the place.

But, one of them caught Lenny's eye. He stopped at a broken down, beat up, rusty brown Oldsmobile Cutlass 4-door with tinted windows. It was from the 80s. *This'll do*, he thought.

26

"Get me the balsamic, there," Bobby said, as rain thumped on the roof with thunder in the background. "I like to give it a little splash while it's on the stove." He was with Lauren in his small kitchen, standing watch as some beautiful chicken and tomatoes sizzled in a pan.

"Where did you learn how to cook?" she asked as she gave him the bottle. "When we were in college I always did the deed."

Bobby smiled. The food smelled banging. "You'd be surprised what you can come up with when you've got no resources and way too much creativity."

"You learned in jail?"

"I learned in prison. For a couple a months I worked in the kitchen," he said as he hit the food with a little vinegar.

"Then why'd you quit?"

"I'm not a quitter."

"So then what happened?"

"I got in trouble."

"This is amazing."

"I know," Bobby said as she tasted his dish.

"No, I mean this is really good."

"I'm aware," Bobby said. "You didn't see that movie? Even locked up, *I* saw that movie."

"What movie?"

"*Donnie Brasco*." And then he explained to her, in his worst Al Pacino accent ever, that the best cooks were men.

Lauren smiled. "I beg to differ. But you definitely get points for this one. In college all you ever volunteered to do was barbecue."

"That wasn't barbecue. That was Adobo."

It wasn't just the seasoning that made the food taste good, though. It was the ambiance, the atmosphere. The one-bedroom apartment wasn't perfect but it was nice.

"I really like what you did with this place."

"It wasn't me. Victor had the whole thing hooked up before I got back."

There was a 50 inch TV, a black leather sofa, a rack with a bunch of bootleg movies that Victor got from some crooked bootlegger he was extorting and the simple yet effective 4-person glass table they were sitting at with a nice bottle of Merlot on it. But she had to ask, "Is he the one who picked out the posters?"

"Actually, no, I got those on Main Street." On the white walls, next to two prison paintings from Bobby's friend Up North and a framed copy of the little league baseball picture of the old Ralph's Pizza team were the one sheets for *Heat*, *Mean Streets* and *Carlito's Way*, Bobby's favorites. The place was a bachelor pad.

However, Lauren told him, "Personally, I think it could use a woman's touch."

"Well then," Bobby said, as he took a sip of his wine. "You can start with the dishes."

But first, after they finished eating, Lauren went to the bathroom. So Bobby, wearing just an undershirt, started doing them on his own.

When she came out though, having brushed her teeth and feeling fresh, she told him, "Stop. I can do it."

"Let's do it together then," he said.

So she grabbed a plate and a sponge. Then she smiled.

And Bobby smiled also.

"What's so funny?" she asked.

"Nothing."

"Something's funny."

Bobby smiled again. "Something sure is."

"What?"

"Nothing. Wanna hear a joke?"

"Sure."

Bobby got serious for a moment. Then he told her, "Women's rights."

Lauren slapped him, across his face.

He smiled as he wiped the detergent off his cheek.

However, she told him, "Tell me another one."
"Okay. Feminism."
But, she didn't laugh. She turned the water off.
She stared into his eyes, and she told him: "Kiss me."
He did. He grabbed her face, and they started making out, passionately.

Bobby lifted her up in his strong arms and placed her on the counter, where they continued. They moaned as their tongues met and she wrapped her legs around his waist. He kissed her on her neck. He breathed on it. He sucked on it. And after a moment, he picked her up again, and they continued necking as he walked her into the dark bedroom and laid her down on her back. The lights were off and they had no desire to turn them on as the thunderstorm outside provided brief flashes of lightning in Bayside that night as he pulled off his wife beater and she began to unzip his jeans.

With her lying on her back, he lifted up her shirt, slowly, kissing her stomach in the process. He unzipped her pants, and told her, "Take your shirt off."

She did.

And he kissed upwards, towards her breasts, and turned her over, onto her stomach. He removed her bra in a single smooth move, kissed up her back, put his mouth on her neck and then pressed himself against her.

He rubbed his body against hers, his front to her rear. And she gladly let him take control.

Because Lauren and Bobby, Bobby and Lauren…
They were meant to be.
They were meant to be together.
However, they didn't just make love that night.
They had the best sex of their lives.

While they eventually climaxed, though—both of them—the storm never did. It poured hard all night long, which only enhanced the mood. They laid there under the covers, under the black sheets on the queen sized bed with a candle lit on each of the black nightstands at its sides, thinking about life. However, lying there in silence, just enjoying that peaceful moment as Bobby held Lauren so comfortably, so securely in his arms, he couldn't hold it in any longer. So he just told her: "I love you."

She paused. She didn't know what to say.

So she just responded: "Prove it."

"I thought I just did."

She smiled. "That was fun."

"I would hope so."

Then, after a moment, she asked him, "What did you do in prison, with no women around?"

"There were a couple, actually. Some of the guards."

"Were they hot?"

"They were linebackers."

She laughed. "I meant what did you do when you had to, you know?"

"Jerk off?"

"I was going to say masturbate."

"Simple. I would tell my cellmate, yo, get the fuck out for a while, I gotta jerk off."

"And he would?"

"It worked both ways. Doing time was all about respect."

"Did you have lotion in there?"

"It was funny, actually. When I was in Elmira? Some Jamaican dude on the tier, some Rasta fuck, that was his hustle. All day long he'd go around trying to sell lotion to people."

"What kind?"

"What kind do you think? There were Bloods whacking off to Coco Butter everywhere."

She laughed again. But then she asked him, seriously, concerned, "How did you get that?" She was talking about the scar through his eyebrow.

"Honestly, I don't know."

"What do you mean?"

"I don't know. I'm not sure. I was having problems in there, me and this guy Bert. We got into a beef with these bikers, Outlaws. They were covered in tattoos. And then like a couple a days later I'm getting a haircut, sitting in the chair, when out of nowhere some psycho Puerto Rican—I mean like, certified, he wasn't a gangster there was just something wrong with him, comes out of nowhere and slashes me with a razor."

"What did you do?"

"I jumped out of the chair and he tried to come at me again with it. I had no idea what was going on I had never even spoken to him before. But we got into it and before you knew it I knocked the blade out of his hand and I stomped the shit out of him. I lost it Lauren I really did. I was just so stressed out and pissed off that I just lost it."

She didn't know what to say. She touched his face. Rubbed her fingers where the scar was. "What happened after? With the bikers?"

"Nothing. After that I got put in solitary and I ended up spending 14 months there. Then I got transferred to Dannemora, another shithole."

"I'm sorry."

"Stop saying that. I already told you."

"I'm sorry."

"You're acting like it was your fault. I told you to stop saying that."

"No. I mean, I'm sorry for saying I'm sorry."

"Oh," Bobby said.

"So tell me."

"What?"

"Where do we go from here, Bobby?"

"I don't know, Lauren. But the only thing I'm positive of in my life, in my entire existence is that I just want to be with you. I don't want to lose you ever again."

"Then you have to stop what you're doing. I can't go through you being in jail again. I won't be able to take it."

"I'm not doing anything crazy. I'm just trying to save a little money, just doing some collections and stuff."

"What do you mean by *and stuff?*"

"I shouldn't talk about it. But I'm not doing anything crazy. I just want to save up enough money to move someplace warm, maybe open up a bar on the beach in the Caribbean."

"But they already have bars on the beach in the Caribbean."

"Then I'll rent jet skis and sell weed to the tourists."

Lauren loved his sense of humor. No one else could make her smile like he could. But she had to ask him, "Where are we going, Bobby? I'm being serious. Where is this heading to? I don't want to get my hopes up anymore or ever again. I have to know."

"Honestly, Lauren? I don't know. But all I can tell you is that, while you're with me, I'm gonna love you."

"Bobby—"

"Listen to me. Shit happens in life, okay? And I don't know what tomorrow's gonna bring, so I don't know where we'll be next year, next month, or even a week from now. But all I do know is that tonight, right now, and every minute I'm with you—I'm gonna love you. I just want to protect you."

She smiled.

"I want to spend the rest of my life with you."

27

Crack! A few days later at Shea Stadium one of The Mets hit one high up, in their direction. The guys told Lauren, Michael and Michelle to get ready.

Bobby and Victor, with Mets jerseys on, stood there ready to try to catch it, barehanded, like the idiot tough guys that they were. But, it flew right over them, and banged off the right field foul pole. Then the baseball fell right back into the stands near where they were sitting and a mob of fans scrambled after it. Except, it rolled right past all of them, and right into Michael's hands.

Victor was beaming. A proud father, he held his kid, holding the ball, up high, over his head. The whole stadium cheered, everyone in it could see them on the big screen. It was the kind of moment a Met fan never forgets.

Once that moment ended, though, as Victor put him down, Michael jumped into Michelle's lap, and Victor shouted out, to everyone who could hear: "That's my kid!"

Bobby and Lauren smiled. In their seats, they held each other's hand. They looked into each other's eyes. Things were looking up.

But Victor, still standing, still on top of the world, stared around at the crowd as Michelle bounced Michael up and down on her lap and told them: "Future Mickey Mantle, ladies and gentlemen!"

With that, their whole section stopped cheering and stared at Victor, in disgust. Lauren didn't understand why, though. So, Bobby whispered in her ear: "Mickey Mantle was a Yankee." And they both cracked up laughing.

After the game they drove home alone in the Pathfinder, just Bobby and Lauren. His hand was on her thigh and one of their favorite songs, *Juicy* by The Notorious B.I.G. played on the radio on Hot 97 when he asked her: "So what do you think? We gonna put some bread in the oven or what?"

"*Some bread in the oven?*"

"What else do you want me to call it?"

"I don't know. A goose in the caboose?"

"What? I think you need to go to joke school."

"Thanks."

"I was being serious, though."

"I know."

"And I'll tell you what—if it's a girl? Which I doubt it will be because I don't think my karma is that bad."

Lauren smirked.

"If it's a girl," Bobby said, "she'll be beautiful like her mother, with those same big, beautiful brown eyes."

"And if it's a boy?"

"If it's a boy I'll make sure he doesn't end up like his old man."

"No."

"No?"

"No. If it's a boy I want him to be just like you."

"How so?"

Lauren smiled at him: "Tall, dark and handsome."

They weren't the only ones in love, though. About a week later Victor took Michelle to the supermarket. Michael came with them also. He always got a kick out of riding around in the shopping cart with his legs dangling out the back. And Michelle, pushing the cart, got a kick out of him too. She always did anytime she saw him enjoy himself.

So Victor, right in the middle of the produce section, seized the moment as Michelle smiled at Michael. He came up behind her, squeezed her around her waist and pressed his hardening brajiole against her ass as he kissed on her neck. He breathed in her ear. "I can't wait to get home."

But she wasn't with it. She pushed him off. "Behave yourself," she said. "We're in public. Set an example for your son."

Then she looked back at Michael with a smile Victor couldn't see and all of a sudden nipples so hard they were about to pop through her shirt.

And when they got to the parking lot, nothing had changed. As Michelle buckled Michael into the car seat, in the back of her brand new shiny white Nissan Maxima, with the tinted windows, Victor again rubbed against her. This time his hands reached around towards her crotch. And as they loaded the groceries, not only did he rub up against her, but he pushed her head down, doggy style, into the trunk.

Michelle loved every minute of it. No one could tear her up like Victor could. Just like in the streets, in the bedroom, he was a boss. He was her alpha alpha male.

But the thing was, that day there in the parking lot, people were watching. Like Lenny Malco, who was in the brown Oldsmobile, 20 cars away.

So when Victor drove her Maxima out of the parking lot, he followed them. With a black baseball cap on his head, his hand still in a brace, and a grin on his face. And revenge on his mind.

28

"This is the plan," Victor told Bobby, Bell, Fat Mark and Leto. "I'm gonna be in the rental, doing lookout and back up. Mark, you're gonna be on the other side of the motel," showing him the location on a map he drew on white computer paper. "You'll be in another rental, keepin' another eye out. Bobby, it's your deal, you're gonna be in the room. You make sure the money's right. You fucking make sure the money's right. And Belly, you're gonna be in the next room, you and Leto, with the product, and the burner. But you two, they're only gonna see your faces if there's drama. You got it?"

Everybody did.

"Questions?"

Nobody had any.

"Good. Just remember, each of us is gonna have a radio, me and Mark and another in the motel rooms, and scanners too just in case. But no matter what, Bell, do not open that door unless you hear the designated knocks. Under no circumstances, if you don't hear 'em, and hear 'em right, do not open that fucking door. But—if you hear 'em wrong? You know what to do. We've done this shit before so let's play it right so we can make sure we can do this again. O.S.N."

To Bobby though, this deal wasn't just about the money. To him, it was also about the camaraderie. Prison life was boring. Prison life was lonely. He missed being in the huddle even more than he missed the action.

Now it was time though, and as J.C. and one of his guys walked into the motel room that afternoon, Bobby put his game face on.

"My bad about the timing, Bobby."

"You were supposed to be here 2 hours ago."

"I wanted to make sure no one was following me. You know how it is."

"Still."

"I did call though, to let you know."

"Whatever," Bobby said. "You got it?"

He did. J.C. pulled a manila envelope out from under his shirt and gave it to him. Then Bobby emptied it on the table and counted the cash that was in it. When he was sure it was right, he knocked three times slow and then two times fast on the door to the adjacent motel room and Bell opened it.

Bobby went in, deposited the cash and came back out with a black duffle bag and put it on the bed. There were 30 pounds of weed in there, high-grade fluff.

"Nice," J.C. said. He looked inside it. Smiled, nodded his approval. "Nice. They're gonna love this stuff."

"So are the bosses," Giardino replied. He was in a minivan with Springer a block away, watching the whole transaction on a mini-TV screen broadcasted from a spy camera J.C. was secretly wearing. J.C. was an informant.

20 minutes later Bobby left with Victor and the cash in a Toyota Camry. Bell and Leto went off with the gun and Fat Mark later on in a Toyota Corolla. Too many people walking out at once was suspicious.

Victor, he went straight to the parking garage where Bobby had the jeep parked. He was feeling sick though, queasy. "I think I'm comin' down with something," Victor said. He had a migraine.

So Bobby asked him, "You want me to drop you at home?"

"Fuck that. Take me to Ralph's. We're late as it is."

"Fucking Giuliani," Greg said.

"What now?" Jackie asked, sitting at his desk, eating a pastrami sandwich, while Greg read the newspaper, the *New York Post* on the couch in the corner.

"We should a whacked this guy when we had a chance."

"So what then? You'd rather have Dinkins?" asked Bert, eating an identical sandwich on the other side of Jackie's desk.

"Of course," Greg said.

"Why?" Bert asked, again. "That lazy fuck? You're telling me you'd want a moolinyan for mayor?"

"Better than a fucking prosecutor for mayor," Jackie told him.

"My point exactly," Greg replied. "In all honesty, I miss Koch, too. And Beame?"

"We lived like fucking kings back then," Jackie said.

"Kings we were," Nino threw in. "This whole Thing." He was at the card table counting money and gambling slips with Lorenzo.

"Seriously, though," Greg said, looking at the newspaper in awe. "I can't believe this."

"What?" Lorenzo asked.

"They're trying to close down Willet's Point again."

"The Iron Triangle," Bert said, fondly. "I bought my first car over there. Bought my first prostitute over there, too."

"Really?" Greg asked.

"Yeah," Bert answered.

"How much did your mother charge you?"

They all laughed while Bert didn't. There was nothing he could do about it though, but not because Greg was a stone gangster. Bert had bodies on him also, but Greg was Italian, and Bert wasn't. Greg was a made guy. Bert just wanted to be a made guy.

Regardless, there they were, just another day in the life, the small yet capable crew commiserating in the back of Ralph's Pizzeria. But as Bert, pissed off, went back to stuffing his face, Jackie looked at his watch. "Where the fuck is this kid?" he asked.

"He needs to learn some respect," Bert replied.

"Then why don't you teach it to him," Greg said. He knew Bert was jealous that Victor was going to get made one day too but he never would.

Jackie though, he just paused, and said: "I don't like tardiness."

The way he saw it, in that paranoid mind of his, if someone wasn't with you they could be plotting against you. Just at that moment though Victor, sick and tired walked through the door carrying a manila envelope and a small black duffel bag.

Bert just looked at him: "You're late."

"And you're a faggot. What's your point?"

They stared at each other as everyone else stared at the two of them. Then Victor told Jackie, "I'm sorry."

"You should be," Bert said.

"You wanna step the fuck outside!?" Victor told Bert as he threw the bag and envelope on the ground.

"Any day, pal," Bert said as he stood up.

"The fuck is wrong with you two?!" Jackie asked. "We're on the same fucking team here. Or did you forget that?"

Neither one of them said anything. They put their heads down. Then Bert sat back down.

"That's what I thought," Jackie said. "You, Victor. Everyone up to date?"

"Fucking Jimmy Neutron at the bakery," he said as he picked the bag and envelope up off the floor, placed them on the desk.

"*Again?*" Jackie asked.

Victor nodded. "I went by there this morning."

"Alright, then. Do what you do best."

"Right now?"

"Fuck it."

"No doubt," Victor replied. "But uh, yo—you mind if I send Bobby instead? I'm feelin' fucking nauseous."

"That's fine," Jackie said.

But to Bert it wasn't.

"That cocksucker."

"What happened?"

"I was about to break that guy's face," Victor said.

"Who?" Bobby asked.

"Bert, that scumbag. He doesn't even know."

"Okay but you're not telling me what for." He was sitting with Victor in the Pathfinder, parked outside the pizzeria on the boulevard.

When Victor started coughing, harshly.

"You alright?" Bobby asked.

Victor though, still coughing, just nodded. "Typical Whitestone jerk-off."

"Dude—you call everyone in Whitestone a typical Whitestone jerk-off."

"'Cause they are, those fucks. Fucking white trash over there, all of them. I hate his guts."

"I told you this years ago. When we were in Elmira that guy was as shady as they came. He was the scum of the scum."

"And what are we, angels?"

"Not at all, but we definitely ain't scum."

Victor agreed. "I feel sick. I'm gonna puke."

"So open the door."

"You crazy? Never disrespect the pizza parlor. Go around the corner."

So Bobby drove around the corner. Victor got out of the car and let it rip. When he regrouped himself though, he asked him, "Come here for a second."

Bobby did. He got out of the car also and they walked a few feet away from it.

"Let me ask you a question," Victor said.

"Sup?"

"If I asked you to help me do a sneak job on Bert? You rolling out with me?"

Bobby smiled, nodded. "Yo—you know I got your back no matter what. If your back is to the wall then mine is right next to it. But this is crazy. Go home and get some rest, Bro. Then if you feel better, this cold kicks, let's go to A.C. this weekend. We did good this week, right? We deserve it."

"Word. You're right. We'll find some nice working girls out there," Victor said.

Then he puked all over Bobby's shoes.

29

That night was no better. Victor woke up at 2 A.M. in a sweat. He took some pills and drank some water. Michelle stared at him next to her in bed hoping everything was okay. But she knew it wasn't.

Down the middle class block, though, Lenny Malco lied in wait. In the Oldsmobile, in a baseball cap, his hand still in a brace just like he had been doing for several days now, just waiting for the right opportunity. He wanted to catch Victor alone.

However, Victor was in no mood to fight anyone. He woke up again sweating. The clock reading 3 A.M., Michelle was nervous as hell. He barely got his face over the toilet before he puked his guts out again.

And Michelle, being the ever-loyal and understanding wife that she was, rubbed his back and did her best to console him. Even if her gut told her it wouldn't do anything.

Victor gagged. He told her, "I have to, I have to go. *The doctor*. Hospital…"

As the words came out, more vomit came out.

Vomit that had blood in it.

Then Lenny got giddy. It was the moment he had been waiting for, *patiently*. Lenny saw the brown garage door open on the front of Victor's building, and as the BMW rolled out, he got ready. Lenny amped himself up. He took a blast of cocaine.

Then watched it cautiously turn down the block, away from him. It was a one way street. But, Lenny didn't immediately follow it. He waited a few moments to make sure there weren't any undercover cops following Victor first, and when he was sure there weren't any, he turned his headlights on. He put the Cutlass into drive.

But, up ahead, the BMW stopped at a stop sign. It just waited there for a second and Lenny, creeping up the block wondered if he'd been made.

He wasn't. The BMW made a slow right and he followed it. To the next stop sign, where it stopped and the brake lights went off. It was parked.

This is my chance, he thought.

So he took off the hat, pulled a ski mask over his face, sped up just enough, lowered his right window and then *jammed* on his brakes right next to the BMW, lifted his 357 revolver and let two shots rip, shattering the 540's driver side window and peeled off like Speed Racer. "Karma, bitch!"

The thing was, though—Victor was in the passenger seat.

30

The sign on the door said Saravano, and outside the room, in the hospital hallway at Booth Memorial near Bobby sat Fat Mark, Bell and the rest of the O.S.N. guys, 6 of the 7 heads who were there that day at the Anchor Motor Inn when he got back from prison, everyone except Petey who had since left for the Marines. Not to mention, Lauren, who was holding Michael over her shoulder, rubbing his back and keeping him calm.

She always wanted to be a mother.

Inside the room, though, it was a different story. Jackie, Lorenzo, Nino and Greg stood around the hospital bed. Even Bert was there too, telling Victor they were going to find the dead man who did this and rip his balls off before shredding them while he watched.

But then, Dr. Cullotta entered. An attractive, tall, 47-year-old redhead with a chart in her hands.

She told everyone they needed to leave.

"Mr. Saravano, I need to speak with you," she said.

Victor nodded, and the guys dispersed into the hallway and closed the door behind them. But Victor, he just stared at the ceiling. With numerous cuts and wounds on the left side of his face and nose from the glass.

And that's when she told him: "Mr. Saravano—Mr. Saravano, I have your results back."

31

"What the hell am I supposed to do here, Jackie? You gotta tell me, what the fuck am I supposed to do?"

It was only a few days later, but already their entire world had changed.

And Jackie, he could only give him the advice he knew that worked: "You got to be a fucking boss, Victor. That's the only answer. The only one that matters. You got to stand the fuck up and fight. Life sucks sometimes but no matter what, you got to stand the fuck up and punch it in the face like a fucking man. Like your fucking father would've. You understand?"

And Victor did, even if he wasn't ready to.

"There's only one choice, that's it," Jackie said. "Be a fucking man's man or be a fucking man's woman. You either get fucked or you do the fucking, you understand?"

Victor nodded that he did, even though he wanted to cry. He wanted to cry tears of vengeance.

"I don't know who did this, Jackie," Victor told him as they stared at the raw body, in the funeral parlor. Before they had applied the makeup to Michelle's blown off face. "But I'm gonna make them hurt. I'm gonna find 'em, Jackie, and I'm gonna make them hurt."

"I know, kid. I know."

And then Bobby hit a speed bump and it woke Victor up.

"My bad," Bobby said as they cruised around in the Pathfinder. "Go back to sleep, you want."

"Nah," Victor said, "I gotta wake up." He was in the middle of a nightmare that he wanted no part of. Partially because he was on a pill binge the last 2 days that messed with his mind.

Normally Victor didn't do drugs like that, not in recent years at least, just a coke sniff here or a weed toke there. But this was different. This got to him. He didn't want to stay home and after the funeral that morning he needed to go out and get some air so Lauren volunteered to babysit for a few days while Victor cruised around with Bobby searching for answers, picking up collections and doling out ass-whoopings to whoever Victor deemed fit.

"I'm gonna find 'em, Bobby," Victor said. "I'm gonna hurt 'em."

But he didn't have to tell Bobby that. The whole time they were driving around the two of them were strapped.

"So somebody wants my fucking head, huh?" Victor said as he stared at his pistol, a black Glock .9 millimeter. "Okay. Okay."

Bobby though, he didn't know what to say. However, he knew going hunting with Victor in this state was a death wish, a suicide mission. All he wanted was a way out of it, but he couldn't let him face this alone. So after the luncheon, after the funeral, he went out with Victor to hit the pavement. Jackie and the team were out there too, searching for answers. After all, they had to wonder—was this just a personal thing? Or was someone coming after the crew as a whole? If so, it affected the entire crime family city wide.

But Bobby, he never left Victor's side.

It wasn't like Victor had ever left *his*.

And then they got a call over their walkie-talkie, from Lorenzo. "Meet up with me, *now*," he said. "At that place, the second one. I'm with that guy."

Bobby's jeep pulled into a parking garage. He parked in a spot, and then Victor got out and walked, but Bobby had no idea where. He stayed put. But all he knew was that he saw Victor check the ammunition in the .38 on his ankle before he got out of the car. Then he put the .9 in his waist, behind him, in plain sight for anybody watching.

Victor didn't give a fuck.

Besides, for all he knew he was about to get whacked. For all he knew it was Jackie himself that set him up. Or Bert. So Bobby was on guard too. But what Jackie told Victor shocked him.

"You gotta calm the fuck down." He was standing there with Lorenzo when Victor approached.

"How can I do that, Jackie?"

"After what just happened? Kid, I got no idea. You know we're all with you. But that don't mean you go around smacking the daylights out of everyone on your route."

"Right now Jackie I don't even give a fuck."

"Well you better give a fuck, because what you do, how you carry yourself? It don't just represent you, it represents *us*. Look, you need time off, I already told you, go take a vacation with your son, lay up in the safe house, do whatever you got to do to clear your head."

"Jackie the only way I don't think about it is to go out there and hit the concrete, I gotta find this fuck."

"Then do what you gotta do, but that doesn't give you a pass to start smacking around everybody in the borough. I got reports that you cracked 7 different heads in the last 2 days, and those are just the ones I know about. You put Jose in the hospital?"

"He came out his face to me."

"For some reason I don't believe that. But regardless, you tell me, how's he gonna work for us with a broken fucking cheek bone?"

"It's a long story."

"I don't give a fuck, and when things calm down you're gonna go to him and make that right. But for now, lay off the fucking drugs. You don't want to take a vacation, fine, but then get your head back in the fucking game. Because if you don't you might not just get yourself arrested, you're gonna get yourself shot. You understand?"

"Drive," Victor told Bobby.

"What did he say?" Bobby asked.

"I told you to fucking drive. Let's get the fuck outta here."

Bobby didn't like Victor talking to him like that but given the circumstances he just ignored it. He put the jeep into gear and went towards the exit of the garage.

"How many pick-ups we got left today?" Victor asked.

"It's Tuesday, just three."

"Who?"

"Fish, Shandeep and Robert at the pawnshop."

Victor shook his head. *Shandeep.* "That dirty fucking turban. Go to Robert first."

They pulled out of the garage.

When they got to the pawnshop, Bobby parked right outside at the curb on Springfield Blvd., off the Long Island Expressway. He unbuckled his seat belt and was about to open the door but Victor stopped him.

"I got this one," he said. Then he got out and walked inside like nothing was wrong. Bobby didn't really think much of it either, until he looked to his right and saw Victor pistol whip Puerto Rican Robert right in the middle of the business. There was no one else there at the time but Bobby figured if there was Victor would have smacked him anyway.

Then Victor got back in the Pathfinder all nonchalant like nothing happened. He put the envelope Robert gave him in the glove compartment and told Bobby, "Let's go see Shandeep."

So Bobby put the jeep into gear and drove off as he asked him, "You think we should ring Mark or Bell or any of them? Have a few more boots with us in case we catch any drama? They offered."

"Fuck that," Victor said. "The only person I drop bodies with is you."

While Bobby was flattered though, pulling a trigger was the last thing he wanted to do today, or ever again. *I promised her,* he thought.

"Bobby, it's gone too far. You have to get out of this, now."

"I hear that, baby. But, Michelle? Jesus, what am I supposed to do? I can't leave him. I want out as much as you do but I can't leave him."

"I know, Bobby," Lauren said.

"He's my Brother."

"I know. Just get home safe. Don't do anything, promise me."

"I'm tryin', baby. I am."

"*Promise me*," she said.

Bobby's mind was in another place. He just wanted to escape but he couldn't.

Victor though, he was on a separate planet. "You really think I'd bury somebody without you? With somebody else?"

"How the fuck should I know?" Bobby replied.

"That's like cheating," Victor said. "You can't trust *nobody* no more." And for the next few miles they drove in silence. No talk, no radio, no nothing. Just them and their surroundings. Just them and their emotions. Just them, just each other.

And that's when Victor recalled, "You know, it's the little things that count. That's what Jackie always told me. The little things tell who a guy is. Where he comes from. Who raised him."

"Jackie also said the guy who doesn't wear a seat belt doesn't wear a condom. You should put one on."

But Victor could have cared less, especially now, and up ahead after they pulled into Shandeep's Gulf Gas Station, Bobby went inside, passed the 1994 dark green Honda Accord with tinted windows idling at a pump and the black hoods out front like ghetto bodyguards in matching light blue jeans and black t-shirts and baseball caps who Victor just wanted to abuse and kick the shit out of for no other reason than they were there.

He just didn't give a fuck. So he lowered the window a little and just stared at them—at the bigger one in particular. While the smaller one was skinny, this guy was huge, tall and jacked, at least 6'5". But when he didn't back down, and stared right back, Victor lowered the window all the way to the bottom, and asked him:

"You got staring problems?"

And when he didn't respond, Victor hopped out of the jeep like it was normal and got right in the behemoth's face: "I asked you a fucking question."

Which made Kareem eye Victor up and down: even though he wasn't scared, he could tell Victor was for real, so he tried to diffuse the situation by asking back, all friendly-like, "Man, where you from, dog?"

Boom. Victor cracked him dead in his face with a thunderous right hand and sent this massive giant crashing through the glass door behind him. Then he turned to the short, skinny one next to him and told him to "Get the fuck out of my neighborhood!" and blasted him with a lightning fast 2-piece that put him on the floor also.

Inside the Honda though, where there was a red bandana wrapped around stick shift, the black 23-year-old in the driver's seat also dressed in light blue jeans and a black t-shirt with another black hat on his head desperately tried to radio someone on a walkie-talkie: "Pramal! Get the fuck out here! Now!"

But when he saw Bobby pistol whip Kareem with his revolver and then point it at him on the floor, as Victor stood next to him, the driver got out of the car with a Glock .40 in hand, aimed and sent two slugs through the doorway into the store, one grazing the back of Victor's right arm, who fell forward onto his face.

Which made Bobby shoot right back. One shot in his direction dropped him behind the Honda and sent his hat flying through the air.

Which made the Puerto Rican cashier in the blue Gulf shirt behind the counter pull out another Glock and unload as Bobby dove behind a rack just as Victor pulled the .38 from his own ankle holster and gave the cashier a receipt.

Making sense of what the fuck just happened Bobby tried to gain his composure.

As Victor calmly got up, knelt down, and put his .38 against the side of Kareem's head and squeezed the trigger. He blew his brains out the side of it and told Bobby they needed to leave.

Except while Bobby agreed and ran straight to the car Victor went to the skinny black kid on the floor outside and put one in his head also, then a second one.

And then ran to the jeep, hopped in and didn't even get the door closed before Bobby flew out of the lot, asking him what the fuck was wrong with him.

However, Victor just stared straight ahead. "Go hard, or go home."

The thing was, though—they didn't go hard *enough*.

In the back office inside the gas station, with the door closed, Pramal, 29, another black guy also dressed in light blue jeans and a black t-shirt and baseball hat had Shandeep, 41, the shady Hindu owner hog-tied face down on the floor with his turban on the floor next to him. He was about to start torturing him for the combination to the safe and the location of his stash spot when Bobby and Victor showed up. They knew Shandeep was dirty. They knew the gas station doubled as a numbers spot. Truth be told, though, to him, it wasn't just about the money. Pramal enjoyed torturing people.

But everything that went down inside the store he saw on the secret security camera hidden behind the register which was torture to him unto itself.

Looking at Kareem's lifeless body on the monitor, trying not to freak out, Pramal took the security tape out, and then took his gun out. It was a giant black .45 and Shandeep, on the ground, crying and scared, pleaded for his life.

Which was futile. Pramal pressed the cold steel to the back of his head.

32

Lauren knew something was wrong. She was sitting on Bobby's couch with Benny and Michael that evening, watching TV, and when he got home all she did was wonder what happened to the dress clothes he was wearing. He was in athletic pants and an undershirt. So she went up to him, and then she saw a speckle of blood on his neck. Then she looked into his eyes.

Later that night Lauren lied with him in his bed, under the covers. She was in Bobby's arms as they watched the 10 O'clock news on the 27-inch TV and a mid-30s African American woman spoke live from the gas station.

"Not even one week ago, in what most residents have previously called a tranquil neighborhood, a young mother of a 4-year-old child was shot and killed in a drive-by. And this afternoon, in what police are saying was an armed robbery gone horribly wrong, 4 people, only one of whom worked at this Gulf Gas Station behind me were found shot to death. The owner here, also one of the victims, was even found not just in a pool of blood, but hog-tied. So, I ask you: where are we going, New York City? Where are we headed and what are we doing? Live from Queens, this is Roberta Seagram for"

Lauren turned it off. She had no desire in hearing the end of it. It was depressing. However, when she looked at Bobby, his jaw was still dropped.

Hog tied? What the fuck?

So she asked him: "Did you have something to do with this?"

But he didn't answer.

So she just said to him, "Baby."

Yes?

"You have to leave this life."

"Leave this life and go where?"

"Anywhere, now. You have to get out now, before it's too late."

"I wish it was that simple."

"Well I don't understand what's complicated about it. If you don't go back to jail for another 25 years you're going to end up dead like Michelle."

"And that's exactly why I can't just pick up and go. What do you think this is, Lauren?"

"You tell me, Bobby."

"I can't leave Victor behind. I can't just pack up and go on him. I have to be there for him. I have to help him."

"Then help him by taking him away from all of this. Bring him and Michael with us, I don't care, but if you stay in Queens there's nothing here for you."

"That's not true. My best friend is here, his wife just got murdered right in front of him, he's got a kid, I can't leave them. I can't leave them, Lauren."

"Well then if you stay in Queens then there's nothing here for *us*. There's nothing here for me and you."

"What are you saying?"

"The same way you couldn't talk to me when you were inside? It's the same way I can't get hurt again. I can't."

"Lauren."

"Bobby. We've got some money between us. We've got passports. We could just go, anywhere."

"You don't know what it's like."

"*What it's like?*"

"To be me."

"No, fuck that. That's bullshit. Because you being you is going to leave you in jail again. And you being you is going to leave me dying from heartbreak."

"I can't leave my friend, Lauren."

"Your friend is a psycho."

"Come on, don't say that."

"Don't you get it already? The longer you stay with Victor, the longer your rap sheet's gonna get."

"Lauren."

"You're going to end up rotting in a cell again and next time you're not going to get out."

"Well did I ever tell you how I got out the last time? Did I ever tell you that story?"

"You got your appeal."

"Bullshit. Victor rigged it. Without him I'd still be in a steel fucking box. I owe my life to him, Lauren."

"No."

"Yes. He paid for my lawyers and somehow he even got Dino to change his story, and don't even ask me how because he wouldn't tell me. And then he got me a job and this apartment so I wouldn't be on parole when I got out. I owe him everything, Lauren."

"The only person you owe anything to is yourself."

"I owe him my freedom."

"Bobby, if it wasn't for him you would have never lost your freedom to begin with."

"You don't know that."

"Oh, yes I do. You're from a good family, Bobby, you don't have to be involved in all this."

"My family? What are you talking about, my family? My uncle? My fucking uncle who testified against me? And my cousins? Those assholes? Give me a fucking break, *my family*. Those hypocrites? The minute shit hit the fan they all disowned me. *Oops, sorry, see ya later*. Fuck them. Victor's my family."

Then they heard Benny wake up in the living room, on the couch, on top of it. As Benny jumped off of it, came into Bobby's room and jumped onto the bed with them.

So Bobby told her, as he rubbed his head: "Benny's my family."

"You know you're acting like it isn't the same for me."

"What?"

"Do you really think my father wants me being with a convict?"

"You don't even talk about him."

"Because when I asked him if I could bring you over for dinner he said no. He stopped picking up my calls. As long as I'm back with you he refuses to speak to me."

"Then how come—"

"How come nothing. It's his loss," she said as she sniffled. Lauren wanted to cry but she was fighting back the tears. "If he can't accept the fact that I'm with you, then it's his loss," she said, as she rested her head on his chest.

He held her.

"Don't kill me again, Bobby. Please, don't kill me again."

33

They were at Victor's apartment, two nights later. Lauren was on the floor in the living room, playing with Michael and his toys, his WWF action figures in front of the TV.

Victor though, he grabbed two Coronas from the fridge and went through the sliding glass door onto the small balcony with Bobby to talk. But first he pulled out a pack of Newports and offered one to him.

"I got my girl here," Bobby said.

Victor shrugged his shoulders. He lit one up for himself anyway. He took a pull, and then he asked him, as rain drizzled in the background, "So what's up?"

"What are we doin' out here, man?"

"Stayin' low, at least until the heat dies down. There's cops all over the place."

"That's not what I'm talkin' about."

"Then what are you talkin' about?"

"I'm talkin' about what the fuck is life supposed to be about? This isn't normal. This kind a shit isn't supposed to happen."

"It goes through my mind 24-7, believe me. Mike's still waiting for his mother to come home."

"This feeling in my stomach, I hate it. I was sitting on the couch all day today just waiting for the cops to show up."

Victor blew some smoke in the air and looked off into the night. He thought about it. "Don't worry. If the hammer comes down I'll take the weight for that. Besides, I'll beat it on self-defense; the most they could get is a weapons charge anyway. You read the newspaper; they were a robbery crew from Far Rock. You think the cops or a jury give a fuck about anyone from that shithole? We walked into a fucking ambush."

"You sure about that?"

"What's your point?"

"All I'm saying is don't sleep on it. Or on whoever was behind it."

"And all I'm saying is I don't really give a fuck anymore."

"You've got a kid, Victor. You have to give a fuck."

Victor just blew more smoke in the air.

They both drank their beers.

Then Victor smiled. "So somebody wants my fucking head, huh?"

"Let's get out of here while we still can."

"What are you saying?"

"I'm saying, yo, you've gotta have at least 3 or 4 hundred grand stacked, cash. Take that money and start someplace new. If at least not for you, for your son."

"So you're saying that you want out? You're getting soft on me?"

"I'm saying we still got a chance. Neither one of us is in jail. Neither one of us is dead. Neither one of us has been indicted for multiple homicides."

"My wife just got shot in her face right in front of me. I can't leave, Bobby."

"You've got a son."

"I gotta see this through."

"It's a big world, Victor. Let's go explore it, like little kids again."

"Like little kids? This is all I am, Brother."

"That doesn't mean you can't be more."

"Let me ask you a question. If something happened to me, if I got whacked, anything—would you take care of Michael for me?"

"What kind of question is that?"

"Given the last week? One I need to ask. Somewhere out there there's a bullet with my name on it."

"Yo, Victor, man. Look, you know we're blood. I don't have to mention that. Anything you need, anything you ever need, I will be right here for you no matter what. But that girl right *there*…"

They looked at her playing with Michael.

"I understand your pain, Victor. As much as anyone other than you could. If you need me to ride out with you, I'm there. You need someone to help you drop a few bodies, I'm there. I'm with you all the way and you know that. But I don't know what to do anymore."

"What did she say to you?"

"She told me get out or goodbye, and I don't want to lose her again, Victor. But I ain't tryin' to lose you either."

Victor thought about it. "So get out then. I'm fucked regardless."

"What does that mean?"

"It means you're fired."

"What?"

"It means get the fuck out. Now's your chance and you might not get another one. So it means I want you to take it. I'm in too deep to get out, Bobby. I know way too much. You understand what I'm talkin' about?"

Bobby did.

"I know way too much, about *other* people. About *other* bodies. And if something happens to me, someone's gotta be there for Michael. The way I see it, sooner or later if somebody doesn't put a bullet in my head I'm sure I'll get indicted for one thing or another anyway."

"You don't know that."

"Yes I do. You were gone a long time."

"So then get out while you still can. It's not like you took the oath yet."

"You're obviously not hearing a word I'm saying. Look, guy, take your girl, and go live on a beach with her. Live the dream. Just promise me that if anything happens you'll look after my son."

"Come with us."

"I can't, not right now. But I need you to do one thing for me."

"Anything."

"When are you leaving town?"

"Whenever you let me. But if possible Lauren wants to hop on a plane tomorrow. Maybe not forever but at least for a little while, till things cool down at least."

"Did you tell her about the other day?"

"Of course not, but she's not stupid. I had blood on my neck when I got home."

"So?"

"So she knows something must have happened she just doesn't know what."

"Whatever. Look, before you go, just do the right thing. Go by Jackie's and tell him you're going on a trip. Don't disrespect him by not saying goodbye."

"I won't."

"You better not."

"I'll go by Ralph's tomorrow. You comin' with me?"

"Tomorrow?" Victor shook his head. "I think you should speak to him one on one, do the man thing."

"I feel you."

"I'll let him know you're comin', though. I was actually supposed to help him with some shit tomorrow night but I went by there before to cancel. I'm gonna take Michael to his grandmother's. Great-grandmother's, whatever."

"In Jersey?"

"Yeah, Newark. Thing is though I don't know what time I'll be back tomorrow, but Michael's gonna stay there for a while. I don't want him around here till I know it's safe."

"I hear that."

"So did Jackie," Victor said as he looked at Lauren and Michael again. "But there's one other thing I want you to do for me too."

"Like I said—anything."

Victor paused.

Then he spoke: "Michael was never baptized. I want you and Lauren to be his Godparents."

Bobby thought about it. He wasn't sure what to say. So, he just told him, "In all honesty…"

"What?"

"I kind of thought we already were his Godparents."

Then Victor thought about it also. But, he wasn't sure what to say, either. So, he raised his beer.

And Bobby raised his as well.

They tapped them together.

As Victor looked into his eyes: "To the end, Brother."

34

An end that couldn't come soon enough. Least that's what Lauren thought. An ending to all of this was all she'd been thinking about lately. There were no words for their situation. None she wanted to speak, anyway.

As they drove home that night Bobby and Lauren just listened to the rain drops. And the entire time, they held each other's hand.

Unlike Victor, who had no hand to hold.

As Michael slept in his bed, peacefully, in the spot that used to be Michelle's, he just stared at his son.

Little Pal, he thought. *Little Pal*.

Victor wanted something better in life for him.

Victor wanted him to become a better man than his father was. *My Little Pal*, he thought. *My Little Pal*.

35

"Let me sum it up for you. First we got you on a videotape making three different sales. Then we got you on a search warrant 'cause of what you said on that videotape when you was making those sales. And now," Springer said, with a smile. "Now, we got you on 50,000 Vicodins."

"Not to mention," Giardino said, "26 in cash and two .45s."

"Plus two kilos of cocaine."

"And we were just looking for Xanax."

"So the question is this," Springer told Lenny, who was sitting in an undershirt, with his biceps bulging, and his good hand cuffed to the small table inside the precinct in the steel box that was the interrogation room. With no hat on and assorted scars from Victor across his face. "Are you aware that you're fucked?"

"Blow me," Lenny replied.

"Maybe after you fill this out," Giardino told him as he placed a notepad and pen in front of Lenny. "Maybe after you write your memoirs on here, you'll find somebody Up North to do that for ya."

"Tell us what we wanna know, Lenny," Springer told him. "It's that simple. You do all of us a favor here. You help us out, and maybe, just maybe we help *you* out. Just maybe we let you go home early."

"How early?"

"You wear a wire for us, you go home right now."

"And who exactly do you want me to wear a wire on?"

"Lorenzo Vissi."

"And when do you want me to wear it?"

"As soon as you get out of here."

"Well I can't do it as soon as I get out of here."

"Why not?"

"Because I'm going to see your grandmother as soon as I get out of here."

"You think this is a joke?" Giardino told him. "You sick bastard. What do you think they're going to do to you when they find out all the time you're facing? They know you can't do time, and so do you."

"Who's they?"

"The fucking Jackie Iacone crew, who do you think?"

And think Lenny did. He just stared at them.

36

On a dark, narrow, neighborhood street, Jackie stood there, holding an umbrella, smoking a cigarette and walking his Jack Russell Terrier.

As the man he was waiting for arrived.

"So what the fuck did you call me out here for at 4 in the morning?" Jackie asked.

"A little gratitude would be nice," Special Agent William Ormalis, 43 and white, replied.

Jackie passed him a letter-sized white envelope stuffed with cash. "Get to the point."

"I figured you'd want to know sooner rather than later."

"Know what?"

"Your kids, they got a problem."

"I don't got no kids."

"Yes you do. Drakis, Saravano. Your little gang over there."

Jackie didn't say anything. He just stared at him.

"I got an update from one of my buddies before, from the 109th. He told me they were questioning some moron from a sting tonight, some DJ-slash-drug dealer they had an undercover working with, buying from. Lenny Malco, name ring a bell to you?"

Jackie gave him a nod. *It does.*

"Point being, they raided his stash house, found all kinds of toys."

"Your squad was involved in it?"

Ormalis shook his head. "You would've heard about it."

"Then why do I care?"

"'Cause the next time you see him he'll be wearing a wire."

"I don't deal with him."

"Yeah but he deals with the guys underneath you, right? Lorenzo?"

"And?"

"He says Drakis and Saravano kicked the shit out of him, put him in the hospital, in aid of racketeering. They're coming after your guys hard, and they're coming after your guys soon."

"Feds too?"

"You're covered, you know that. But it turns out there's an NYPD task force whose only goal in life is to dismantle your operations. They got ambitions."

"Who's running it?"

"Ray Springer."

Jackie thought about it. "Why does that name sound familiar to me?"

"He's one of them detectives who took down those Irishmen a few years ago, The New Westies or whatever the fuck they were calling themselves. You better watch out."

"Watch out? Why? *The New Westies?* Those guys weren't Westies. Those guys were morons."

"Yeah but it ain't just that. Here's the ticker. This guy, Springer? His partner now, his running mate, this other clown, Giardino, Mike Giardino. He was on that task force that took down those Giannini fucks out in Ridgewood."

"Baldo's boys?"

"Him too."

Fuck, Jackie thought.

"They're going around trying to wipe out all the satellites, the farm teams, the connected crews all over Queens, and your guys are next. They got a whole chart and everything. But for whatever reason, my friend, for whatever reason they want your guys bad, more than the others. And they think by getting to your guys they'll get to you, to the top guy in the neighborhood. Just like they did in Ridgewood."

"Well which one of my guys do they want the most?"

"Get this—Drakis."

"Drakis? Why?"

"They think he's the weakest link, and the Lenny kid's saying that he was buying product from him, a lot of fucking product from him."

"So? Why does that make him the weakest link?"

"They think he was at that massacre the other day."

"*What?*"

"At the gas station. They're gonna try to flip him."

The cops wanted Bobby to become an informant.

But more importantly, they thought he was weak enough to become an informant.

Not something Jackie was happy to hear.

37

"You know, I gotta tell ya," Jackie said, "I appreciate the respect you're showing me coming down here, you understand?"

"Of course," Bobby replied, in the back room of the pizzeria. It was just the two of them there, around 2 P.M.

"And I also respect *you* for coming down here. In times like this? It takes balls. *Do you fucking understand?*"

"Jackie, I spoke to Victor about it. I told him—"

"Stop," Jackie said. "You don't need to get into it."

"I just don't want you to think—"

"Stop it, I told you. Shut the fuck up. Let me talk."

Okay, Bobby nodded.

"You know, I helped you out."

"And I'm grateful, extremely."

"Motherfucker I even gave you a job. I gave you a good job. You work for Victor, and Victor works for *me*. And *he* needs you. So *we* need you. He's your friend, isn't he? So that makes you my friend, and you're leaving us. You're not being a good friend."

"It ain't me, Jackie. It's my woman."

"You think I give a fuck? I think you're a fucking asshole."

"I'm just gonna be honest with you. I gotta do what's best for *me*, Jackie."

"I can see that. Thing is, though, Victor came down here this morning making his case for you, pleading. Telling me he had to let you go for the simple reason that you never did nothing to him wrong. So even though I don't understand it, I gotta say, you're covered."

"Thank you, Jackie."

"Well, don't thank me just yet."

"What's up?"

"I need a favor. Call it a going away present. You ever wanna come back, that is."

"Whatever I can do for you, I will. You know that."

"Good. Victor was supposed to help me with this thing tonight. I had to let him out of it though, this shit with Michelle and all. So you're gonna fill in for him."

"*Jackie.*"

"What?"

Bobby thought about it. "Alright, what is it?"

"Nothing major. We just need some faces some people don't know. New faces, you understand?"

"You need me to hurt somebody?"

"Nah, nothing like that. I doubt it. But there's this thing going down tonight, this meeting with these Albanians. The Rudaj people, you heard a them?"

Bobby had. "The Corporation." They were the Albanian mob, a gang actively trying to become the city's 6th crime family. They were for real.

"Long story short," Jackie said, "it's a big meeting, they're trying to put a deal together, one that would make us some money indirectly too, but it ain't my crew meeting with them, it's our guys up in The Bronx. But they asked me for a favor, just to have a few faces there so they know not to fuck around. But more importantly, faces they haven't seen before."

"And where do I come in?"

"You don't. You're gonna be a lookout. You're gonna drive my guys up there and then you're gonna sit in the car and wait where Greg tells you and radio them you see anything suspicious. That's it. Easy, right?"

"I guess. Where's this taking place?"

"New Rochelle. But listen to me, and listen closely. You make sure you keep the fuckin' engine running, God forbid. Do you understand?"

"100 percent."

"Good. But you'll be compensated. If the deal goes through we'll give you a couple of bucks just for showing up. Consider it going away money."

"I don't want the money, Jackie."

"You don't?"

"I do this, I'm doing it out of friendship, to you."

The statement made Jackie happy. "There's my boy."

"But I gotta ask—why do you want *me* for this? There's gotta be a thousand other guys who'll work for quick cash."

"But there ain't a thousand other guys I could trust, Bobby. I knew your father, you know?"

38

Bobby walked into the apartment wearing a smile so bright it made her smile too.

"What?" Lauren asked as she boiled some pasta.

"Remember how I said let's leave this weekend? So we had time to say goodbye and all?"

"Yeah, so?"

"What if I told you let's leave tomorrow instead, first thing?"

"What if I told you if you're lying you're a scumbag?"

He wasn't.

"Are you serious?"

"Of course I'm serious, pack a freaking bag already."

"I have to go to my place. I have to get my stuff."

"So do it. We'll send some postcards when we get settled."

"Settled where?" Lauren laughed. "Where are we going?"

"Who cares? All together I've got like 26k stashed away, we'll pick a place at the airport."

"Wait, what? How, where did you get 26k?"

"You don't wanna know."

"Actually, I kind of do." Lauren smiled. "I'm curious."

"Trust me, you don't. But look, I heard Costa Rica's nice."

"Florence, Bobby. Florence."

"Beaches, Lauren. Beaches."

She understood. She smiled.

"There's no better place for freedom," he told her.

"Wherever you wanna go—let's just go."

"It doesn't have to be forever. Let's just go somewhere warm and cheap and warm and cheap for a few and then go from there."

"Let's go."

"We could open a small business or something."

"Let's do it."

"Let's, I already spoke to Victor. He said if we had a business plan to open a bar or a dog groomers or something he'd front us the money to get started."

"*Bobby.*"

"I know, I'm just saying. Options, Lauren."

"We'll be fine. I've been working, we'll be fine."

"Okay. But then there's the dog. What do we do?"

"We're not taking him with us?"

"I mean, shouldn't we get settled first?"

Lauren thought about it. "Well…"

"What?"

"I'm not positive, but I'm pretty sure. I think I've got someone to watch him."

"Who? Lisa? Please don't bring your sister into this."

"Shut up."

"As long as you don't bring your sister into this."

"I'm not. I wouldn't. But, look. I've got a friend, from the vet. I'm sure I could get Benny housing for a few weeks."

"You're sure?"

"Pretty much. He owes me a favor."

"He?"

"Don't worry, he's gay."

"Who said I was worried?"

"Your face said you were worried."

"Whatever. But…"

"But what?"

"Is he gonna put him in a cage? I ain't trying to see this dog go in a cage."

"From what I understand, gay guys prefer closets."

Bobby smirked. "Something's off about this."

"What?"

"I don't know. I don't know about it."

"You don't trust my judgment?"

"I don't trust your friend."

"Bobby."

"Lauren. Look at you. You're beautiful. You're gorgeous. You're everything. How could anyone in their right mind be gay around you?"

She was flattered. "What?" Her heart melted. She couldn't believe he said that. So she wrapped her arms around his neck, she stared into his eyes, and then, she just asked him: "Why are you being so good to me?"

Bobby grabbed her around her waist, and he smiled. "Because, honestly?"

She smiled too. "Yeah?"

"You give the best blowjobs."

39

It was that evening. It was their final goodbye. Although, Bobby didn't want it to be.

"Relax," Victor told him. "I'll meet up with you guys when I get everything straightened out."

They were at the park, at 169, O.S.N. Bobby came by to say peace to some of the guys but he didn't tell them he might never be back, at least not for a couple of years. He just said he was going away for a little while.

But, he had to be honest. "Victor, I don't know."

"About what?"

"I'm torn. I feel like a fucking jerk leaving you out here, especially now."

"Don't," he told him. "If you were a jerk you'd know about it. I'd let you know about it."

"Would you?"

"Of course I would," Victor said. "But the thing is, this life? This life ain't for you. Go live the dream with Lauren on a fucking beach on a fucking deserted island somewhere. 6 years inside, I think you deserve a little sunshine."

"But what if there's a contract on your head? What if something happens to you and I'm not there? I gotta live with that."

"You also gotta live with the fact that what if something happens to you and someone else has to look after Lauren."

"Still."

"Still nothing. I'm the one telling you to go, me and nobody else. 'Cause if something happens to me, Michael's gonna need you."

"I'm sayin', though."

"Just go, Bobby. You're fired, I already told you."

"Then what about tonight?"

"After tonight," he said. "And take this with you."

Victor pulled out a knot of $9,900 from his pocket and gave it to him. All hundreds.

40

It was nearing 10:00 P.M. and nobody was around. Except Bobby, next to his jeep, smoking a cigarette, down at the end of the dead end. Anxiously waiting, checking his watch.

Then Bert pulled up, in his Jaguar. He shut the engine off and when he began to get out Bobby walked up to him and tossed his Newport.

"What are you doing? Let's get outta here already."

"It ain't me, college boy. He's sending Greg and Lorenzo with us too."

"What about Nino?"

"Nino's a bookmaker. You're gonna be the driver while we handle this fucking thing."

"So then where are they?"

"Relax, they're on their way."

"Fine," Bobby said. "And what the hell did he want us to meet all the way over here for anyway?"

"Don't tell me you're the only one who hasn't noticed the heat this past week."

But Bobby was unfocused. He pulled out the pack of Newports and asked Bert, "You want one?"

"I don't smoke."

"Neither do I," Bobby said as he turned the other way towards Bert's car to light another cigarette without the wind interfering.

However, the lighter kept flickering. It was one of the cheap ones that you get for less than a dollar at the store, and after a bunch of tries to get the flame up, just as the Newport caught fire, he lifted his eyes at the Jaguar, and his eyes opened wider than he thought possible. *What the fuck!?*

In the reflection of the window he saw Bert lift a black semi-automatic to the back of his head.

And in an instant Bobby spun around and tackled him, the gun landing in the grass 2 feet away and the cigarette right next to Bert's face.

"What the fuck!?" Bobby said as he wrestled him.

"Fuck you!" Bert told him as Bobby gained control.

Bobby got him pinned down. He was younger and stronger and had much more to lose. "What the fuck, asshole!? I fucking knew it!" Bobby said.

"Fuck you!"

"I'll kill you!"

"Go ahead," Bert said as he struggled, hopelessly. "You're a fucking dead man walking."

"What's that supposed to mean?"

"Figure it out."

"Jackie order this?"

"Your mother ordered it."

My mother? Bobby thought, instantly enraged.

"Where are you?"

"Bobby?" Victor asked, driving. He looked at his cell phone but didn't recognize the number. "Where you callin' me from?"

"I'm at a payphone. Where are you?"
"Why?"
"We need to meet, *now*."

Bobby was seated in his car, constantly checking his mirrors. Then when he saw Victor pull up, in the Maxima, he held the gun in his lap, Bert's gun, tighter. It was pointed towards the driver's side, beneath the window. He was ready to blast someone through the door. As Victor hopped out of his car though, Bobby put it in his waist and did the same.

"Let's go for a walk," he told Victor as they moved a few feet from the jeep.
"What happened?"
"You sure you didn't tell anybody you were coming to see me here?"
"You said not to. What the fuck happened?"
"I got Bert in the car."
"What?" Victor looked at it but didn't see him. "Where? You're supposed to be in New Rochelle."
"I didn't say he was alive."

Bobby popped the glass window on the trunk. Then he rolled back the black leather tarp that covered its belongings. And then Victor saw Bert's bloody, stabbed-up body. Bobby shanked him, did him up, prison style.

"Jesus," Victor said.
"I put out my cigarette in his eye."
"Why?"
"He tried to give me a moon-roof."
Victor smiled. "And you call *me* crazy."
"You are crazy."
"Not as much as you," Victor said.
"I beg to differ."
"Really?"
"Yeah."

"Then why the fuck are you driving around with a body in your trunk?"

"'Cause I didn't wanna leave him in the street."

"And this is better?"

"Of course."

"How?"

"'Cause I wasn't sure how his body popping up would affect you. For all I know you're next on the parade. For all I know Bert's the one who killed Michelle. And for all I know Jackie ordered all of it. So for all I know maybe it's better if maybe he just disappeared."

Which made Victor grateful.

And which also made Victor think.

"Okay, here's what we're gonna do," he said.

"Sup?" Bobby asked.

"We're goin' to Jersey."

"*Jersey?*"

"Now, right now."

"Bro I gotta catch a plane in the morning."

"And you're driving around with a body in your trunk like it's nothing. Look, when I went to Michelle's grandmother's earlier she gave me the keys to her cousin's summer house out there. She wanted me to take Michael out there."

"What part?"

"I don't know, a half hour before Atlantic City. Thing is though her cousin's in Florida."

"So you wanna bury him out there?"

"No, dick. Her cousin likes to fish. He's got a boat."

It was a long drive. Almost 2 hours of constant paranoia. Not so much for Victor, he was in his Maxima, driving the crash car. Bobby though, his whole future, and Lauren's too, depended on him not going more than 5 miles over the speed limit. Those New Jersey Troopers, they hated cars with New York plates.

So Bobby had to concentrate.

The whole way out there, Victor listened to old school rap music, not blasting, just a low level on the radio. While Bobby drove in silence.

And finally, after 1 A.M., they reached their destination. Victor drove down the quiet, old block of one-level vacation homes. Some of them were occupied, some weren't, a few had boats docked in the waterway behind their backyards. Mostly, however, the whole block was asleep. *Thank God.*

Regardless, Victor told Bobby to pull into the gravel driveway while he circled the block again in the Maxima just to make sure nothing stood out. If there was a sting operation or even any dumb drunk white kids who might call attention to them.

There wasn't. So he pulled into the driveway as well, doing his best to block the view from the house next door so there'd be less of a chance of someone seeing them haul a corpse out of the Pathfinder. Then Bobby went inside with Victor to disable the alarm and use the bathroom. They got something to drink and ate some granola bars.

Then they checked out the boat. It was a 27 footer that would get the job done. Victor turned it on and they were both relieved that it had a full tank of gas.

After which they went back to the cars. First, Victor popped the trunk on the Maxima. And then, Bobby asked him, "What the fuck is this?"

"I'm a grown ass man," Victor said, in all seriousness. "I gotta be prepared."

But Bobby just looked at him like he was crazy, even if he was right. In the trunk of Victor's car there were two baseball bats, a bag full of baseball equipment and some chains and padlocks, the kind you use to lock up bicycles with and two 45 pound plates. The Olympic kind you bench-press with.

"How long you been driving around like this for?"

"I don't know, 5 years maybe?"

"In both of your cars?"

"Ever since I started working for Jackie, working for him full time at least."

"He told you to travel like this?"

"Nah. But then one day when he had his guys do a surprise search on my old car they were pleasantly surprised."

"What did he say to you?"

"Nothing, he just laughed," Victor said, as he went into the baseball bag. "If anything he was happy to see I was thinking ahead."

"Sometimes I think you were born in the wrong era."

"Likewise." Victor took two pairs of baseball gloves out of the bag. He gave one to Bobby. "Put these on."

They did. They put the gloves on and took the accessories onto the boat. After which they went to the Pathfinder.

"Here's the fun part," Victor told him. "They teach you the best way to carry a body when you was Up North?"

"Nah," Bobby replied. "But at least once a week I heard a conversation about the best way to dispose of one."

With that, they opened the Pathfinder's trunk, picked up Bert, and smiled at each other as they dropped him onto the gravel.

"Oops," Bobby said.

He laughed. He shut the trunk, and Victor grabbed Bert's legs as Bobby grabbed his upper body and they lugged him onto the vessel in the dark.

However, Victor told Bobby, "Don't get this thing dirty. I'm taking Michael fishing on Saturday."

"You need a Coast Guard license or something for that?"

"Only if you get caught," Victor replied.

They were about 9 miles out and no other boats were in sight. "I think we're good here," Victor told him, as he brought it to a stop. "Let me see what you did." Victor went over to the body that Bobby chained up while he was driving. He inspected it. It was naked and Bert's clothes, money, watch, beeper and keys were piled next to it, as well as his gold necklace.

"Good?" Bobby asked. "You look like you're enjoying the view."

Victor didn't say anything though. He just checked his pockets. He was looking for something but didn't have it on him. "Fuck," he said. "I forgot."

"What?"

"You got a knife on you?"

"Always. Why?"

"Hand it to me."

He did. It was a 3.5 inch blade, the one on his waist that he shanked Bert with.

"Nice," Victor said. Then he squatted down next to Bert's body with it.

"What are you doing?"

"Being professional." Victor began stabbing Bert's corpse over and over again in the chest and gut, all the spots that Bobby missed. A total of 13 times as blood splattered everywhere. Then he stood up, proud of his accomplishment.

"Seriously—what the fuck is wrong with you?" Bobby asked.

"Sometimes the chains get loose."

"How?"

"Who knows? But it happens."

"Then what the fuck does this have to do with anything related to that? You're a sick fuck, you know that?"

"Like I told you, it's called being professional. God forbid the chains get loose, I've now punctured his lungs and stomach. He won't float."

Oh, Bobby thought.

Victor smiled. "You can't be lazy with this kind a shit." He offered the knife to Bobby. "You wanna take it for a spin?"

"I already did take it for a spin."

Victor stared at him: "You said you'd never leave me hanging, Bobby."

Bobby smirked. "Fine." He took the blade from him and squatted down just like Victor did. "Fuck it." He gave him one nice jab to the chest and left the knife standing upright. "Happy?"

"Very," Victor said with a smile.

Then Bobby smiled also, and he told him, "Honestly—I would hate to have beef with you."

"I wish I could say the same," Victor replied.

And they laughed as they threw Bert over the side.

41

No laughter here, though.

Even though she should have been happy.

She was smart enough not to be.

On the floor next to Lauren were two big suitcases. Her purse, a packed book bag and two small duffel bags.

She should have been happy. But Lauren just stared at the clock. She was lying in bed. It was almost 2 A.M. and Bobby wasn't home yet.

She tried to call his cell phone again but it went straight to voicemail. She had a terrible feeling in her gut.

42

"I'm gonna say it again. You guys should really come with us. I don't understand why you won't."

"I already told you, Bobby. I can't leave with loose ends untied."

"Then I gotta be honest with you, *again*. I gotta convince you, 'cause I'm gonna feel like a fucking jerk leaving you behind. I'm gonna feel like a fucking scumbag when I get to the airport."

"Yeah, well, *again*—you're gonna feel like an even bigger scumbag if you lose your girl again," Victor told him as he went through the old kitchen in the old summer house, through the cabinets and refrigerator, looking for food. There wasn't much, just some canned stuff. However, he told Bobby, sitting on the old brown couch from the 1980s, "Look, I'll be fine out here, believe me."

"You don't know that."

"Yes I do," Victor said.

"Karma doesn't have a statute of limitations."

"So what?"

"What if something happens to you and I'm not there? How do I live with myself?"

"You live with yourself by watching after my son, the same way I'd watch after one of yours. But you don't got none. So you live with yourself by then making one of your own and watching them grow up together, like we did. Except you guys'll have the money I'd be leaving behind."

"That's not what I'm talking about."

"Just go, Bobby. This life isn't for you."

"But it's yours?"

"It's the only one I know."

"Is that what you're gonna tell your son when he comes to visit you and you're doing life?"

"Why would I be doing life?"

"What if that shit comes back from the other day? Or what if some other shit comes back? You know God damned well eventually *something* will. Maybe you should take a little breather for a while."

"Then what do I tell Jackie? I just killed 3 or 4 people in a gas station? I gotta lam it for a while? I gotta play it cool, like nothing happened."

"You're crazy."

"Look, Bobby. Go set up shop somewhere, someplace warm. Then when you get settled, maybe in a few weeks I'll come down there and we'll see what's what."

"Whatever," Bobby said.

"Yeah, whatever," Victor replied as he went into the freezer. Where he found some frozen steaks. "How hungry are you?"

A little while later they were eating, on the old couch in front of the old TV, the kind with dials instead of buttons. Some rib eye steaks with brown rice and tomato slices, there wasn't much else to put on the side.

But, "This ain't bad," Bobby said.

"It was either that or eggs."

"Well dig in, Brother. You're barely touching your food."

"I don't know. I'm not that hungry." Victor hardly made a dent in it.

Bobby was scarfing his down though.

"You can have the rest of my steak if you want."

"You sure?" Bobby asked.

"Yeah, I'm good. Maybe I'll go to a diner later on or something."

He didn't have to tell Bobby twice. He stuck his fork on Victor's plate and airlifted the rib eye onto his own. But then he told him, as he chewed, "You know, that whole maybe last 2 years I was locked up…"

"What?"

"I used to dream at night. Fantasize. All I ever really wanted sometimes was just a giant cheeseburger with fries."

"Well I'm sorry if I couldn't accommodate you."

"Victor, you have accommodated me just fine."

"I tried."

"No, seriously, man. The way you looked out for me? The way you're still looking out for me? Shit, the way you hooked that apartment up for me before I came home? I can't tell you how much I appreciate that. I love you, man."

Victor smirked. He tried not to laugh.

"What? I pour my heart out to you and you think it's a joke?"

"It's not that," Victor chuckled.

"What then?"

"I got a confession to make."

"So then confess it already."

"I had that apartment hooked up like 15 months before you got out, when I first took over the place."

"What?"

"Yeah. It was my private spot. I used to take milfs from the gym there after their Zumba classes."

Bobby found it funny. "Well then I'm sorry for cock-blocking on you."

"You have no idea."

"Asshole. Why didn't you ever tell me that?"

"I never told *anyone* that."

"Why?"

"For one, I didn't want to get you upset in case you were never gonna see a woman again. And two, I didn't want it getting back to Michelle. The only people who knew about that spot were my hoes."

"Well at least you put it to good use."

"Yeah. You remember Rolando's mom?"

"Villanueva?"

"Yeah."

"What about her? You hit that?"

"No. But I blew a load on her sister's face."

Bobby laughed. "Damn. How old is she now?"

"I don't know. Maybe like 46, 47? She was trying to act pissed that I didn't warn her first."

"What did she say?"

"Who cares? I know she enjoyed it."

Bobby was happy for him. "You're a fucking scoundrel, you know that?"

"What can I say?"

"A lot, but it's definitely good that you don't."

"Well you know how that goes. You can't trust nobody no more."

"Yeah." Bobby thought about it. "It's fucked up, though."

Victor looked at him: *What?*

"Trust," Bobby said. "'Cause when you're a kid, when you're coming up, you think you can trust everybody."

"Tell me about it."

"I used to think about it in the can, all the time. 'Cause when you're a kid, you think you got like 40 people behind you. But then when you grow up, you realize that there's only a handful of people you can really count on, if you're lucky."

Victor didn't even say anything to that. He just gave Bobby a dap.

So Bobby told him, "I remember when the lawyer tried to remind Dino of that, of how we were kids together. I couldn't take it, man. I couldn't believe it, sitting there watching him testify against us."

"It was like something out of a movie."

"That shit broke my heart, man. I loved him, I really did."

"He tried to bury us, Bobby."

"Still. All the things we went through together? I still laugh at them, even sometimes at night alone in my cell I'd smile to myself. Just trying to be thankful for the good times I already had even though I thought I'd never have any more again. I'd try to stay positive but it just felt hopeless sometimes. I was just numb, Victor. I just became numb."

"You had to."

"Still, though. I didn't want to."

"You know, when Kojo died we were wondering if Dino would show up for the funeral, if he'd at least send a card or anything."

"Did he?"

"Nah. Kojo's mom said she never even got a phone call."

"You asked her that?"

"She brought it up herself. I gotta be honest, though. When I was living with her for a while after that? I mean Kojo died not even a month after I got out."

"I know."

"Jackie offered to put me up again but I couldn't just bounce on Miss Kojo like that."

"It was the right thing to do."

"For both of us. I mean I think she was lonely and I was too. I never even knew my mother, man. And I think she was just getting to know her son."

"After he was in the wheelchair?"

"Yeah. The whole tough guy, wild-man image got stripped away. And then, the funniest thing was, he was still out there shaking people down. He used to roll around, I mean literally roll around with a pistol on him."

Bobby laughed.

"Miss Kojo laughed too. We laughed about the good times. I'd stay up with her at night here and there and we'd just drink and laugh about all her son's craziest stories."

"Damn. How long were you there for? Before she passed away?"

"I don't know, a little under 6 months. I remember 'cause right before she passed was when I knocked up Michelle. Then that's when I started working for Jackie full time."

"Damn." Bobby just thought about it. But then he asked him, "You think she knew about that time?"

"Who? What time?"

"Miss Kojo. Halloween."

"No. I mean if she did she never said nothin' to me about it."

"Well thank God Dino wasn't there for *that one*, though."

"No shit, Sherlock. What were we, we were 16, right? We would've got charged as adults. We'd be getting out in our 40s."

"You think Kojo ever told anyone about it? I mean not to tarnish his memory or nothing but I heard he was doing a lot of drugs before he died, when he was in the wheelchair and everything."

"Bobby what I think is that Kojo was a stand-up guy. What I think is that Kojo took it to the grave with him, the same way we're taking it with us. So let's do each other a favor and not discuss it again."

"You're right. But I gotta ask you. You don't have to answer, I don't even expect you to answer but I gotta ask you in case I never see you again after tonight, for my own curiosity if not for anything else."

"What?"

"How many is this for you?"

"You're losing me."

Bobby cocked his hand, like it was a gun. "You know." He was talking about bodies. "Not counting the other day, how many is this for you?"

"Not counting Halloween?"

"Fuck it. Counting Halloween."

Victor smiled. "Let me see," he said as he thought to himself.

"You have to count?"

"You were gone a long time, Bobby."

"Jesus."

"Not counting the other day, and not counting tonight?"

"I didn't know tonight was mutual."

"Well I'm here with you, aren't I?"

"This is true."

"I showed you how to be professional."

Bobby agreed.

"But before the other day, I had four."

"*Four*? Who were the other three?"

"I did some work for Jackie."

"Fuck."

"What can I say? Some things went wrong."

"You're out of your mind."

"Not really. He showed me how to be professional."

"And how to drive a boat also?"

"Actually, that was Kojo. He hotwired one out of the marina that time, The Bayside Marina. It was nuts."

"Jesus Christ."

"I'll tell ya one thing, he was definitely smiling down on us."

"I bet he was."

"You missed out, man."

"Believe me, I know."

"That guy was a maniac."

"Jesus?"

"No. What? Kojo. Kojo, I loved him but he was a maniac," Victor said, fondly. "I mean, who the fuck hotwires a boat?"

"Kojo does."

"Word. I fucking loved him."

"You and me both. You and me both."

"Yeah, but what about you, though? You got any skeletons I don't know about? Or you still playing catch up?"

Bobby smirked. "There was one asshole, in the joint, when I was up in Green Haven. We got into a fight. I hit him too hard though and he fell down a flight of steps, hit his head. Really, it wasn't intentional."

"It never is."

"Believe it or not other than being happy no one ever found out about it, I actually felt bad about it."

"Well, I'll tell you this much. When I was living with Miss Kojo? It felt nice. I felt great about it. It was an escape from all this madness."

"I hear that. Believe me, I do."

"She was like the mother I never had. Matter of fact, she *was* my mother."

"Well, at least you had a father."

"I guess. Till I was what, 12? Minus the 4 years of that he was in prison."

"Still."

"Yeah, still. Here I am some kid waiting 4 years for my dad to get home, then 2 weeks after he does they find him in a trunk. Talk about a mind-fuck."

"I remember, that was foul."

Victor shook his head. "Fuckin' Colombians." He was talking about the bastards who killed his father.

Bobby didn't know what to say.

"I remember, Bobby, it was horrible. That was the worst moment of my life. It was, I fucking spazzed out after that. Then the next thing I know I'm doing 3 months up in Spofford with Kojo." It was the juvenile jail up in The Bronx in New York City. "What a fucking summer that was."

"Honestly, that's one bid I wish I was around for. The three of us together probably would've had fun in there."

Victor's face brightened. "Word, take Fat Mark and Bell with us too. I'll tell you one thing though, mad as I was, I was gangster up in Spofford. Me and Kojo, we held it down in there. None of those moolies fucked with us."

But Bobby thought about it. He wasn't sure what to say. So, he pondered his upcoming question, and then he asked Victor, "What do you think is more important? Having a mother, or having a father?"

Victor shrugged his shoulders. "Life doesn't get any easier, Bobby. You just get number."

"But regardless."

"Regardless my ass. The world doesn't owe anybody shit and the sooner you realize that the better off you are. You just gotta appreciate what you got and that's that. Every time I hear people complaining, bitching about shit, I just wanna bitch-slap the shit out of those fucking pussies. You just gotta appreciate what you got and that's that. That's that."

"But still."

"What?"

"Having a parent missing from your life? It fucking sucks."

Victor sighed. "Amen, Brother. Amen."

"Yeah. But you're talking about appreciating? One thing I'll tell ya, one thing that I did definitely appreciate, when I was locked up, when I'd just lay there and stare at the ceiling at night?"

"What?"

"I mean, shit. The last time I saw my pops I was 6 years old. He got bodied too, Bro. I don't even really remember him. I just got a couple of pictures. But when I was locked up, sometimes I'd just think about it. I'd think about that summer when we were kids, that summer before your dad went away, when your pops took us to all those Mets games. I gotta tell ya, I appreciated them, really appreciated them, especially then."

"I remember that. We had season tickets. I remember that, I remember that a lot, those games were fun."

"They were fun. But my mom? When I was locked up I really began to think, man. I took out so much of my anger on her growing up and I felt horrible for it. Especially after she passed when it was too late to tell her I was wrong, that I was sorry? Fuck, man."

"She was a good woman."

"Thanks. Thanks, I mean that."

"All good."

"I know. But you know who I always liked? Who I thought was nice? Back in the day, what was her name, Rebecca?"

"Jackie's niece?"

"Yeah, she was cool."

"She was cool. And it was funny too, 'cause when I was living with Jackie, people were always trying to be nice to me."

"No shit. You were living with a notorious heroin dealer."

"That's not what I mean. What I'm sayin' is that, like, half the time the goons on Francis Lewis were just tryin' to be nice to me to get in good with Rebecca. Everybody always had a crush on her. One time I had to back some stalker down coming off the Q13."

"Well if it makes you feel any better I had to deal with a couple of stalkers with my mom when I was younger, too. People trying to be nice to you, shit, people were always trying to be nice to me too."

"Like who?"

"One time Mean Gene at the deli, you remember him?"

Victor did.

"That old fool? One time Mean Gene at the deli, one time he goes to me, I was like maybe 16 or 17, and he goes to me, 'Hey, Bobby, don't forget to tell your mommy I gave you ten percent off.' And I'm like, *yeah*, you fucking Jew."

Victor laughed. "Well, I guess that's just another thing to be appreciative of."

"What? The Jew discount?"

"No. Just, you know, these crazy motherfucking characters than inhabit our ecosystems."

"Big words for a loan shark."

"I'm being serious. These nuts out there? They're the ones that make life interesting. You gotta appreciate 'em."

"You've got a point."

"I know," Victor said.

"Yeah. Matter of fact though, you know what I was always appreciative of? It was when we were on trial. I gotta tell ya, I was always appreciative that that judge let me out so I could go to her funeral, my mother's funeral, when we was on trial."

"Word, he didn't have to do that, not on a murder at least. The prosecutors wanted to keep you in a fucking cage."

"I know," Bobby told him. "But I couldn't believe Mark and them hooked that up for me with Lauren. I was shocked. I wanted to give Jackie a hug right then and there but Lauren told me he said not to say shit about it."

"I was dying when I found out. When you told me? Jackie was the fucking man for that. I mean, I don't know what the hell happened tonight, but over the years he's done a lot for us. He's done right by us. For me especially, I can't thank him enough, I could never thank him enough. After my pops died he took me in, he gave me a bed. I don't know what happened Bobby, and I'm gonna find out, but all I can say is he always looked out for me. He schooled me. If it wasn't for him I got no idea where I'd be right now. I'd probably be dead or doin' life."

"I know, I know. But still."

"What?"

"You should've seen it. I go in to use the bathroom and Lauren pops out from behind a fake wall."

Victor smirked. "You think the guards had any idea?"

"They couldn't have. They inspected the bathroom to make sure there weren't any windows or weapons in there or anything before I went in."

"You must have been thrilled."

"Of course I was thrilled." Bobby paused.

Bobby took a long pause.

"And then two months later she told me she was pregnant."

43

Lauren tried, but she couldn't take her eyes off the clock. It was now 3 A.M.

Lying in bed, fully dressed and on top of the covers, she called Bobby's phone again.

But again, it went straight to voicemail.

All it said was: "Call back. Don't leave a message."

44

"So this is it, Brethren."

"Yo Victor I'm just gonna be real with you, Bro," Bobby told him as they stood outside the summer house, in the dead of night, next to the Pathfinder. "Fucking people tried to kill both of us more than once in the last 7 days. If you don't try to go somewhere else, right now, not later, right now at least just for a little bit, you're stupid. You're stupid."

"I told you, maybe in a few weeks."

"Well then maybe you're crazy too."

"I don't want to sound like a dick, Bobby. Believe me, I don't want to sound like an asshole. But other than your girl, you don't got shit. No offense, but you don't got shit other than that. Well, maybe you got some clothes and a few dollars now. I mean, hey, you even got your freedom now. But that's all 'cause of me, not you. And me, I got businesses to run, I got people who work for me, I got employees, I got mouths to feed. And more than that, I got balls, Brother. Ain't nobody running *me* out of town."

"That's not what I'm saying, or not saying. Look, I know you wanna get made and all, I know you always wanted to be like your pops, and that's good. But I know more than anything you don't wanna leave your son with shit like he left you with shit. Take your kid and go, man. You got money, yeah, so cash out while you can and go spend it, don't be a fool. I know you always secretly, or really not so secretly, I know you always wanted to take over Queens and then take over the entire city. But fuck that. Just take your kid and go while you still can."

"I can't, Bobby. I can't."

"Why? Why?"

"Look at me. Look. And just trust me when I tell you that there's things outside of this, that, I don't know, I can't get into it. Not right now at least."

"After everything we just went over?"

"Trust me, okay? Have I ever steered you wrong?"

Bobby just stared at him.

"Trust me, Bobby. I can't go. I can't get into it, but I can't go. But you go in my place instead, and call me when you get there."

"Whatever, man. I think you're stupid, but whatever."

"Whatever."

Bobby looked at his watch: 3:32 A.M. "Look, I gotta head out, man."

"Do you even know where you're going?"

"Costa Rica."

"No, dick. Do you know where you're going to get back to the highway?"

"I'll find it."

"Whatever you say. What the hell do you wanna go to Costa Rica for?"

"'Cause Florence doesn't have a beach."

"Florence?"

"She wants to take me there."

"Oh. She lived out there, right?"

"Yeah. She says she wants to show me the Christine Chapel."

"Dick."

"Pussy."

"No, dick. It's the Sistine Chapel."

"The who?"

"*Sistine*. Not Christine. *Sistine*. You're disrespecting my whole history."

"My bad."

"It's all good. But look, you gotta leave already. You got a nice trip back."

"So what?"

"So nothing," Victor said. "Look, take care of that girl, alright? I mean that."

"I will. I am."

"Don't break her heart, okay?"

"I won't."

"I'm being serious, now. Take care of her, take off, and get the fuck away from all of this madness."

"That's what I've been saying, but you're not hearing me."

"Sometimes it's what somebody doesn't say that's more relevant than what they do."

Bobby thought about it. "Well then, let me just say then, that, even though I think you're a fucking asshole? Truth is I don't know where I'd be without you. Everything you've done for me? Aside from the shit you've done for me that was fucked up."

"*Guy*."

"All I can say is thanks, man."

"My pleasure."

"I mean, you're still an asshole, but thank you."

"Bobby, wherever you go in life, just remember to be professional."

Bobby smirked.

Then they hugged each other. They embraced.

"Thank you," Bobby said.

"Go," Victor told him. "Go. It's getting late."

And Bobby knew it. So he got in his car. He started the engine. And then he lowered the window, and told Victor, "You got the other set of keys, right?"

"Yeah."

"Alright. But yo, if I don't leave this thing outside the gym I'll call you and tell you where it's at."

"Don't call me."

"Why not?"

"Beep it to me. Beep me. Send the address on my pager, use the code though."

"You got it."

"Use the code. Use the code, Bobby."

"You got it. I'll put the key in the sun visor."

"Go, Bobby. Go."

"I'll see you on the other side, Brother."

"See ya," Victor told him.

And Bobby pulled out of the gravel driveway.

He was free.

Cruising down the highway, in the heat of the night. Windows open, music playing, not blasting. It was at just the right level, one that put a smile on Bobby's face as he enjoyed the peace that came with the fresh air.

Then he took his cellphone out too, and was about to turn it on, to call Lauren—but then he just decided to stop for a second, and let the song continue. It was a rock station on the radio in New Jersey, 104.3, and they were playing the classics.

At that moment, Phil Collins, *In The Air Tonight*. And Bobby could feel it, in the air that night. He couldn't wait to get home, get Lauren, and get on a plane and get to a beach and fuck her brains out on it.

He had survived a lot, and he deserved it.

But then the music changed, to Billy Joel's *She's Always A Woman*, and he knew it was time. He turned his phone on.

Back at the summer house though, Victor just lied in Michelle's cousin's bed. The lights were off, the house was empty. There was nothing much to look at.

Not that Victor would have looked at anything anyway though. He was depressed.

He was reflective.

He just stared at the ceiling, contemplating his situation.

Facing the reality that his days were numbered.

But at the same time, plotting how to get the most out of them.

Not for him, but for his son.

Little Pal, he thought. *My Little Pal.*

"Free at last," Bobby said. "Free at last."

Things were looking good. Everything was on the up and up. And then he reminded himself. "*Stay focused.*" *Don't end up like Carlito when he gets whacked on the platform.*

So as he cruised down the highway, he tried his best to take the smile off his face. *Don't get ahead of yourself*, he told himself. *Someone tried to put a bullet in your head, don't forget. Don't get comfortable.*

Bobby was a survivor, though. And then, as he called Lauren, as he dialed her number into his cellphone, his smile came back. Hearing her voice pick up was like feeling the whisper of an angel.

Even if she was pissed: "Where the hell are you? I've been calling you all night."

"I'm sorry, baby."

"Are you?"

"Yeah. Look, I can't get into it now."

"What happened? Are you okay?"

"Yeah, I'm just, I'm driving. I'll talk to you when I see you."

"When are you getting here?"

"I'm like an hour away, maybe. Maybe a little more. Are you ready?"

"Ready and waiting, let's go already."

"Alright, but look, I gotta meet you somewhere else."

"What? Why?"

"I can't get into it, Lauren. Just do what I tell you. Where's your car parked?"

"It's in the parking lot, in the back."

"Is there anyone else parked back there? Go look."

Lauren did. It was empty, except for her Acura. A white 4-door Integra, 1998 model.

"Okay," Bobby said. "Then get ready to go down there and put the bags in the car. I want you to meet me somewhere else."

"You're making me nervous."

"Don't be. I'm gonna send someone to help you."

"Who?"

"Mark, maybe. If he picks up." It was almost morning.

"Are you sure?"

"Don't ask questions, okay? Just do what I tell you, Lauren. It's for the best."

"Okay."

"But don't tell him or anyone else where you're going. There might be someone else with him. I'll call you back and let you know. But just let them get you on the road safely, onto the Clearview or something, then when the coast is clear just bounce on them."

"You're making me nervous."

"I told you, don't be. Just let him help you get your stuff in the car and on the road and then bounce. You can do this, Lauren."

She inhaled. And she exhaled. "Okay. Where should I meet you?"

"24th Avenue. Off of Bell, by Bay Country down there."

"Where you used to live?"

"Yeah, the apartment complex down there. Just park on 24th, I'll find you."

"Okay."

"Do one more thing for me though."

"Anything."

"Set out a change of clothes for me. Just put out a t-shirt, some jean shorts and sneakers."

"Underwear too?"

"Yeah, and socks, make it comfortable. I'm showered and all, I just wanna change though. I'll change in the car. As soon as we meet up we're out."

"Showered?"

"Just do it, I can't get into it."

"Okay," she said, happily, optimistic and all. "I love you."

"I love you too, I mean that. I fucking love you, Lauren."

"I love you too."

"You're the best thing that ever happened to me. I love you."

Lauren smiled. "I know. Just get here already."

"Alright. Keep it tight."

"Ha." Lauren smirked as Bobby hung up the phone, and went back to focusing on the road ahead.

Then he called Fat Mark.

"Yo," Bobby said.

"What's the word?"

"What are you doing?"

"Getting my dick sucked," Mark replied, as a black chick went up and down on his lap.

"Phenomenal. Are you in the neighborhood?"

"*Yeah*," Mark moaned, as she slurped. "I'm at the crib."

"Alright, good. I need you to do something for me. I need you to drop everything, now, right now and do something for me."

"What happened?"

"I just need you to do something for me."

Twenty minutes later Fat Mark pulled up to the back of the gym in his gold Toyota Camry. He got out, swaggered to the back door and knocked on it to find Lauren behind it with their bags.

He helped her put them in her car, and she gave him a hug. Then he followed her as she rolled out onto Francis Lewis Boulevard and kept up with her till she turned down Northern Boulevard and hopped onto the Clearview Expressway.

Seeing in the rearview that he didn't continue with her, she got right off at 35th Avenue, drove straight down to 26th, made a right, turned left down Bell Boulevard and turned right again on 24th. She went down to the end of the block, but stopped before crossing the adjacent street and going into the dead end.

Instead, she parked in the shadow of the Bay Country apartment complex, a group of nice, small buildings that reminded her of fancy projects, next to a small basketball court that the guys in the neighborhood always called The Clay Courts.

And she just sat there for a few minutes, taking it all in.

When she first started hanging out with Bobby in college, before they ever hooked up, when they came back to the city one weekend he brought her there to show her where he used to play as a kid.

And then, as they sat there next to the basketball court on the swing sets, before he brought her upstairs to see his apartment and meet his mother, that's where and when he kissed her for the first time. And she gladly kissed him back, right as the sun began to set. She always thought it was magical.

They were best friends who became lovers.

But that was a lifetime ago. Now she was just parked there in the dark, and after she was sure that no one else was around on the narrow, quiet street, she decided to call her man. She told Bobby that she got there safely.

And then she just went back to waiting.

With a semi-bad feeling in her stomach.

She just wanted to leave already. Like Bobby, she just wanted to put all of this behind her.

Hearing that she got there safely though was music to Bobby's ears. It was past 5 A.M. now and he was getting closer to New York. He knew because he could smell an increasing level of pollution in the air. Yet, he kept the windows down regardless. There was nothing like the mean, dirty streets of the city. And then, when he hit The George Washington Bridge, the funk hit him full blast.

He loved it. *Home sweet home*, he thought. Maybe not for much longer, but he had a smile on his face as big as a pie in the sky. He was at peace.

After crossing the G.W.B. he took the Cross Bronx Expressway through The Bronx, down to The Throgs Neck Bridge. Hardly anyone was on the roads, it was Saturday morning and the sun was starting to come up.

Bobby was exhausted, but as he crossed the bridge into Queens, looking out at the beautiful, dirty water on both sides, he was just happy. Everything was working out.

After years of struggle, as the color of the sky started to change into multiple fluorescents, everything was just starting to work itself out, and he was thrilled.

The Throgs Neck Bridge led him onto the Clearview Expressway and he got off at 26th Avenue. Before he knew it he was driving through the old neighborhood, just taking everything in and knowing it would be some time before he'd be back, if he was ever back. But he was happy with that. And then, as the sky turned an orangey-blue, half-awake but fully alive, Bobby turned down 24th, slowly, looking for his bride. And as he cruised down the block, Lauren saw him coming from the opposite direction.

So she checked her make up. It didn't matter what time of day it was, she had every intention of looking dope for her man.

And Bobby, coming down the block, smiling, pulled up alongside of her, and just stopped his car, rolled down his window, and looked at her, as she looked back at him.

"Hey you," he told her.

"Hey," she smiled back.

He got out of his car, shut his door, and opened hers.

Lauren then got out.

She threw her arms around his neck and stuck her tongue in his mouth with everything she had.

So much so that she didn't even hear the birds chirping in the trees. All she heard was:

"Get on the ground motherfucker! Now!"

What the fuck?! Lauren thought.

Springer, Giardino and 6 other cops came out of nowhere with their guns pointed at them as two undercover cars came flying down the block from both directions with red lights flashing.

"I told you to get on the ground, cocksucker!" Giardino barked, as he and Springer's troops got closer to them, circling like sharks.

And as Lauren looked on in terror, Bobby began to put his hands up and stepped away from her. Just looking Lauren in the eyes, not knowing what to say.

One of the cops charged Bobby and knocked him onto the ground, *hard*. It was unnecessary roughness, typical pig bullshit.

"No!" Lauren screamed. "No! What are you doing?"

"Placing your boyfriend under arrest," Springer said. "For murder."

As his cop dug his knee into Bobby's back. He pushed the side of his face into the street and made sure the pavement dug into Bobby's pores.

He put him in cuffs.

Giardino though, going through Bobby's jeep, just said, "Looky, looky, what do I have here?" He pulled Bert's gun out from the center console and held it up like a prize.

As Bobby, on the ground, in physical pain from being rushed by New York's finest just looked at it.

Then, with his dirty, street-covered, shameful face, he looked at Lauren.

She was crying.

45

"What, *the fuck*," Jackie said.

"I haven't spoken to him yet. They just picked him up this morning."

"What, *the fuck*."

"Just tell me what you want me to do, Jackie," Victor said. The two of them were alone in the back of the pizzeria, a little after 6 in the evening. Jackie was at his desk, Victor was standing in front of it.

"What else did she tell you?"

"Nothing. She just said the cops came outta nowhere, searched him and found the pistol. Then they took him in, that was it."

"You sure?"

"Yeah. They had his phone tapped. They probably got all our phones tapped."

"No shit they got our fuckin' phones tapped! How many times have I fuckin' told you that?"

Victor paused. "Look, I'm on nobody's side but yours, Jackie. What do you want me to do here?"

"What can you do? It's a fuckin' mess."

"Then how can I help clean it up?"

"You gonna find Bert for me?"

Victor remained silent.

"Exactly," Jackie said.

"What are our options?"

"I don't know. Maybe I'll just go into Rikers and strangle this fuck myself."

"Just because Bert hasn't turned up doesn't mean something happened to him."

"Then what?"

"I don't know. Maybe he lammed it."

"Doubtful."

"Then…"

"Then what?"

Victor thought about what he was going to say next. "All due respect, Jackie, but you really think something happened between the two of them?"

"Of course something happened between the two of them!"

"But how do you know that? What if Bert flipped or something and we're looking at this the whole wrong way?"

Jackie's anger elevated. "Are you questioning my judgment? Are you questioning my fucking troops?"

"No, Jackie, I'm just—"

"Are you?"

"No," Victor said. "It's just—I don't want to disrespect you, Jackie. You know I look at you like a father. You've done so much for me, you raised me. But Bobby's my Brother and if

I can prevent it I don't want you getting mad at him. He's one of us. He's a good guy."

Jackie calmed down. He thought about it for a second. "So then let me ask you. You're old enough to make your own decisions. You know you're moving up the totem pole. We've had this discussion. I've been schooling you for years, my little friend."

"I know, and I'm grateful."

"So then how would you like to handle this? What do you think is the right move going forward on this?"

"The right move?"

"Yeah. The right move."

Victor paused. "The right move is whatever move you say, boss."

Jackie smirked. He stood up. He came around the side of the desk, and stood face to face with his protégé. He smiled at him, like the devil, into Victor's eyes, and with his old hands, grabbed the sides of Victor's muscular upper arms. And he told him—

Knock, knock, knock... there was a soft knock on the door. Jackie let Victor go. They both stared at it.

"What?" Jackie asked.

Pepe opened it. The elderly little pizza maker walked in a step, and told him, with his Sicilian accent, "Ah, Mr. Jackie?"

"What? What the fuck do you want?"

"Ah, Mr. Jackie. You gotta to see this, onna the TV."

On the old, small television, standing in front of the gas station reporter Roberta Seagram told the New York underworld what was going on:

"Sources within the Police Department tell us that Robert Drakis, currently being held in Central Bookings, will not be arraigned until Monday morning when the courts open. However, Mr. Drakis is no stranger to the legal system. Only 26

years old, just over four months ago he was released from prison after serving 6 years for killing a college student in a bar fight in Albany. In addition, what is more shocking is that police sources also say that he is an up and coming mafia associate of the Bonanno Crime Family, pictured here (she is replaced on screen by a surveillance photo of Bobby, Jackie and Victor standing in front of the pizzeria) with Damian 'The Victor' Saravano, a former middle weight prize fighter and New York Golden Glove, who also is said to be a budding mafia associate, who also went on trial with Drakis in the bar fight but was acquitted; and John 'Little Jackie' Iacone, a reputed powerful North Queens gambling kingpin and alleged capo regime within the Bonanno Crime Family who went to trial but was acquitted during the 1980s on heroin distribution charges related to the Pizza Connection investigations."

"Yo Pramal, you seeing this?"

"Every drop of it," he told the driver from the gas station robbery. The driver whose head was bandaged, covering the streak the bullet left along the side of it when Bobby took a shot at him.

They were sitting in front of the TV in two shithole recliners, in the living room of a shithole housing project apartment, with a half broken air conditioner in the window pumping what it could and one of their homies cooking crack in the kitchen while another put it into nickel bags on the ratty couch next to them. Not to mention, there were two old revolvers on the coffee table and red bandanas everywhere. Some red and black graffiti on the walls, low rap music playing in the background, the driver and the cook were even in red t-shirts. They were members of the Bloods gang.

But while the driver was in shock, Pramal fumed. There was more red in his eyes than that entire room. However, he didn't say a word about it.

He just massaged the sawed off shotgun that was in his lap.

Because like Victor, Pramal also ran a crew. Pramal ran a set. And members of it were missing.

46

"As of right now they're just charging me with the gun but they say they got me on trafficking too and they're gonna pin those murders on me."

"How? How could they do that? How could they pin those murders on you that you didn't even do?"

Bobby, in a green jailhouse jumpsuit, one that said DOC on the back, and Victor, sitting across the small table from him in the packed, noisy Rikers Island visiting room with 49 other inmates and their families and various criminal associates in there, had to be careful what they said.

"They said they got a witness. They said someone saw my Pathfinder fly out of there after the shots went down, out of the gas station."

"So what? There must be a million Pathfinders that go in and out of that gas station every day. Every hour."

"That's what the lawyer told 'em."

"And how'd they take it?"

"They said but how many gas stations are numbers spots for Jackie Iacone?"

Fuck, Victor thought. "What else did the lawyer say?"

"Just that he feels like they're gonna charge me with a whole bunch of shit they haven't even gotten to yet. They're tryin' to make me flip."

"On who?"

"Who do you think? They said they know I didn't kill all those blacks by myself and they know I was there because I work for Jackie. The lawyer told them they were crazy."

Victor shook his head. "Fuck."

"What?"

"Nothing. I don't wanna be the bearer of bad news, but…"

Bobby was concerned. "Lauren?"

"We'll get to that. Something else, though."

Bobby looked at him: *What*.

"You remember that guy? Your friend?"

"Who?"

"The one who I said, uh, in front of the park that time, that you should be happy?"

Bobby thought about it. "The one who I wanted to go with you but you wouldn't let me?"

"Yeah, him."

"What about him?"

"Bad news, real bad news."

"Say it already."

Victor touched his shirt, rubbed it right in the middle of his chest. He was telling Bobby that Lenny was wearing a wire. "Know what I'm sayin'?"

"All due respect, Victor, but I got my own problems. Look at me. What the fuck does that have to do with me?"

"Everything."

"How? I mean not to be a dick or anything but I don't even know him."

"That's what's fucked up about it. He's gonna say that, or, I mean, uh, he already said that you were there that day, for the delivery. For that pizza delivery. They're gonna charge the two of us for that, for the delivery he got."

"You fucking kiddin' me?"

"I wish I was. He's sayin' that we sold him food, even though we didn't."

"Jesus, God." Bobby sighed. "So that's what those pigs were talking about."

"What?"

"They said they got a witness against me selling pies, but they wouldn't say who."

"Yeah well I spoke to my attorney also. He says they're just waiting for the right time to take me in on it, probably a couple other things too. They're gonna fold us into a RICO, C.C.E. charge, whatever, maybe."

Bobby leaned back in his chair. "Jesus."

"What can I say?"

"Nothing."

"I'm sorry," Victor told him.

"Yeah."

"No. I'm sorry, Bobby. I really am. The last thing I wanted was for you to get caught up in my bullshit all over again."

"Yeah." Bobby almost laughed. "I mean, what the fuck, right? Just like old times."

"Hopefully not."

"Whatever. Are you sure about this asshole? How do you know?"

"I just know," Victor said.

"How?"

"I just do. Look, just sit tight, man, we'll figure this out."

"Sit tight? Where the fuck am I going?"

Victor shrugged his shoulders.

Bobby sighed. "You still haven't told me."

"Told you what?"

"Lauren. How is she? How's Lauren?"

Victor didn't know what to say. He just looked away.

"How is she?"

Victor looked back at him: "Not good, man. It's not good."

47

Lauren felt horrible. She felt sick. She was lying on her side under the covers at her sister's and just wanted to be left alone. She didn't want to face it.

Lisa, though, 4 years older, just looked at her, and came in the room anyway. She was worried. She sat down on the side of the bed and rubbed her back. "Hey sis," she said. "Let's go to the movies or something. You gotta get outta bed, sweetie."

"I'm tired," Lauren replied. Tired of all of it.

48

From the outside it didn't look like much. Except for the red awnings, nothing about the restaurant stood out. It was in the middle of a nondescript intersection in working class Maspeth, Queens. The kind of nondescript intersection, not far from Brooklyn, that looked like you could find prostitutes there at a discount.

But you couldn't. Anyone who knew anything either about food or the underworld knew that the CasaBlanca was owned by one Big Joe Massino.

At 5'10" and a massive 300 pounds, Big Joe, otherwise known as "The Ear" was the head of The Bonannos and the last of the old time crime bosses still free on the streets. Sure, there were new dons popping up all the time, but all of Joe's contemporaries—all of the real, old school gangsters—were either dead or incarcerated. All of them who wore a crown at least. He was the last official boss standing.

However, in their absence, Big Joe rebuilt the once weakened Bonanno family into a powerhouse. There was a time, in the 1980s and early 1990s that law enforcement had written them off. The Bonannos were history, a running joke even in wiseguy circles. They had been infiltrated by an undercover FBI agent and became a laughing stock.

Although, as Big Joe stewed in federal prison in the late 1980s, he quietly consolidated his power. And then, when he got out in 1992, he quickly began their resurgence.

From the shadows he stressed discipline and secrecy and beefed up his family's longtime interests in gambling, loan sharking and extortion—and drugs. And now, at the end of the decade, except for the larger Genovese Family, as all of the other New York crews were ravaged by informants and infighting The Bonannos had become not just the second strongest criminal group in New York, but possibly, the country. They were an underground army of over 100 seasoned, deadly men.

Massino didn't build his team and take things to that level by being stupid, though. He was cautious. A surveillance and gadget wiz, above the table they were eating dinner at in the half empty restaurant, on the ceiling, sat two metal boxes.

Scramblers meant to disrupt the recording of any conversation taking place beneath them if someone was wearing a wire at his table. To anyone in the establishment who didn't know any better, however: they were smoke alarms.

But Massino, 56 and rotund, didn't notice anything out of the ordinary as he twirled spaghetti into his spoon and *The Godfather* soundtrack played in the background. All around the restaurant there were pictures of famous actors and nice mirrors for self-centered Italians to look at themselves in. It wasn't crowded, but it didn't matter. Massino just focused on his guests: his loyal captain, Jackie Iacone, and his tested consigliere, Luigi Carcaterra, who told them:

"In all my years, I never seen anything like it. Such disrespect."

"They wanted to hurt him for that," Jackie said. "Least that's what I heard."

"Well, you know what they say?" Joe asked.

They both looked to their boss for his answer.

"No matter what," Massino told them. "No matter what, you can never trust a cock-blocker. Fucking weasels."

"It's true," Jackie said.

"Loyalty is everything," Massino said. "Loyalty. Without that, there's nothing. But it also takes brains, heart, balls. It takes all different kinds of meats to make a platter."

"You just hit it on the head," Jackie said—as he stared at Massino getting huskier by the mouthful.

"But without loyalty?" Massino told them. "None of it matters. Without loyalty, none of it matters," Massino said, as he slurped his spaghetti, adding to his already massive frame. "Without loyalty, the platter ain't worth a dime. Nothing, nothing. Without loyalty, there's no flavor. There's no reason for it to even exist. Loyalty is the ultimate, the most important ingredient."

Jackie and Luigi agreed.

As the boss finished up his meal though, Lorenzo came back from the bathroom and sat back down with them. At which point the boss asked Jackie, "So, you seen the upgrades yet? I got some new stuff in the kitchen."

Jackie hadn't. He shook his head.

"C'mon, lemme show ya," Massino told him, and the two of them picked the napkins up off their laps, stood up and placed them on the table.

Massino walked towards the back with Little Jackie, half his size but just as vicious trailing behind him. Past some diners, a few waiters, and one final waiter who, when he saw Big Joe walking towards him, held open the door to the kitchen.

"Gratzi," Massino said, as they walked into the metal room, passed some busy Mexican dishwashers, went right to the back, to the chef. He was prepping some deserts. A little cannoli, some pastries, chocolate cream puffs, too.

Big Joe picked up one of the puffs, told Jackie "Try it," and gave it to him.

Jackie did.

"Nice, huh?"

Jackie enjoyed it. "Very. You guys making these *here*?"

Massino took a handful and devoured them in one shot. "Of course. We get the ingredients from all over. But *here*, we mold 'em." The pun was intended.

"They're beautiful," Jackie said, as he picked up two more.

Before he could eat them though, Joe told him, "C'mon." He picked a few more up into his hand, popped one of them into his fat mouth and walked around the corner in the kitchen to the walk-in freezer all the way in the back. After which, he opened the freezer door, turned on the interior light, and looked at Jackie, who just nodded in return.

Jackie went inside, Joe followed. He shut the door behind him, and asked him, his captain, "Do you remember what I said to you when I gave you the power down there?"

"Keep it quiet," Jackie said.

"Keep it fucking quiet, I told you. I gave you one of the best territories in the city, and all I told you was to keep it quiet. That's it. But now you got these cowboys running around. I told you to keep it fucking quiet."

I know.

"You think I built this thing by making noise? We got to where we are by keeping it quiet, and that's how it's gotta stay. But now I'm hearing about fucking shootouts? This ain't the 80s no more."

Jackie just looked at him. "What do you want me to do?"

"Get your house in order."

Jackie nodded.

"It's true that that kid from the nightclub went bad?"

"To my extreme distaste," Jackie said.

"Can he hurt youse?"

"Me, not so much. I never discussed nothing with him. Barely even spoke to him. But my guys, yeah."

"Our guys, or just your guys?"

"Two of ours. More of mine."

Massino thought about it. "Just keep it quiet. Do whatever you gotta do, but keep it quiet. Make it disappear."

"That's what I was thinking. But then there's the other thing. The other thing, with the other kid. My kid."

"We've been here before."

"I know. I'm well aware. But the truth is I don't know what to do. On this one, you gotta tell me. I'm not asking for permission, I'm asking for an order."

Massino thought about it. "Has he changed at all? Recently?"

"With that thing that happened? With the wife?"

Massino thought about it some more. "She was a Puerto Rican, right?"

Jackie nodded.

"Well that says it all right there."

"Ever since, this kid's gone crazy."

"I heard. He wired Jose's jaw?"

"Something like that."

"Jackie I gave you the power down there for a reason. Not 'cause you made the most money. 'Cause you had the most brains. 'Cause you was sharp. 'Cause you could make decisions."

"Which is why I'm coming to you, I got to. I gotta make sure whatever decision comes down on this one is the right one."

"Then all I can tell you is you better get ready for a lot of heat, more than ever before. You do this, you're gonna be covered after this, just know that. So whatever you do, you be smart. You keep it quiet."

"That's the thing. I hate to say it but the cash flow might go down after this. If we're gonna be laying low and all it definitely will. Expect less samoleens."

Massino wasn't happy. "And this kid is your blue chip, right?"

"One of 'em at least. He makes money hand over fucking foot." Jackie held his hand up, in the shape of a gun. "And, he's capable." Victor could be called upon to drop bodies when needed.

"Then why are you even still considering this? We need all the guns we can get. There's a reason we got the strongest mob right now."

"Something I'm deeply proud of."

"Jackie, our friend out there, at the table, the older one. He tells me your whole crew wants you to make him. Wants me to make him."

"I mean, his father was one of us. They all knew him. He was on the crew. Some of us made our bones together. But, ever since the tragedy? They especially want to see you make him. All of a sudden stones got hearts."

"Then maybe you should reconsider. All the heat this is gonna bring down?"

"That's the thing. This life, boss? You know how unpredictable it is, more than anyone. And you're telling me it's time to clean house."

"And?"

"And I just feel that, you know? If we, if you make him? I feel that one day, it's just more of a possibility that one day, he's gonna know who did that thing. Who did that guy. He's gonna know who popped that cherry."

"So then you'd have to tell him. If he's gonna be part of our family? If he's gonna be one of us? Before he gets baptized, you'd have to tell him. A capable kid like that? We can't have no problems. You'd have to see how he reacts."

"I know. But like you said, he's capable. *Very* capable. He's proved that."

"So?"

"So, say I tell him. And even if I don't, say somebody flips one day. Especially if my crew's gonna be indicted now? And who knows who else with us?"

"You know well as I do that this is the only family never had a rat, and it's gonna stay that way."

"I don't mean to sound bad, bo. Look, I'm not saying it'll be somebody from my bunch, even our bunch, but I'm just saying. You know how it is. How *This Thing* goes. Say someone talks one day? And then he hears about it from them on a witness stand instead? There's no telling how this kid'll react, whether it's me that tells him or someone else that tells him. And then what?"

Massino thought about it. He thought about it hard, as he popped the last cream puff in his hand into his fat, slobbering mouth. He thought about it even harder.

And then, he, Massino told him: "And then loyalty."

49

Lorenzo was driving, and Victor knew better than to ask where they were going. It was just something you didn't do. It was just one of those things. Jackie told him to get in, and he did.

Into the backseat. Jackie was riding shotgun and Lorenzo was driving Jackie's big, silver Lexus LS 400 for him when they pulled up to Victor in the parking garage and picked him up. Because while Lorenzo was his bodyguard, Victor was his pit-bull. His favorite enforcer. He was what Lorenzo, when he was younger, used to be, albeit on steroids. And the way Jackie saw it, Victor had what it took to one day go farther in the life than any of them ever would. *If he doesn't knock up another Puerto Rican.*

He had boss potential, but Lorenzo, he would probably never go beyond captain of his own crew, if he ever got that far. Because Jackie, like everyone else, always knew Lorenzo would be way too busy with his women for that. He was a playboy.

But Jackie, himself, he had no desire to ever go beyond captain. Maybe consigliere one day, but he knew that anything beyond captain was a guaranteed ticket to the big house. Unlike most wiseguys who dreamed of being the boss one day, Jackie's greed had a limit. He didn't need the stress.

So they drove. They cruised down Northern Boulevard, they waddled through traffic. Lorenzo went slow, suddenly making turns, trying to make sure they weren't being followed. The whole time Jackie looked in the side view mirror, also doing his part. And then they crossed over the border from

Queens to Long Island on the boulevard, where the NYPD had no business to keep following them.

Before Victor knew it, Lorenzo pulled off down a side street, near a small, grassy park with a pond and soccer moms everywhere. Little kids all abound. And Jackie told him, "This is good." Lorenzo pulled into a spot, parked, and Jackie told Victor, "C'mon."

They both got out of the car, while Lorenzo stayed inside with his eyes open. Jackie and Victor though, they went for a walk, around the pond.

"This Christmas," Jackie told him in stride.

"Huh?"

"This Christmas. The big guy. He's opening the books."

"You saying what I think you're saying?"

Jackie stopped walking, after which Victor did too. "Let me ask you a question."

"Anything."

"Do you want to take a step up in the world?"

"I've been wanting to take that step up my whole life."

"Then now's your chance. I spoke to the man last night. I put your name in the hat."

Victor was elated. "Jesus. I'm honored. Thanks, Jackie." It was vindication for all the years of hustling, beating and killing he did on Jackie's behalf.

But then Jackie told him, "Don't thank me just yet."

And Victor coughed, violently.

"You alright?"

"Yeah, I'm just—" Victor coughed up again, bad. "Fuck," he said, out of breath. He cleared his throat, as Jackie watched on, cautiously. "I don't know, been feeling fucked up lately."

"You look fucked up, which makes me wonder, you sure you're ready to take a step up?"

"100 fucking percent. I've been banging out with you since I was a baby, you know that."

"Well then here's your chance. But."

"But what?" Victor asked.

"You're gonna have to do some more work first."

"I don't give a fuck, you know that."

"Then listen to me. Listen to what I'm gonna tell you now."

"I'm listening."

Jackie started walking again, and Victor kept up with him.

"Some guys in this life, kid. They get to where they are 'cause they're the right person's kid. They get their stripes passed down off their father's shoulders. Nepotism and shit, you understand?"

"Of course, spoiled brats."

"Exactly, silver spoon motherfuckers. Something I would never have on my crew. But you? I'm proud to say that I'm proud of you because you're stepping up not 'cause of who your father was. I'm proud of you 'cause you're stepping up 'cause of who *you* are. I'm proud of you, proud to say that you earned this. I felt so proud recommending you last night, talking to the man last night. And I'm sure your father would've been proud, too."

"Thank you, Jackie. That means a lot. You got no idea, that means a lot, Jackie."

"Well, like I said. Don't thank me just yet."

"What happened?"

Jackie stopped their walking. "It's not what happened, it's what's gonna happen. 'Cause these charges that are coming at us right now? I don't know when, but they're coming."

"So what?"

"So like I said, I spoke to the man. And the man says, and I agree, that before we bring anybody new into this house we gotta clean out the house we already got."

"Which is why you need me to do some work."

"Which is why I need you to do some work."

"Who?"

They started walking again, as Jackie told him, "I got the okay. The DJ. I want it done immediately."

"You got it. You know you got it."

"It's more than that. It's gotta be quietly. He's gotta disappear."

Victor almost laughed. "What? How? Is that even possible? I mean, no disrespect or nothing, but can we even do that?"

"Yes."

"Immediately, though?"

"Yes."

"Jackie, like I said, no disrespect, but hear me out."

Speak.

"After the number I did on him? How are we gonna make it quiet? He's not going nowhere alone with me."

"I'm 10 steps ahead of ya. What do you think, I wanna end up like Tommy Agro? You remember him?"

"Yeah. The documentary about him anyway."

"Well I don't. You see that guy over there, who's driving right now? He's workin' on it. He's gonna bring him down to the club. He thinks he's gonna be giving turntable lessons to some kids, nightclub advice, the sons of friends. You understand?"

"Alright. But what if he won't go with him?"

"Then you do a roll-up on a Huffy if you have to. But if he does get him there? Then you do it there, and then you make him go away. Roll him up in a fucking rug if you have to. You got it?"

"You know I'm down. But, I still got one question."

"So ask it."

"How's he gonna start givin' DJ lessons? I'm pretty sure I broke his hand."

"You didn't, I checked. You fractured his metacarpals."

Victor smiled. "A boxer's break from a boxing great."

"Yeah, laugh."

"Oh, I will. I did good work."

"To a tee. But then there's the other thing. Your boy, who just got nabbed."

"What about him?"

"You do this? You're giving him back years of his life."

"That's how it feels."

"That's how it is. That and one less charge to pay the lawyers for."

"I know."

Jackie paused. He stopped their walking. "You think he'll be eligible for bail after?"

"I doubt it. Not with the gun at least."

"Well then what I want you to do is make him think you're doing everything in your power to help him make bail."

"Why? I mean, I will, but why?"

"'Cause if he does? You're gonna do him, too."

"What?"

"I know you like him. I'm sorry."

"But, what? Why?"

"You've asked enough questions."

"But why? What the fuck?"

"Watch it, Victor."

"No disrespect, Jackie, I don't mean it like that, you know I don't mean it like that. But what the fuck? What did he do?"

"Enough."

"What? How can I do that? He's my best friend. He's my Brother."

"Which is exactly why you should be happy it's you doing it and not someone else."

Victor was pissed. "You mean like Bert?"

"You got something you wanna say to me?"

"I don't know, Jackie. You tell me."

"Bobby say something to you?"

Victor thought about it. Then he looked back at the car, and saw Lorenzo staring right back at him. And now he realized why Lorenzo was there, in a public, family friendly place, when they could have discussed this anywhere else. Lorenzo came as backup.

Fuck it, Victor thought. "Matter of fact, he did."

"What?" Jackie got annoyed. "What did he say?"

"When I went to visit him. He told me Bert tried to give him a moon roof."

"Then where's Bert now?"

"In the ground."

"Motherfucker."

"I didn't even know if I should say something to you or not."

"You didn't?"

"For all I knew I was next. For all I knew it was Bert who killed Michelle."

"Kid, if I wanted you dead, you would be."

"Then why'd you want Bobby dead?"

Jackie looked at him. Then Jackie started walking again. "Word came to me that he was cooperating."

"What?"

"That's what I heard."

"Then why didn't you bring it to me instead? What did you bring it to Bert for?"

"You had enough going on. Michelle, everything, you had enough on your plate."

"Where did you hear that? About Bobby?"

"A reliable source."

"I don't believe it."

"Now, neither do I."

"Then why the change of heart?"

"'Cause he got arrested. He was cooperating he wouldn't of got arrested."

"Then why do you still want me to do him?"

"'Cause there's no reason he should be making bail. A loaded gun charge, and a suspect in a mass murder?"

"It could still happen. He could still make bail." Victor was lying to himself.

"Not on the gun charge, not with a witness disappearing in the case. And not with him just coming fresh off a murder beef."

"Well I'm sure when he gets sentenced that kid's family's gonna be there testifying again."

"Exactly. You think the judge isn't gonna slam him hard?"

"He'll take it on the chin. He's not gonna say anything."

"You sure about that? He didn't look too happy when he got home."

"He did his time, Jackie."

"A lot of people did their time."

"So what are you asking me to do here?"

Jackie stopped their walking. "I'm asking you to play along. You go see him, you don't talk about nothing specific. You be cautious. But you play along, and you see what he does, how he moves. You feel him out. And you try to get him out."

"And if and when he gets out?"

"If he gets out on bail? Like we said, you do him. Simple."

Victor thought about it. Could Jackie be right? Could Bobby be selling out?

But Jackie just looked at Victor, struggling at the whole concept of Bobby going bad, turning his back on everything and everyone he ever knew. So he just told him: "That's the life, kid. That's the life you chose. And once upon a time, a long, long time ago? It was the life your father chose. We chose it together. He knew the risks, and so did I, and so do you. So I'm gonna ask you, one final time."

Victor was disappointed. "Go ahead, Jackie."

"You want your wings, kid? Here they are."

50

It was beautiful out. The sun was shining. On the monkey bars, kids were climbing. On the grass there at Crocheron Park, in Bayside, couples were laid out on blankets, enjoying not just each other's company, but the weather too, taking in the last days of summer.

Victor didn't always get up early but these days he was having trouble sleeping. And today, Victor just sat there, on one of the benches, by the little league baseball fields.

Sometimes he would come here with Michelle, and just think, *This'll be the place where Michael's gonna hit home runs one day. He's gonna be a star.*

But that wasn't today. It was beautiful out, but that wasn't today. It wasn't his day. It hadn't been in some time. Maybe it had only been a matter of days, barely even weeks, but the last two felt like forever.

Victor checked his beeper, but there were no messages. He checked his phone, but he had no one to call. Then he checked his watch, and the time read 10:30.

He didn't want to leave, though. In his world that was once filled with madness, now by loneliness, he had found a moment of peace.

Then he coughed again. His migraine came back. It was a reminder to get up.

Victor pulled the sunglasses down from on top of his head, covered his eyes with them and popped some pain killers.

From one waiting room, to the next fucking waiting room, Victor thought. He sat there in the doctor's office rotating his eyes from his watch to the clock on the wall to remind you how high up the doctor was on her horse, and to the medicine cabinet, wondering if there was anything in there he could have Fat Mark sell for him.

Fuck it, Victor thought. 15 long minutes had gone by. So Victor opened the draw. Nothing in there though but plastic gloves and band aids. He opened the cabinet above the sink next. Not much there either, nothing of any value at least. Just syringes and other things that would be useful to heroin addicts.

He didn't fuck with addicts.

He just strung them out. He didn't really give a fuck anymore. So he picked up the phone off the wall jack. He dialed a number.

As Doctor Cullotta, the tall redhead walked in, carrying some paperwork. "What are you doing?"

"I'm checking on my son," Victor said, as the phone rang in his ear.

"You can't use that phone. Patients aren't allowed."

"Then what's it here for?"

"It's for the doctors, for us. Now please put it down."

"When I'm done."

"Mr. Saravano, please put the phone down."

He ignored her. Then the answering machine came on. Just a standard one, but he didn't leave a message. He hung up. "Like I told you, when I'm done."

"Mr. Saravano, if you'd like to be treated here, you're going to have to respect this office."

"And if you'd like my business here, you're gonna have to respect my time. You tell me to be here at 11, it's already 1:30. I don't know what the fuck it is with you people."

"Would you like to continue this appointment or not Mr. Saravano?"

He settled down.

"Mr. Saravano, please take a seat."

He did.

"I have to ask you, is everything okay?"

"Is everything okay? What do you think? I'm in a freaking doctor's office waiting for my latest fucking death result."

"Mr. Saravano you are not dead yet. You've still got a chance."

"Is it a good one?"

"Judging by your charts here," she said, as she looked at the papers in her hands. "Have you been taking the medicine?"

Victor put his head down.

Then, after a moment, he picked it back up.

He looked in her eyes, and he smiled: "I mean, we're all going to the same place anyway, right?"

51

No pain, no pain, no pain, Bobby thought, doing push-ups in his cell. The floor was cold, the space was tight, he could barely move around. But all he knew was if he was doing a bid he needed to be strong, as strong as possible.

No pain, no pain, no pain, he thought, doing push-up after push-up, with no shirt on. He needed every one he could get. The stronger he was the less likely people inside would test him. The lawyer told him all in all, if it was only for the gun charge, he might be able to plea out and only serve a year. If he was lucky. Really lucky. If the cops were just bluffing on the weed and murder and rackets charges, and if he could get through his sentence with good time, without any infractions on the inside, if he was a model prisoner.

No pain, no pain, no pain, he thought.

But, he wasn't just thinking of himself.

He was thinking of Lauren. He wasn't losing touch with her this time. He was doing his time as quickly as possible, and leaving with her the day he was released—if the parole board allowed it at least. Whatever it took he was making it his mission to reform himself. To be worthy of her again, if he ever once was.

No pain, no pain, no pain, he thought.

He thought of Lauren.

Lauren, though, she just thought of her future.

Not of her surroundings, of her future.

Lisa's bathroom was nice, almost like a hotel bathroom. Everything in it was shiny white.

To Lauren, though, sitting on the toilet, it resembled a jail cell. There she sat, the door closed, closed off from the rest of the world. Thinking about Bobby, but still, but more, thinking about the world.

Then it was time.

She lifted it up, and she checked it.

She checked her pregnancy test.

She checked her result: Negative.

Some women, with a man in jail, might have been relieved. Lauren, though, she didn't know what to think. The only thing she knew for certain was that she had spent way too much time thinking as it was.

She turned to the right and stared out the window.

It was a big world out there and here she was closed off from it.

52

"Don't do it, Victor. I'm telling you, don't do it," Bobby said, discretely.

"And if I don't?" Victor spoke discretely too. "If I don't? Then what? All the bullshit this guy's making up? Who knows what this scumbag has up his sleeve?"

Bobby leaned back in his chair. He looked around. 49 other prisoners in the packed and noisy visiting room. Guards posted around the perimeter. Family members and random losers seated across their visiting tables. And here he was, a former college athlete, a scholarship student, in a jailhouse jumpsuit whispering for his freedom.

Again.

"Look, man," Bobby said. "I realize that I fucked up. I get that, okay? I get the fact that I'm gonna do time on this one, okay? Whatever though. I can rock with it. Even though I'd rather not, I can rock with it, I'll be fine. But I'm telling you, I got a bad feeling about this. You know how much heat it's gonna bring down? If he is what you say he is?"

Victor looked around. "It's been confirmed."

"So what? You didn't deal with this guy, right?"

Victor shook his head.

"So say you do a few years for assault? You could plead out to that. So what? Just do a short bid and get out. And when you get out? *Get out.*"

"And how do I know it's gonna be a short bid, Bobby? I can't leave it alone."

"Do you really want to be in here with me?"

"Well maybe if I do this you won't be in here at all. He lams it, I help him get out of town, they'll give you bail. Eventually you plead out instead, maybe do a year on the gun and goodbye. You're out free and clear. I gotta get you out of here."

"You're out of your mind."

"And you're locked up, I'm not yet."

"Victor you know Goddamned well they're not giving me bail on this."

"I'm not so sure on that. If it was just the gun?"

"I don't know what the hell you're smoking. Did you forget the fact that I'm a suspect in multiple homicides?"

"So what?"

"So everything. It's a high profile case, not to mention I just beat a fucking homicide. It was in the Capeci column for Christ's sake, *Gangland*. They're gonna want it solved. And now a cooperating witness is gonna skip his court date? I'm not getting bail, no way. If anything it's gonna be harder to get bail. I'm sitting here for at least the next year, that I already know."

Victor, though, he was happy to hear Bobby say that. He didn't want to believe for a second that Bobby would become a snitch. To him, it was the lowest form of life. So, he just leaned back, and looked around. He smirked.

"What?" Bobby asked.

"Nothing."

"Something's on your mind."

Victor smiled. "You remember the first time we came here? When we were 17?"

"How could I forget?"

"I remember," Victor said, fondly, "when we were in the bullpen, in Bookings. I remember just being in there, us and Kojo, Bell and Dino—just laughing."

"I remember too." Bobby smiled. "We shot up those moolies from Hollis."

"It was fun."

It was, Bobby thought. "What's your point?"

"We've gone full circle. Paintball guns to real guns."

"Not I said the cat."

"Yeah. I found out what happened with that guy, the scumbag. The older one." He was talking about Bert.

So Bobby just looked at him: *What*?

"You were right, that guy was behind it."

Bobby sighed. "I fucking knew it."

"I think I did too, I just didn't wanna believe it."

"That motherfucker. Neither did I. That motherfucker. Why would he do that for? I was always loyal to him, always. What would he do that for?"

"He thought you were getting weak. He thought you were weak."

"That cocksucker."

"Someone told him you folded. You know what I'm sayin'?"

Bobby did. "It's not true."

"I know."

"If I was gonna do that I would've done it a long time ago. I would've done it 6 years ago."

"I know. You don't have to remind me, I know."

"So what then? What do I do now?"

"You watch your back. For all I know someone's gonna come at you behind these walls."

"Great."

"And you sit tight."

"For what? For the first knife in my back? Jesus, Victor."

"That's not what I'm saying."

"What then?"

Victor thought about it. "Your prints were on the gun, right?"

"I assume."

Fuck. "Look, Bobby. I'm gonna go out, and I'm gonna do this thing. Then I'm gonna handle your lawyers, and I'm gonna get you the best deal possible. I'm gonna do everything in my power to get you the shortest time possible. All in all I'm gonna take the weight for whatever possible. Then as soon as you get out, hopefully you won't be on parole. But as soon as you get free? You're gonna take my son and start over someplace new. You're gonna raise that kid to be the man that neither of our fathers ever were. The man that neither of us never became. But the man that you could still become. You're gonna take that kid away from all of this and make a new life and make sure he's got a shot, away from all this garbage and destruction."

"That's great, Victor. But what are you, gonna run away from your responsibilities now?"

"Bobby—I was gonna run away from my responsibilities, I would've stuck the wire up there myself."

"Classic, Victor."

"I'm sayin'."

"And so am I, I'm fuckin' serious. You, big, bad, boss of the neighborhood, what're you gonna be a pussy now and run away from your responsibilities? You're talking all this shit about me raising your kid, how about I start asking where the fuck are you in all of this raising your kid?"

Victor stared at him for a moment.

Bobby waited for an answer.

Then Victor gave him one: "I'm in a casket."

"The fuck is wrong with you, talking like that? It should be you he's trying to fire. You're telling me you're gonna be a coward and run away? You're gonna run away from your son, from your responsibilities?"

"I'm telling you that I'm sick, Bobby."

"Sick in the head."

"No. I'm telling you that I'm sick." Victor coughed, harshly—unintentionally. "I'm sick."

"What are you saying?"

"I'm saying that I'm sick. I got the bug, Bobby. I'm dying."

Bobby just looked at him. He didn't know what to say.

"I got the bug. I got HIV."

"Fuck. I'm sorry, man. I'm so sorry."

Victor just waved him off though. He was too macho for sympathy. "What are you gonna do?"

"I don't know. I don't even know what to say."

"How could you?"

"But, if it's not AIDS yet? If it's HIV? Then you're not dead yet, right? Don't you still got a chance? You're not dead yet. You gotta be a father, Victor."

"It's not in my future."

"What are you talking about? Are you listening to yourself? With science nowadays? They got medications now."

"Not for what I got."

"Yes they do. Don't give up on me, Victor. You're all I got, man."

"It ain't me, Bobby."

"What then? 'Cause you're all Michael's got too. You gotta stay strong for him."

"He's too young to know what's goin' on."

"But one day he's gonna be old. You want him to think you were a coward? One day he's gonna be old."

"And I'm not."

"Stop saying that. You don't know that."

"Yes I do. 'Cause I got cancer also."

"What?"

"In my stomach." Victor paused. "That night when Michelle got shot? We were on our way to the hospital. I was throwing up blood. We were goin' to the emergency room. I didn't know what was goin' on but I felt like I was dying and I was. I am."

"Fuck. I'm sorry."

"Don't be. I had my chances. I had my shot. Despite all the bullshit I had my shot and I rode it out to the fullest. I lived a good life."

"Fuck. Still."

"Still. I still lived like a king."

"I know. But still."

"Still."

"Yeah. How far along is it?"

"The cancer?"

"Of course."

"The doctor says I got 6 months if I'm lucky, really lucky. I'll be dead before you get out. But here's the thing."

"What?"

"I went to my lawyer's office."

"Who? Peters?"

"That's him. Good old John Peters, wheeling and dealing. And I made you and Michelle the executors of Michael's will."

"You mean Lauren?"

"Shit. Yeah, you and Lauren. 75% of what I have is goin' to him. The rest is goin' to you."

"Thanks."

"Who else was I gonna give it to?"

"I don't know? Mark?"

"That fat fuck? He would've spent it all at Roy Rogers."

Bobby smiled. "I'm just sayin'."

"Those guys have been taken care of. All the money I put in their pockets? They're fine, and if they're not it's 'cause they're stupid. But look."

"What's up?"

"I'm going back to see Peters again, end of this week when he's back from vacation. I'm gonna do a videotape."

"You're doing porn now?"

"Fuckhead—listen to me, this is important."

"Doggy style always is."

"As long as it's not Greek. But look, I'm gonna make a videotape, separate videotapes absolving you from every serious crime that you could ever get charged with. I mean, it's not like you've ever committed a serious crime, but just in case, so you can't get charged with somethin' I might've done myself. Know what I'm sayin'?"

Bobby did. "Thanks. I mean that."

"Whatever. I'm sure you'd do the same."

"You know it."

"That's what I just said. So I'm gonna make that tape, those tapes, and I'm gonna do that thing. And I'm gonna do whatever else I can to get you short time. And then I'm gonna focus on making as much money as possible to leave for you guys. That's why I couldn't leave before, Bobby. I wanted to know that Michael was as set as possible. So he'd never have to get into any of this shit. This shit business. When I got out I went back to hustling 'cause I didn't have shit and I had a kid on the way. It wasn't a choice. I didn't know how much time I had left I just took the best option I had. That was being with that guy. You understand?"

"Not really. You could've kept boxing. Everybody said you were gonna be a champ one day. You had skills; you were a Golden Glove for Christ's sake."

"I told you to listen. You're not listening."

"I'm not? When you told me you were buying a gym I thought it was a boxing gym. I mean, shit, inmates were paying you commissary to give them lessons in county, up in Albany. I remember, do you remember? You were hilarious."

Victor smiled. "Bobby, you don't get it. I couldn't keep fighting."

"Why?"

"'Cause I got HIV, dick. I would've never passed the blood test."

"Oh. My bad."

"Dumb ass," Victor said.

"Thanks."

"Anytime."

"Yeah."

"Seriously," Victor told him, "you're an asshole."

"I know. If you don't mind me asking though—when did you find out?"

"When Michelle got pregnant. We went to get physicals. Then we found out. She had it too."

"She did?"

"She did."

"Damn, man. I'm so sorry, man. I'm so sorry, Victor."
"Don't be," Victor said. "This life we lead? It's crazy."
"Yeah. I gotta be honest though, Bro."
"What?"
"She didn't look like she had it. I mean, you were looking a little fucked up lately, but she looked fine. She looked great."
"She was a dime piece."
"I know."
"She had those good genes, guy. And Michael got those genes, too. For whatever miracle that kid was born clean. For whatever reason, if there's a God out there, he didn't give it to him. He's got a fair shot in life. But that's why it's so important you get out so you're there to guide him."
"You got it, Brother."
"But watch out for this guy, for that guy. I'm gonna talk to him and all, but still."
"He doesn't know?"
"About the bug? Me being sick?"
"Yeah."
"Never. I never told him nothing. Michelle and I, we kept it between the two of us. Other than Peters you're the first person I'm telling. But when you get out, you watch your back, Bobby. I'll do what I can, I'm gonna talk to him, really talk to him, but you watch your back. You understand what I'm sayin'?"
"Honestly, Victor. Not to be an asshole, but if you're taking off? Do me a favor and take him with you. If anything do it for Michael."
"I can't do that."
"Why? Do me a solid, man."
"I can't."
"Why?"
"Because."
"Because what?"
"Forget the fact that he's been like a father to me."

"Forgotten."

"And forget the fact that he's been like a grandfather to my son."

"I'm sorry. Forgotten."

"Bobby for better or worse the guy raised me, man. Took me in after my pops died. Even before that, he took me in when my pops took off, when he went away. I can't do that to him, Bobby. He's done nothing but be there for me through thick and thin."

"You're right. I'm sorry I didn't mean it like that it's just that, you know."

"Nah I do, it's fine. But the truth is? It ain't even about that."

"What then?"

Victor paused for a second. He thought about his next words. "You keep this between me and you."

"Of course."

"No, seriously. I'll get in a lot of trouble."

"Like you have so much to lose."

"Yeah. He's gonna make me, Bobby."

"What?"

"Yeah."

"Seriously?"

"Yeah, you believe that? And I want him to make me. I'm gonna be a made guy, Bobby. After all these years, after everything, you believe that?"

But Bobby couldn't believe it. He couldn't believe what he was hearing. "I mean, like I said. Not to be an asshole, but does it really matter? Now, at this point?"

"You should be congratulating me."

"Congratulations. But what the fuck? Isn't your son's well-being more important?"

"Of course it is. And one day my son's gonna grow up, and when he looks back, I want him to know that in the short time I was granted on this Earth I became something. I was a somebody."

"But you already are a somebody. You fought at The Garden. You knocked people out. Not to mention you run that whole zip code. Everyone in Bayside eats 'cause of *you*, not them. You are already are somebody, Victor. You're a fucking boss."

"Thanks, I mean that. Thank you."

"No problem."

"But, look. It's a dying man's wish, Brother. Let me go out on top. It's all I ask."

Bobby sighed. *Okay*, Bobby thought. Nodded it, too. "Okay. You're right, man. I'm sorry, you're right, you earned it. Congratulations."

"Thank you. Honestly Brother it's just the one thing I wanna take with me. How I wanna be remembered."

"I hear you," Bobby said. "When's it gonna happen?"

"From what I'm led to believe? Merry Christmas."

"Will you still be okay then?"

"That's the thing. I don't know."

"So then why don't you talk to him, to that guy, then? Reach out to him; maybe he could do something for you."

"That's what I was planning, after I take care of this guy, I was gonna talk to him. If I'm checking out anyway I don't see why anyone would give a fuck. I'll make as many videos as possible."

Bobby smiled. It was a nice thought. "I'm sure the feds'll be happy about that."

"Fuck the feds. Fuck all those pigs. But listen, let me just get my button, and if I'm able just let me enjoy the holidays with my kid. Then after that, I'll tell the cops the gun was mine. Then you should get outta here."

"Brother, you don't have to do that. Take as much time as you need to. I'll be fine. I can do the time, you know that. Take as much time as you need. It's all gravy, man."

"I appreciate that. But if I'm fucked up? At that point? I'll probably be out on bail on a medical anyway so it shouldn't matter."

"Oh."

"Yeah," Victor said. He checked his watch. It was going on 2 P.M. So he told him, "Look, man. I gotta get outta here. Couple things I gotta do."

"Of course. Live it up, man. Ain't no need for you to be in here with me."

"Yeah. I'm picking Michael up from his Grandmother's, gonna have dinner with them. Tomorrow though I'm bringing him by Lauren's. I mean Lisa's. But she's, Lauren's gonna watch him for me, for a day or two."

"You spoke to her?"

"Right before I came to see you."

"You were with her?"

Victor shook his head. "I called her."

Damn. "You know she still hasn't accepted my calls? She won't speak to me."

"I'm sorry."

"Nah, it's my fault."

"Look, I'll talk to her."

"Thanks."

"I'll tell her, I'll straighten everything out."

"Just don't make her an accomplice."

"I won't. I'll see if I can get you back in her graces."

"Thanks, Victor."

"It's the right thing to do. Gotta have honor, know what I'm sayin'?"

"If you want to look at it like that."

"Yeah." Victor checked his watch again. He knew it was time to leave, but he didn't want to. So he just told him, "You know, it's crazy, man. This is some heavy shit. Having death call you?"

"I can imagine."

"No, you can't. It's not like getting shot at. It's not like having someone put a contract on you. It's not like having beef in the streets. It's having beef with the unknown. Beef with yourself. Beef with something inside of you, raging at you, destroying you little by little. It's scary, Brother. But I gotta tell you, in case I drop dead tomorrow—I'm sorry."

"Sorry for what? You've done nothing but have my back."

"Not at all. Bobby I'm sorry for bringing you into all of this, for letting you get back involved, especially since I knew my time was limited. I'm sorry for letting you into this shit business."

"Victor. I mean, it's not like you knew about the cancer though, right? I made my choices. I'm a man. I made my choices and I gotta deal with them, that's all. There's nothing to be sorry about."

"Yes there is, I feel like a jerk. When you were telling me you were gonna feel like a jerk that day at the park? It wasn't true. I was always the jerk. I should've looked out better for you."

"Looked out better for me?"

"A man admits when he's wrong. It should be me on the other side of this table. I feel like dirt. I feel like an asshole."

"Victor, you should feel like my Brother."

"How?"

"Because, everything you've done for me? With most of these fucks out here it's every man for himself. But just you sitting here, being straight with me? After everything we've been through together? Victor, the way you stuck by me when I was inside? And before, everything you did to get me out? I mean, whether you had nothing to lose or not, I don't know, but who gives a fuck? You were still there for me. Shit, my own blood, my own family, they all turned their backs on me, so fuck them. They're not here with me now. You're here with me now."

"Do they even know you're here?"

"In all honesty, I could give a fuck. The last time I got arrested they acted like I was garbage, like they had never made a mistake before, like they were perfect. You were the only person who was always there for me. Other than Lauren? Every time my back was to the wall growing up you were the only one who I ever knew was there for me 100 percent. And now looking back? You're the only person, Victor. You got nothing to be sorry about. Other than Lauren, and I shouldn't even say other than Lauren, 'cause that female shit is a different kind of loyalty, but other than her? You're the only person who was always loyal to me 100 percent, who I could never have a doubt in. You're the only one. The only one loyal 100 percent at least. Victor, my own blood turned me down, they disowned me. But you know what? Fuck it. *I* disowned *them*. You're my Brother, Victor. You, you and no one else. You're my Family."

"Nice speech."

"I try."

"Yeah. But you know what they say, right Bobby?"

"What?"

"About blood, and loyalty?"

"What?"

"You know, Jackie used to always tell it to me, all the time. He used to tell it to me, and it was—it's true. Because blood?"

"What about it?"

"Blood? Blood doesn't count for much."

"It doesn't?"

Victor shook his head. "Nah." Then he stood up, to end the visit, and Bobby did too. "'Cause at the end of the day," Victor said. "At the end of the day? At the end of the day all blood does is make you related. But loyalty? It's loyalty that counts the most, more than anything."

"Why?"

"'Cause at the end of the day?" Victor looked like he was going to cry. "At the end of the day, all blood does is make you related. But Loyalty? It's Loyalty that makes you Family."

53

"No," Victor said, as he lifted Michael out of his lap, and put him on the floor. "He needs to learn how to work. He needs to know what it means to sweat."

"He's only 4. He's baby."

"No. The earlier he learns the better off he'll be. C'mon, *Little Pal*. It'll be fun."

Abuela Marialita shrugged her shoulders. "You're the father," she said, as she sat at the round, dark wooden table in the small New Jersey kitchen. "Michael, always listen to the father."

Even though she appreciated Victor's gesture, the respect he always showed her, she still thought he was too young to work. *He should playing*, Abuela Marialita thought. But she was old school Puerto Rican. Whatever daddy said went.

At 87 though, she was actually Michael's great-grandmother. Her daughter, Michelle's mom, died from a heroin overdose years before. But Abuela Marialita was a great lady, and a smile came to her old, wrinkled eyes as she watched Victor and Michael do the dishes together. Victor standing, and Michael standing on the stool next to him.

Victor might not have been able to teach him much, not at this age at least, but he wanted him to remember whatever values he could. The quickest way to lose Victor's respect other than to be weak was to be lazy. Even if he wouldn't be around to see it, he still wanted his kid to grow up to be a boss one day. It ran in the family.

"You should be proud of your poppa," Abuela Marialita said. "He teaches you to be man."

As Victor and Michael looked at each other, as soap got all over their hands and shirts.

They smiled at each other.

That bond between father and son.

Victor was happy to pass it on.

Tonight was different, though.

Michael always sat in the back seat, in the car seat. Michelle insisted on it. It was the correct thing. It was the safe thing.

Tonight, though, as Victor began to buckle him in in Abuela Marialita's driveway, outside the small house that Victor paid for so she could live better and he could launder more of his money, Victor just said *Fuck it*.

She waved to them from her doorway, blew a kiss to Victor in the front seat of the repaired BMW as he backed out of the driveway and smiled and waved to Michael in the rear who smiled and waved back in return.

As they drove down the block of small houses in a better part of Newark, New Jersey, a real shitty, crime ridden city that Abuela Marialita refused to leave, even though Victor offered to put her up somewhere else, even in Puerto Rico if she desired, as long as he could wash his cash there… Victor turned the corner, and pulled over. He didn't get out, though. He just reached into the back, unbuckled his son, and had him hop through the middle into the front seat. Victor buckled him in, smiled at him, and gave him a high five. "Tonight you ride with the big boys."

"What cartoons do they watch?"

Victor smiled.

Other than a few lifestyle programs and this new show they had on called *The Sopranos*, Victor didn't watch much TV. His passion was always music. Sometimes he would dream of them finding a cure to his disease, and him one day opening a nightclub, maybe even managing some musicians. Not just financing their careers but also having his underlings break the heads of any DJs who refused to play their songs on the radio or in the clubs.

Opening his lounge, Covers, was a step in that direction. A step towards bigger and better things.

Michelle's death and his latest diagnosis derailed those plans.

But still, he knew his kid had it in him to one day grow up to be something. To be a somebody, a somebody who used his mind, more than his fists.

Bobby was right. Victor needed to spend as much time with Michael as possible. He still wanted to get made, and he would get made, he would talk to Jackie, and do this piece of work for him and somehow convince Jackie not to have anyone kill Bobby in jail, but Bobby was right. He needed to be there for his son. And the truth was he had stacked enough money already so Michael could go to school and not be on welfare. And even more so, was the truth that Victor enjoyed doing the dishes with him. Abuela Marialita even took a picture of the soap covered occasion so there would always be a memory of it. So, *Fuck it*, he thought. *If I'm gonna school my son, might as well be on music*.

"You know what it is that makes a song great, *Little Pal*?"

"What?" Michael asked as they drove down the freeway, listening to the characters from *Sesame Street*, Big Bird, Bert and Ernie.

"When it comes from something real. When it's real," Victor said. "You know what that means?"

Michael smiled. He nodded.

Victor smiled too. "What does that mean?"

"It means mommy made it."

Fuck, Victor thought.

Twenty minutes later the *Sesame Street* CD ended. He let it play till the end, for his son, who he tried his best not to look sad in front of. He needed to be strong, always, so his son would be strong, always. But now it was over. So he put in another CD, this one of his favorite singer, and asked, "You ever heard of Jimmy Roselli?"

"Is he friends with Big Bird?"

Victor smiled. "I named you after him."

"Big Bird?"

"Jimmy Roselli. His real name was Michael Roselli, Michael John Roselli. His dad was a boxer, too," Victor said as he put on his favorite song, which also happened to be his dad's, even Jackie's favorite song. Wiseguys in general, they loved it. It was their anthem. So Victor told him, "This song I'm playing right now? My father used to sing this song to me."

"When?"

"Sometimes at night. Sometimes at night when he tucked me in at night he'd sing it to me." *Or at least the night before he turned himself in and went to prison*, Victor thought.

But then he thought with more clarity. *Little Pal* was a song about a father just talking to his son, about what would happen if he ever had to go away. About who would take care of him, his *Little Pal*, and how he should act with them, day to day.

That night before Walter turned himself in, though, he didn't sing his song to him like he usually did. Instead, Walter Saravano just spoke to him.

And now, almost two decades later, facing a fate worse than that prison term that once confronted his father, Victor Saravano recalled it, that last night with him.

As the guitar strings pulled, his eyes got watery and *Little Pal*, Jimmy Roselli's old, crooning, beautiful version of the 1920s hit began Victor recalled the last real night he ever spent with his father.

Walter hated leaving Victor with a babysitter at night.

That's why Victor grew up in the social clubs all around Queens and the rest of New York City. Not having a mother figure in his life, Walter would bring Victor with him wherever he could, whenever he could.

Walter hated leaving him with people who he didn't consider family. Even when he had to leave him with the babysitter, on those late nights when Walter had to go out and do his thing, Walter did whatever he could to come back and tuck in his son at night, even if he had to go right back out on the streets after Victor fell asleep.

Walter loved his son. That's why it broke his heart knowing he had to leave him in the morning. He was happy he would be under the watchful of Jackie, living with him, while he was gone, but still. Walter knew this wasn't going to be an easy 4 to 8 years.

And that night, when he came home, he found his son already asleep, in his bed, with the lights off. Walter came in the room anyway though and sat down on the edge of the bed and just looked at him. Victor looked at the wall next to it.

Unbeknownst to Walter, when he sat down, it woke him up.

Not knowing this, Walter just touched Victor's shoulder. He rubbed it. "*Little Pal*," he said. "*Little Pal*."

Nothing.

Victor knew the next day was coming but had been telling his father he didn't want him to leave for some time now. He didn't want to be alone. His father was all he had.

"Uncle Jackie's family, too," Walter would tell him.

But it wasn't the same. Not to Victor, anyway.

Something his father always knew. Victor was super smart for his age. So Walter rubbed his shoulder. "*Little Pal*," he said.

Nothing.

FOR BLOOD AND LOYALTY

So Walter just spoke, almost sung the words that were in his heart. With a pain in his voice that came from not having an easy start. Walter brushed Victor's hair to the side, as he told him,

Little Pal, tomorrow, tomorrow, I've got to go away.
But Little Pal, my Little Pal, I promise,
Just hold your head, and there'll be a brighter day.
But in the meantime, my sweet child, promise me,
Promise me that you'll do whatever it is
That you hear your Uncle Jackie say.
And God forbid, God forbid, if it happens that
I never come back, that I'm always away?
When you get old enough to understand,
No matter what you do—
Don't get into these rackets, my Little Pal.
Be a better man.
And when you do get old enough to understand?
If your father's place is taken by another man?
No matter what, please, don't ever forget me, Little Pal.
And don't ever forget that I love you, my Little Pal.
And don't ever forget to be happy, my Little Pal.
And in those moments, when you are happy, my Little Pal?
Just say a few words for me, Little Pal.
Because then you'll grow up to be
The man that I should have been.
Damian—
I hope you become the man I could have been.

54

Victor laid in his bed for 45 minutes before he got out of it, just staring at his still asleep son, holding him, thinking. Caressing his hair and reflecting. Grateful for the first good night's sleep he'd had in some time.

Life wasn't perfect, and for Victor, life wasn't anywhere near happy but he was at peace. Looking, staring at his son sleeping there, peacefully, getting to know who Michael was over these last few years, he knew in his heart that Michael was going to grow up to be the man that both Victor and his father should have been.

In part because unlike Walter who was robbed of his stash and murdered by rival dealers Victor was leaving enough cash behind for Michael to start a life with and then some. He had hustled hard these last five years. He had more money on paper than anyone knew. He had done well, financially at least, and his son would reap the rewards of that.

But he didn't get that by sitting around on his ass. He got that by getting up, by grinding, by being constantly on the move, so when Michael woke, it was to the smell of sausage and eggs. "There he is," Victor said as he stood over the sizzling in the pan. He watched him walk into the kitchen in his *X-Men* Wolverine pajamas.

Victor sat him down at their round glass table and served him a nice plate. Eggs, sausage and bacon with fruit salad on the side. "Here you go, *Little Pal*." He poured him a small glass of orange juice.

75 minutes and 2 cartoons later, Victor made Michael take a shower.

After he was done, Victor himself hopped in and when he got out he gave himself a clean shave. Then he got ready.

Michael watched TV in the living room, and Victor focused in the bedroom. He put on lightweight light blue jeans, a white tee-shirt, and sat down on the edge of his king sized bed. Where he put on a pair of size 10 Timberland boots, and laced them up tight, but not too tight. They were tight enough to stomp someone's head in if he had to but still loose enough that he was able to stick his 6-inch buck knife inside the left one and a small Smith & Wesson snub-nosed .38 revolver inside the right.

You never know, he thought.

He had a stash of .38 caliber Rugers hidden away also but got rid of them right after the gas station debacle, tossed them into the water near The Whitestone Bridge late the next night. No need to ever get caught with one and have it traced back to that massacre. So for today he grabbed one out of his other batch.

Aside from sleeping next to a 12 gauge, Victor always kept a bunch of guns on hand, ready whenever he might need them.

Gold and guns, Jackie always told him, *gold and guns. The two things you never sell. The two things you stack.*

But the Smith & Wesson in his boot was special to him. 5 shots, lightweight and perfect for anything clandestine. Perfect for times like these. He'd been target shooting with it recently and loved it. A cop could pat him down while it was inside his boot and still not find it. Nobody looking for it could see it. And he never told anyone other than Bobby and Michelle that he carried it.

So Victor stood up, went to his dresser and put his money roll and keys in his front pockets. Then he put a second knife, a tactical one on his belt and his beeper on the other side of the buckle and put his gold Rolex and gold bracelet on his wrists.

After which he put a pair of black baseball gloves into his back pockets, a thin gold chain with a lion charm on it around his neck, and slowly, hesitantly, knelt down next to his bed, clasped his hands and closed his eyes to say a prayer for the first time in years.

But he couldn't get the words out. He hated hypocrites.

Victor opened his eyes, looked to the nightstand to his right and picked up the picture of Michelle that sat on top of it, next to his gold pinky ring and gold wedding ring. Then he kissed it.

For Blood And Loyalty.

"What's the most important thing in life, son?" Victor asked as they cruised down Francis Lewis Boulevard in the BMW. "Tell me."

Michael smiled.

"Respect, son. You gotta carry yourself with it, always. It's a 24-7, lifetime job. Don't ever forget that. You gotta always carry yourself with respect. 'Cause if you don't? Ain't nobody gonna respect you in return, and if you're not going through life with respect, it ain't worth going through at all, you feel me?"

Michael had no clue what he was talking about.

But Victor, he was okay with that. He smiled, and rubbed his head, sitting next to him in the front seat.

"Respect, Michael. It's about respect."

Michael smiled. Victor never stopped.

They pulled down Lisa's block in Fresh Meadows. Victor stopped outside Lisa's building, one similar to his. 5 floors, unassuming, no doorman. Brown bricks on the exterior. He walked Michael to the front door, holding a small duffel bag with some of his son's stuff, some money for his guardians in it that he couldn't report on his taxes and a small *X-Men* book bag with some coloring books inside. Michael liked the *X-Men* ones.

But when Lauren came downstairs to get him, Victor asked her for a moment of her time. He wasn't just dropping him off to her. He wasn't shrugging his responsibilities.

In return all Lauren did was ask him why he was wearing jeans and boots in the summer. It was 75 degrees out.

"I got some work to do today."

"What kind?"

"I'm doin' a construction project. Supervising it."

Lauren looked at him cynically. "You're wearing jewelry."

Victor shrugged his shoulders.

Whatever, Lauren thought. She thought he was an asshole for giving up his boxing career.

The thing was though Victor had no intention of insulting her intelligence. Even if she didn't exactly see it the same way, or didn't see it that way any longer or at least for the time being, he still saw her as a sister in law.

So they went upstairs, and Michael sat down on the living room couch to watch cartoons as Benny ran amuck and Lisa got ready to go to the park with them. There was a nice one nearby.

Then Victor and Lauren went outside, and started to walk down the block, where they had a talk.

Well, Victor talked. Lauren didn't know what to say.

"It's all good," Victor told her. "How could you?"

"I don't know," Lauren said.

All she could do was hug him.

He rubbed his face. He slapped himself lightly. "Wake up," Victor told himself. "Time to go to work."

He popped a DMX CD into the dash, sat there in his car for a second, and let the dark, hardcore, violent rap music amp him up as he focused, looked out on the road ahead of him. Victor inhaled and exhaled real good, a technique Jackie once taught him, like the father figure he always was. In times of stress, it always helped Victor clear his mind, focus on the task at hand. In short, he got himself together. Then Victor looked at Michelle's picture, kissed it, and put it behind the steering wheel.

He drove out of Fresh Meadows.

Given the life that he led, the people, the sharks that he was involved with, he always had to wonder if today was going to be his last. It took a strong stomach to do what he did and be able to sleep at night instead of staying up wondering if the cops were going to kick your door in as the roosters crowed.

Which gave Victor an edge he needed to succeed, because being constantly on edge, looking over his shoulder, he was always ready to break somebody's face in. It was what he lived for.

And on this day, it was after 11 A.M., and there he was at a red light on Northern Boulevard. The sun was beaming, cars were all around him. A McDonald's was on his right. Then next to him, on his left, a Lincoln Navigator pulled up on his driver's side.

They were playing rap music too, a couple of hard-headed looking Latinos in their late teens or early 20s. Victor suspected they were gang members, Latin Kings.

But not real Latin Kings.

The guy in shotgun was wearing a yellow t-shirt and black baseball hat. From up above in the truck though, on 22-inch chrome rims, like an egotistical, immature, hadn't been locked up yet drug dealer who needed an ass whooping bad, he looked down on him.

"Your mommy buy that car for you?" the one riding shotgun asked Victor.

Victor smirked. He couldn't believe what he had just heard. Especially on a day like today, after the last few weeks he'd just had. He couldn't believe it.

But Victor kept his composure, if anything, for Bobby's sake. He inhaled, he exhaled. And then, cool, calm, and collected, he turned his head to the left, and looked up at the wannabe next to him.

Who grilled right back at Victor: "Whassup, nigga?"

He was obviously trying to make his bones in life. He had something to prove. But Victor didn't. Instead, he just looked forward, out the front window, and smiled.

Then Victor picked up his black .9 millimeter.

Victor pointed it at him.

"Rock and roll," Greg said to himself, as he saw Victor come up the ramp in the public parking garage in the BMW. As he saw Victor drive right past him, out of his view.

A few minutes later, Victor, in sunglasses and a dark blue Yankees cap walked down a stairwell near the car and hopped in the shotgun side of the Buick Greg was driving. It was a 1990 LeSabre, 4-door, dark blue. Dark blue, comfortable velour seats also, with a bench seat. Victor took off his glasses, and shook his hand.

Greg, with his massive paw, squeezed and crushed it in return. Without letting it go, Greg eyed Victor up and down, the jewelry mostly. "I don't get it."

"What?" Victor asked.

"You kids today. What if somethin' goes wrong? You must have 30 G's worth a shine on ya. What if somethin' gets damaged?"

"Nothing's getting damaged. We're doin' society a favor over here."

Greg smirked. He let his hand go. "Society could give a shit, rookie." He patted Victor on his cheek, like he was his son.

There wasn't a thing Victor could do about it, or would do about it.

As Greg turned the engine on though, Victor asked him, "Snap?"

"We're not goin' to Snap."

Victor got puzzled. "Then where we doin' this?"

Greg put his fat finger to his lips. *Shhh*. He smiled, and he turned the cassette deck on. An old Frank Sinatra tape played as they rolled out of the parking garage.

And 75 minutes later, the feeling in Victor's stomach had only gotten worse.

Greg drove out there cautiously making unnecessary turns and going extra slow on the expressway so nobody could follow them without him noticing. He didn't feel like going back to the joint. More importantly he felt like getting the job done. It was a thing of honor. He truly loved his boss, Jackie too.

Before Victor knew it Greg got them all the way out to Lindenhurst, on the South Shore of Long Island. "This is Colombo territory, isn't it?" Victor asked.

"The Colombos are a fucking mess," Greg said. He stopped at a light on an unassuming point along Wellwood Avenue, a quiet stretch surrounded by middle class mom and pop stores. Then he looked at Victor: "*We* run shit."

His protégé agreed. Victor loosened up a little, felt more at ease as Greg turned a corner, pulled into a small parking lot behind a small lounge, one with tinted windows, like his. "So what is this place, a social club?"

Greg parked up next to the only other car in the small 6-spot lot. It was a big, 4-door, silver E-Class Benz. Not that Greg gave a fuck though. He just turned off the engine, and then he looked at him again. "Today? It's a church."

Victor nodded.

"You ready?"

55

"What do you mean you're not coming with me?"

"I don't know, Lauren. Do I really wanna watch this guy's kid?"

"We were going to spend the day together."

"Yeah, but—"

"But what? You can see Fernando any time you want, Lisa. We're going to the park, we planned it. We're bringing the dog. I can't handle both of them by myself."

"Lauren."

"It's beautiful outside, let's just go."

"Look, sis. You wanna stay here, you can stay here as long as you want, you know that. But this guy, Victor. I've heard stories."

"Whatever," Lauren said.

"I just don't wanna get caught up in anything. And now he's got his dog here?"

"Whatever," Lauren said.

"I'm sorry."

"I told you. Whatever."

Lisa walked away. She went into her room.

Lauren though, she almost lost it. She was angry, frustrated. But then she looked at Michael. And she got herself together. Then she squatted down.

Which made Michael smile. He went over to her, and he closed his eyes. He hugged her.

So she hugged him back, like a mother would.

56

Greg shut the door, the car door. He stretched to the sky, and inhaled. He took a deep breath. "It's been a while," he said, as Nino greeted them, opened the back door to the lounge but didn't step outside. "Long fuckin' time."

"Since when?" Victor asked.

Greg smiled. "I was away when youse guys did that thing."

Victor shrugged his shoulders.

Greg followed. He swung his arms around a little, loosening up. "It's been a while since an old guy like me had some excitement, know what I'm sayin'?"

"Who gives a fuck?" Nino asked. "Get inside already."

Greg was being nonchalant about the work in front of them. Not that he cared, though. He had always taken a liking to Victor, he knew he had balls and that's what he valued most. So he continued ignoring Nino. "I gotta say, I feel good, kid. Ya gotta stay young, you know what I'm sayin'?"

Victor did. *There's a reason this guy did 20 fuckin' years in the can.*

"What the hell is wrong with you two? Get the fuck inside before somebody sees you."

57

"Lettuce and tomatoes?"

"Check," Michael said.

"Boar's Head ham and cheese?" Lauren smiled.

"Check," Michael repeated, as he took them out of the cooler and put them on the sheet.

"And last but not least, Wolverine and Cyclops," Lauren said, as she took his action figures out of her purse and handed them over. The two of them were sitting on a white sheet, Indian style, with Benny in between, taking in the sun and ready to dine in the middle of Crocheron Park. It was nice.

She fixed them some sandwiches and fed Benny slices of meat and dairy while she did it. Lost in the moment though, she didn't see Michael take the disposable Kodak camera out of her bag.

"Smile," he said.

Lauren did. She moved her head next to Benny's and was sure it came out nice.

Then she grabbed the camera and took one of him with the dog instead. "Say cheese."

"Parmesan!"

Goombahs. Lauren found it funny. As she snapped a few more photos though, a nice-looking, blonde white woman in her late 40s walked by, with a novel in her hand, and asked if she'd like her to take a picture of all three of them.

"Sure, thanks."

"I'm Elaina, by the way," the woman said as she took a picture.

"Lauren."

"Hold on." She moved back a few steps, and then a few to the side. "Let me take another, I don't think it came out good." So she snapped another photo. "There. That one might be better," she said, as she gave the camera back.

"I hope so."

"You from around here?"

"Nearby," Lauren said.

"I love Bayside, don't you?"

"It's nice, gotta say."

"Yeah, the weather's been great lately. I love the summertime."

Lauren just looked at Michael.

"The summertime's when all the best stuff happens, don't you agree?" Elaina asked.

Lauren responded hesitantly. "Yup."

"Yup. If you don't mind me asking, how old's your son? He's cute."

Lauren wasn't sure how to respond. She'd never been asked that before.

But Michael had heard it before. "She's not mommy. Mommy's on vacation."

The woman looked at Lauren. She stared at her. "So that's what you told him?"

"What?" Lauren didn't like where this was going.

"I'm not here by accident, Ms. Bassi."

Lauren, startled, looked around. She moved backwards, away from this woman. A chill ran down her spine.

"I'm with the Federal Bureau of Investigation. I'm with the FBI, Ms. Bassi."

"What? What do you want? I don't know anything."

"I didn't say that you did. But your boyfriend there? If he ever wants to see the light of day again, he better start telling us everything. That is, unless you're okay with a child growing up in the foster system. And that is, unless you're okay with your man there dying in the prison system. I heard the Bloods have an open contract on him."

Michael looked at Lauren. "What are Bloods?"

Lauren didn't answer. Instead she just looked at him too, and put her arm around him. And then she looked at the agent. "In front of him, in front of a child, you do this?"

The agent smirked. "Oh, here, I almost forgot." She pulled a business card out of her novel and handed it to her. Then she smiled, and waved at Michael. "Take care, kid. Enjoy your youth."

58

"Well at least you're feelin' better," Lorenzo told him.

Yeah, Lenny thought, as they drove down the highway in Lorenzo's brand new silver Cadillac coupe.

Well at least he thought it was Lorenzo's brand new silver Cadillac coupe. Instead it was a rental, this way Lorenzo could be sure there was no way there'd be a hidden recording device in it, courtesy of the cops, or the feds.

"You gotta understand, Lenny. There was no other way around it. It had to be done."

"Still, though. I didn't know they was gonna rob you guys. I was innocent. I am innocent."

"Not at all, you were still part of it."

"I'm sayin', though."

"Doesn't matter, you didn't stop it. At least raise a red flag. You see what I'm sayin'? Even if I wanted to help you I couldn't, it had to be done."

"This guy went overboard, though, I'm just starting to feel better."

"Yet another reason why they call it setting an example."

"Still. Still. I still got my hand wrapped. My leg? I can't book a club for at least another few weeks."

"Well you're gonna be okay for today, right?"

Lenny sighed.

"This is Nino's, his goumada's nephew here. You gotta show him the ropes. Show that proper respect."

"I know."

"Look, Lenny. You do good, start doing some good things on the arm, you never know."

"As long as you guys do."

"We do. If we didn't you wouldn't be around no more. Very least you would a got chased, know what I'm sayin'?"

Lenny told Lorenzo he did. But Lenny told himself he'd kill every last one of them the moment he got the chance. *Scumbags*.

Music played from the speakers above the small dance floor. Frank Sinatra worked the room. But in the back office, they only heard it in thumps through the wall.

"So where are you, over in Dix Hills now, right?" Victor asked.

"Yeah," Nino told him.

"Long drive from here to there?"

"Not so bad. You thinkin' a goin' out East eventually?"

"I honestly, I don't know," Victor said. "This whole Long Island thing, it's too spread out for me."

Greg chimed in: "Kid's got a point. I don't know how the fuck you do it."

"What?" Nino asked.

"The suburb, suburban life," Greg said.

"It's nice, it's quiet. I got a grandkid out there now, playin' soccer and shit."

"You better be careful," Greg told him.

"What?" Nino asked.

"You keep it up out there?" Greg said. "Surrounded by fresh cut grass? You're gonna end up getting soft, lose your edge."

"I don't need an edge," Nino replied. "I'll always have an edge. I got a brain."

Greg smirked. "And I got a fucking gun. What's your point?"

"So what is it exactly that the kid wants to know?" Lenny asked.

"He wants to be a DJ," Lorenzo told him.

"No. I mean, he say why?"

"He didn't say a fucking thing to me. Nino just goes this kid wants to be a DJ, better have someone school him then. So I called you."

"I can't front. It's a tough life, lots of competition."

"We could do something about that."

"I figured."

"No shit you figured. Look, the kid just needs a good teacher, alright? So don't you fuck up on me in there. You're getting another chance here. Don't fuck up on me in there."

"I won't," Lenny said. As he looked out the window, hoping the cops wouldn't let him down.

As Lorenzo checked the rearview, confident he had ducked the tail that was following them.

"I don't know," Nino said. "You think he's ready?"

"Your kid," Greg said, "your answer."

"I wanted to bring him along but I don't know. Maybe on the next one."

"How old is he now?" Victor asked.

"21," Nino said, "22 in a month."

"You should've brought him," Greg told him. He looked at Victor. "'Bout the same age as you, right? Your first?"

Victor smiled.

Greg raised his eyebrows. He looked back at Nino. "You should a brought him along. How often we all get together for something like this? Especially nowadays? He could a learned from the masters."

"Yeah, 'cause you're so smart," Nino said.

"Hey, fuck you, bo," Greg told him.

Nino found it funny. "Look, it ain't that."

"What then?" Greg asked.

"It's just that, I don't know. I don't know if he's 100 percent committed, for Our Thing. Now, does he have what it takes, for Our Thing? Yeah, I think so. But I don't know if he wants it, not for the right reasons, anyway."

"So what? Bring him along," Greg said. "Let him find out. Bonanno bonding."

Nino thought he had a point. "Maybe next time. Maybe next time. He's gotta earn his right to earn his rights."

Greg swiveled in his chair. He turned to Victor. "I remember how your pops used to get down. Walter was a monster."

Victor was flattered. "I walk in his image."

"He was a good guy, your father," Nino said. "Everybody liked him, we all did. Especially Jackie, they were tight."

"I know," Victor said, "I know. I just wish I had more time with him."

"Well," Greg told him, "this is where he would've wanted you to be. With us, where you belong."

"It's true. You ever need anything, kid, you know we got you a hundred."

"I know," Victor said. "It goes both ways. I can't wait to belong."

"You already do," Greg replied. "You were born into this. You were made for this. Don't worry, your time's comin'."

Hopefully, Victor thought. "I'll tell you though, Nino, you wanted to bring your kid along, I wish you'd a brought your kid along."

"And why is that?" Nino asked.

"Just that, I don't know," Victor said. "He's hilarious. I remember when he smacked that pissboy at Caffé on the Green that time. Your son's hilarious."

"He's right," Greg said. "Your son *is* hilarious. We could use some more laughs around the pizza parlor. I don't know what's been goin' on with Jackie lately."

Nino shook his head. "Hilarious? What a fucking mess that was. There was nothin' hilarious about it. Hilarious or not he caused a whole fucking sit-down over that, the Gambinos were pissed."

Greg still found it funny. "That's what happens when you hire pissy pissboys. Fuckin' jerk deserved it."

"Yeah—" Nino paused. He was looking out the small back window, the one that faced the parking lot. "Hold on, is that it? That's it," Nino said, seeing Lorenzo's Cadillac pull up next to his rented Benz and Greg's rented Buick. They were using them to transport the body parts.

So Victor put on his black baseball gloves. He loosened up real quick. He cracked his neck.

"So many beautiful Italian singers out there and all this guy does is play Sinatra, Sinatra," Lorenzo said, standing with Lenny outside the back door. "Sinatra, Sinatra, Sinatra. I don't get it."

"Personally, I like Como."

"'Cause you're a homo. Congratulations."

Nino opened the door. "There he is," he said, happy to see Lorenzo. "The Flushing Dumpling." They gave each other a hug, kissed on the cheek.

Then Lenny extended his hand to shake Nino's.

But Nino just looked at it. Then he looked into Lenny's eyes. He didn't shake it. "This way," Nino said, as he ushered them inside.

They followed him, Lenny behind the two of them, as the door swung closed behind them.

"Youse guys want something to drink?" Nino asked as he walked toward the dance floor, where the bar was.

"Ehh, wouldn't mind a little seltzer, this place got it," Lorenzo said. Then he looked over his shoulder. "Malco, you want something?"

Lenny did. "Tell you the truth, I wouldn't mind a"

Bing! Victor jumped out from the shadows and clocked him over the head with a metal baseball bat, a TPX special. Lenny dropped right to the ground and started convulsing. Victor didn't care, though. He banged him once more in the forehead, then hammered him again right in the same spot.

Lenny stopped moving.

Victor dropped the bat down and flipped him over, onto his stomach. He knelt down over him, over his back, lifted up his head into his hands, and looked at Greg and smiled. "Monster, huh?"

Victor snapped Lenny's neck. He broke it. He dropped it to the ground.

Greg got all giddy. He was proud of him. "Kid's got chops." He looked to Nino and Lorenzo. "You see that? Kid's got chops."

"Alright," Victor replied. He stripped off Lenny's shirt, and just like they thought, found a wire underneath it strapped to his chest.

Lorenzo looked on in disgust.

Victor disconnected the wire from the mini-recording box hidden inside his underwear and handed them to him.

Lorenzo asked Nino, "Where's the tool box? I gotta smash this thing."

"Behind the bar," Nino said.

FOR BLOOD AND LOYALTY

Victor and Lorenzo went over to the bar and found some drop cloths, some metal saws, some bleach, duct tape, plastic gloves, a few small suitcases and a metal box filled with all kinds of tools.

"What the fuck?" Victor said.

"What?" Lorenzo asked.

"You guys couldn't get the electric ones?" He was talking about the saws.

"You use those," Nino said, "you're gonna splash blood all over this place. Put the cloths down; try to be neat about it."

"Still," Victor told him, "it's gonna be a pain in the ass, then."

"So what?" Lorenzo said. "What'd we tell you 'bout bein' professional?"

For the obvious reasons, Victor didn't give a fuck.

But everyone else did. Except for Greg, he didn't really give a shit either.

Victor had to ask though, "I don't see why we can't just toss the prick off a boat."

Nino responded, "You really wanna be drivin' around with a load in your trunk? God forbid you get pulled over."

Lorenzo agreed. "We gotta Samsonite this prick, sooner the better."

"Exactly," Nino said. "Get to work."

"What, you're not gonna help me?" Victor asked.

"Kid," Greg said. "What kind a mentors we'd be if we made it easy for you? C'mon, just get this done and we'll tell Jack what a good student you were."

"My fuckin' teacher now," Victor told them.

Lorenzo put the recording device on top of the bar and was about to smash it, but then just decided to use a screwdriver and open it up, so he could be more clean about it.

Victor though, as he dropped down with the saw to do Lenny, he started to feel queasy.

The guys knew something was up.

He was knelt down, the saw was up against Lenny's leg, but he wasn't cutting.

The guys thought the sight of the body was making him nauseous.

"What, you're acting like you ain't done this before," Greg said.

It wasn't the body. It wasn't the dismemberment. Victor's stomach was starting to bother him again. It was the cancer being glorified by his HIV. He had the saw lined up next to his knee, but he wasn't moving.

"Victor," Greg asked, "you alright?"

He was burning up. His migraine rushed back. He fell over to his side. He was half out of it.

Nino didn't buy it. "If this is some ploy to get out of your job, get the fuck outta here."

"Shut up," Greg said. He went over to him with Lorenzo. "You alright?"

After a moment, he started to come out of it.

Just to make sure though, Greg gave him a quick slap across the cheek.

Victor's eyes opened right up. He grunted. He moaned.

Even Lorenzo was concerned. "What, all your energy go to the asshole?"

Victor tried getting up, on his feet, but he felt weak. "Greg. Help me."

"What is this shit?" Nino asked.

"I thought I told you to shut up?" Greg said to him. He looked at Victor. "Here, kid." He helped him up.

Victor leaned against the wall. His stomach felt hollow.

"Victor," Greg said, "snap the fuck out of it."

Victor tried to get some words out but was having trouble. Weakness and nausea took over. "I gotta," he mumbled. "I gotta, I gotta use, I gotta use the toilet. The bathroom."

"Kid," Nino said. "Don't you know the first fuckin' rules of this by now?"

Victor managed to look at him. *What?*

"You gotta use the can," Nino said, "you use it ahead a time, so you can be relaxed. You don't know that by now?"

"Gimme a fuckin' break," Greg said. "The bathroom? Gimme a fuckin' break. Couple a few times down the plank, that shit don't matter no more. Go ahead, kid, take your shit."

"Kid's getting soft," Nino said, as Victor walked into the bathroom, his hand on his stomach.

It wasn't a big bathroom, just two urinals and two stalls to their right. Victor went into the stall closest to the urinals and the door, but didn't even lock the stall door.

He nearly fainted, almost tumbled over. His body was attacked by a sudden bout of fatigue. He held on to the top of the stall to keep from collapsing. He was barely able to sit down.

And when he did, when he got his pants down, he exploded like an upside down volcano. It felt like fire was coming out of his ass.

Damian "The Victor" Saravano, an alpha male his entire life, looked down, into the toilet, and saw a pool filled with blood.

It was bad. His body started feeling weaker, the fatigue increased. But it wasn't just any kind of fatigue. It was the kind of fatigue that makes you dizzy. It was the kind of fatigue that makes you want to lie down. It was the kind of fatigue that makes you just want to give up.

He was hunched over, pants around his ankles and head in his hands, running on empty, barely awake. In his day one of those guys whose mind was always as sharp as the edge he lived his life on, here he was, not even noticing that the bathroom door was opening.

Lorenzo went to the urinal closest to it, unzipped to take a leak, and asked, "Vic, you alright?"

Victor didn't respond.

"Victor," Lorenzo said.

Victor wasn't listening. Victor was in a funk. Victor felt like his managers, his diseases, the ones controlling more and more of his life had thrown in the towel on his behalf.

He couldn't take it anymore. He just didn't give a fuck anymore.

"Victor."

No response.

Lorenzo zipped back up and decided to knock on the stall door. When he did it opened a bit.

"Yeah?" Victor asked, weakly.

"Victor, what the fuck? You alright?"

He was feeling dizzy. He shook his head.

Lorenzo looked away, toward the bathroom's door, and shook his head also. Then he looked back at Victor. "My man, you think you're gonna be able to help out or not? We gotta get moving."

Victor just shook his head. Still out of it, he didn't even notice that now the stall door was opened all the way.

"It is what it is, then," Greg said.

Victor lifted his head up, but only to see Greg standing there, holding a black semi-automatic at his side, pointed at the floor.

"I'm sorry, kid," Greg said.

"What?" Victor asked, weary. "What the fuck?" He started to come out of it. "What is this, the fuck are you doing?"

"I'm sorry," Greg repeated. He aimed the gun at him.

Lorenzo was to his left, towards the bathroom door, almost out of Victor's view, and Nino was standing on the side of the stall, in front of the urinals with a black .9 millimeter identical to Greg's in the back of his waist. But this work was Greg's to do, not theirs. He took it upon himself to pull the trigger, as usual.

Even though Greg enjoyed pulling them, however, he had also enjoyed Victor's presence over the years, so he told him, "Before I do this, I just want you to know. I'm a gonna do what I can to look out for your kid. This isn't personal."

"Fuck you," Victor said, fully awake. "Fuck all of you."

"Like I said, it's not personal."

"And like I said, fuck all of you, you crusty motherfuckers. I've been bangin' out with you guys since I was in diapers; you turn on me like this? Sitting on the toilet of all fuckin' places?"

"Just fuckin' do it already," Nino said.

"Fuck you the most, Nino," Victor said right back.

Nino shook his head. "Greg, do it already."

"I don't even get any last words?" Victor asked. "You do me that dirty like that?"

"You wanna say somethin', say somethin'," Greg said. "Or don't."

Nino thought Greg was crazy. "We only got so much fuckin' time, Greg. Do it or don't, I'll fuckin' do it for you."

Greg looked at Nino. "Shut the fuck up." And Nino did. Then Greg looked back at the dead man on the toilet.

"Thanks," Victor said.

"Like I told you, it ain't personal."

"You gonna at least tell me why this is happening?" Victor asked.

"It's not worth getting into," Greg said. "Say your piece or don't, but we got things to do."

"So that's it?" Victor asked him. "You're gonna point that thing at me, not even give me a reason?"

Greg shook his head. "You gotta get somethin' off your chest, kid, now's the time. I'm being generous."

"The time? Generous? So no fuckin' dignity, huh? This is how I'm gonna be remembered? Least let me pull my fuckin' pants on. Everything I've done for you people you're not even gonna even let me die with a little fuckin' dignity?"

Greg understood where he was coming from. "Alright. But I'll tell you this: you can have your dignity. But before you do, you take that hawk off your waist and toss it over here. Don't think I'm fuckin' stupid, now."

Victor rolled his eyes. "Whatever." He took the knife on his belt and lobbed it by Greg's feet.

"Good boy," Greg said. He kicked it over by where Nino was. "Now put your fuckin' pants on."

"Thanks." Victor put his hands near his pockets, near his boots. "But before I do, before you shoot me, if you can, do one other thing for me, Greg. If you can."

"What?" Greg asked.

"Before you shoot me, at least tell me why. At least do that, Greg. Tell me why this is happening."

Greg replied, "Look, you know I always liked you, kid."

"I liked you too, Greg. I still like you. You don't gotta do this. Least give me a chance to right whatever wrong this is over."

"Can't do that, Victor. Pull your pants up."

"Why can't you do that, Greg? Why don't I at least get a chance? I ain't one of those humps out there. Don't treat me like that, Greg."

"It's not me, Vic, or any of us. It's orders."

"Orders?"

"Orders, Victor. Orders are orders."

"Jackie's orders?"

"Orders, kid, orders."

Victor shook his head. "Whatever. Just tell me one thing, though. Give me one honest answer."

Greg looked at him: *What?*

"Was it you guys shot Michelle?"

"Absolutely fucking not," Greg said. The question made him angry. "What do you think we are, half assed gangbangers? We don't do drive-byes. This is Cosa Nostra; we don't do fucking drive-byes, Goddamnit. Now pull your fucking pants on or don't. How the fuck could ask me something like that? Jesus, Christ. Pull your fucking pants on now or I'm gonna leave you on that fuckin' seat."

"There's no need to be angry, Greg. It's all I wanted to know." Victor reached down to his pants. "It's the only thing, Greg. You gotta understand."

He had a point.

"Fine," Greg said. "You're right, I do. But you gotta do one thing for me too, though."

Victor looked at him. "Like I got a choice."

"If there's something after all of this? I'd like to think there is, but who the fuck knows, but if there's something after all of this? Do me one thing."

"What?" Victor asked.

"You see your pops? You tell Walter that I could a stopped it, I would a stopped it. You tell him that I loved him."

Lorenzo shook his head.

"Fuckin' asshole," Nino said. "You're a fuckin' asshole."

Greg looked at him. "I thought I told you to shut the fuck up? Shut the fuck up."

Then Greg turned back to Victor, and when he did:

Victor shot him.

Boom. Right in his chest, with his .38, the one that was in his boot.

Greg flew back against the wall, dropped the gun and dropped against it to the ground.

Lorenzo looked at him in shock.

As Victor came off the toilet with his pants around his ankles and took a shot at him, too.

Lorenzo caught the bullet in his left temple, dropping him.

Nino couldn't get his gun ready in time. He should've rushed him.

As Victor dove to the floor, used Greg as a cushion, something he planned from the toilet, knowing full well he wouldn't be able to maneuver with his pants down; he bounced off of Greg, looked up at Nino and banged him with two shots, right in his upper body. One of them pierced his heart.

Nino dropped dead.

Victor looked around. He laughed. He could barely believe he pulled that off. "You crusty motherfuckers." Victor laughed. He looked at everyone from the safety of the floor. "You crusty motherfuckers." Victor was ecstatic. He kept on laughing. "You crusty motherfuckers, any you fucks even still alive?"

Nino and Lorenzo were dead. Greg was breathing heavier than ever. He was staring at Victor, in pain, a man less tough would have been dead, but Greg wasn't. He coughed up blood instead. His eyes could move but his body could barely wiggle. He was almost frozen like a stiff.

So Victor got up, held his pants up with one hand and gave him a boot to the face, knocking Greg on his side. He dropped his .38 into the sink, picked up Greg's gun and double checked the other two bodies. They were dead like he thought.

Victor smiled. He was proud of himself. So he wiped his ass.

Then he zipped up, buckled up, and returned his focus to Greg.

Greg was staring at the bottom of the toilet bowl, almost paralyzed.

"Greg," Victor asked with a smile on his face, "what the fuck?"

Greg coughed up more blood. "I guess you got me, kid."

"You guess?" Victor laughed. "Yeah, you keep on guessin', don't ya. Guess all you want."

Greg looked at him. He tried to talk, but only blood came out.

"What?" Victor asked.

Greg was wheezing. He was barely alive, but managed to tell him, "I meant what I said before, kid."

"Don't call me 'kid'. Don't you dare call me 'kid', especially after this, you crusty motherfucker."

Greg leaned back, fell back onto his back, just stared at the ceiling and smiled.

Puzzled, Victor smiled also. "Something funny?"

Greg almost laughed. "Fuck it. I'm a gonna die, might as well be by you."

"Yeah," Victor said. "Tell me, Greg. Why the fuck did Jackie order this?"

Greg looked at him. "He didn't."

Bang. Victor kneecapped him, with his .38.

The bullet made blood splash out of Greg's leg as agony laced with blood rained out of Greg's mouth.

"Motherfucker. Why the fuck did Jackie order this?"

Greg coughed up more blood, as he said, "Fuck you."

Boom. Victor shot him again in whatever was left of that same kneecap with Greg's semi-automatic. His .38 was out of bullets.

"Let me tell you something, Greg. Let me ask you, actually, 'cause you know I always liked you too. You ever known me to not be a man of my word?"

His leg was throbbing. Everything was throbbing. Well, whatever he could still feel was throbbing. "The fuck is your point?"

"You don't tell me everything I want to know, and tell me quick, I'm gonna make it painful, real painful. Just 'cause I like you."

"Fuck yourself, kid."

Bam. Victor shot him again in the same spot. "You like that, huh?"

Greg was in agony.

So Victor shot him again one more time, right in that same spot. "Tell me what I wanna know, *now*."

Greg coughed up some more blood. He was close to choking. But, he was still Greg DePalma. "Like I already told you, *kid*. Go fuck yourself."

Victor smiled. Even though he was pissed off, he had to respect Greg's gangster. "You know, I'd chop off your nuts, I would. But my only fear is that by the time I tried to feed 'em to ya, you'd already be unconscious."

Greg got a kick out of it.

"Is that a smile I see?"

"What can I say, kid? When I got released? I was proud the way you'd done gone and grown up. I'm still proud a ya."

"Good." Victor shot him in his ankle.

Greg cried out in pain.

"Make it easy for us both, Greg. I don't wanna do this to you. Nino, it would've been easier. Bert, I was planning on sneaking up on his ass anyway so who gives a fuck. Make it easy."

Several moments of pain later, Greg started to get his bearings. He tried to talk but it was hard for him.

"What?" Victor asked. He knew Greg was trying to say something.

Then, he was able to. "Tell you the truth? I was gonna whack out Bert too. Fuck it."

"Fuck it. Tell me what I wanna know, Greg."

"All in all, kid." Greg's breathing got worse. "All in all, kid, I done a little over 20 and a half. Anybody ever tells a story 'bout Greg DePalma, it ain't gonna be with a piece a cheese at the end."

"But they are gonna say the reason I went on a fucking murder spree is 'cause you didn't tell me what the fuck I wanted to know. Why the fuck did Jackie order this, Greg? Tell me, tell me or else I'm gonna go home, strap on a vest, grab a fucking machine pistol and I'm gonna walk up in the CasaBlanca myself and let loose."

Greg stared at him. "You wouldn't do that."

"I would."

"You wouldn't. You'd be finished."

"I already am finished, Greg. I'm more finished than you know. And just to prove it, just so you do understand why I don't give a fuck, why it means nothing to me right now to go over there and turn Joe's place, his pride and glory into fuckin' Kosovo, and stick his head on a fuckin' stake? I'm gonna tell you how finished I am, just so you do know, just so you do understand. And then you're gonna start talkin'. Then you're gonna tell me everything, Greg." Victor paused. "Questions?"

Victor couldn't believe what he had just heard. Cruising down the expressway in Nino's Benz, he couldn't believe it. He just smoked a cigarette and blasted the air conditioning with the windows down. He was fuming.

He got stuck in traffic on the way back too, almost strangled the hippies in the car next to him. They were so happy, a bunch of teenagers lost in the magic of youth. But Victor didn't do anything, though. What was more important than him having Greg's blood splashed all over his pants and shirt, if he should get stopped by the cops—was that he had a job to do, the most important job of his life. He had to focus.

The first thing he did after getting off the expressway was go to the garage. He ditched the Benz. It was a nice ride but the BMW had his other gun with a full clip in it. Plus, it also had a fresh set of clothes in it. He took them out of the trunk, changed, and went about his business.

By the time Victor showed up to Ralph's, he was refreshed, kind of. He was feeling sick again but he didn't give a fuck. This was it. This was the beginning of the end. This was the way it had to be and he knew it.

He called his son on the way to talk to him one final time in case shit went wrong, before he went there, but this was it. He could feel it. If he didn't do what he had to Bobby would never leave jail alive. Then Lauren would die inside and who knew if his *Little Pal* would even survive.

There was a contract on Victor's head and Victor couldn't let them fulfill it.

Parked out front, Victor patted himself on the face. He looked at himself in the rearview mirror, and he said a prayer. He held some rosary beads in his hands and he spoke to Michelle. He spoke to his father too, even to the mother he never knew. He had to do what he had to do.

Victor got out of the car, and walked inside. The door was wide open, he didn't even have to pull it open as he strode through like the seasoned killer with nothing to lose that he was, and except for little 75-year-old Sicilian Pepe behind the counter, his middle aged helper next to him, the place was empty.

Victor asked them, "He here?"

By the look on Pepe's face, he knew that he was.

He ignored Pepe's pleas not to and went straight into the back office and slammed the door shut behind him.

Jackie was on the phone. He was standing and talking on it, alone.

When he saw Victor, when he saw the look on his face, he hung up. Jackie was startled. "What happened? Where's the guys?"

Victor didn't say anything.

"The fuck happened?"

"What the fuck do you think happened?"

"I don't know, you tell me, Victor. Did you do it?"

"You're really gonna sit here and keep playing me like a patsy?"

"The fuck are you talking about, *patsy?* The fuck are you talking about?"

"You killed my father."

Jackie's jaw dropped.

"It was you."

"Victor—"

Victor pulled the nine out from behind his waist and pointed it at him. He squared it right between his eyes.

Jackie started to back up, put his hands up, but Victor just walked closer to him.

"Tell the truth, Jackie. Tell me the truth. Why did you do it? Really, why?"

"Victor, I don't know what you're talking about."

"Really?"

"Yeah, really. Your father was my best friend, you know that."

"And then let me guess. I've been like a son to you too, haven't I?"

FOR BLOOD AND LOYALTY - 227 -

"Of course you have. I raised you, Goddammit."

"And that's exactly why this sucks so much."

Boom. Victor put one in his kneecap.

Jackie dropped to the ground, screaming, holding his leg in pain. "Victor, what the fuck!?"

"Why did you kill my father? Tell the truth."

Jackie cried: "I don't know what the fuck you're talking about."

Boom. Victor put one right above his other kneecap.

Jackie cried in pain some more.

"Jackie, I already know you did. I know it was you that pulled that trigger."

"And how the fuck do you know that?"

"'Cause you were his best friend. Who else would've done it?"

"Victor—"

"Jackie, I don't got time for this shit. So you tell me right now why you did it, or when I filet Fat Joe's fat ass I'm gonna say you were the reason why I put a slug in his rectal cavity."

Jackie paused. Jackie stared at him.

"I know it wasn't the Colombians, Jackie. The same fuckin' Colombians who you had the nerve to tell me that you guys even got revenge on. You even showed me the fuckin' street in Jackson Heights *that you did it on*. You cocksucker. I know it was you and the guys, you cocksucker, so you tell me now, and you tell me *why*."

Jackie knew the jig was up.

Jackie knew that there was only one option left.

So Jackie gathered himself together, and he told him: "Alright, Damian. You motherfucker, you. You really wanna know the truth? Okay, I'll tell you the truth." Jackie paused. "Fuck it, I did it. I fucking did it. I put two in the back of your father's head and never thought twice about it. Happy?"

Victor smirked.

BOOM. Victor shot him in the nuts.

This time Jackie *really* cried in pain.

"Tell me why, Jackie, that's all I wanna know. That's it. Everything we been through together, I think you owe me just that much."

He moaned. "I can't."

"You can, or else I'm gonna look Rebecca in the eyes when I rape her."

"You bastard."

"Tell me, Jackie. Do us all a favor over here."

"You fuck."

"Yeah, I'm the fuck."

He screamed for help: "Pepe!"

Victor shot him again in the groin. "Good luck with that."

Jackie calmed down. The bullet made him.

"Tell me, Jackie. Why did you do it? Before I kill you, just tell me why."

Jackie stared at him.

"Well?"

"Fine."

"Fine what?"

Jackie winced in a whole lot of pain.

"Fine what, Jackie?"

He managed to get a few words out. "When your dad got out, back in '85."

"What happened?"

"He was away for slingin' junk, right?"

Yeah.

"Around when he was getting out that's when all that Pizza Connection shit was goin' on. Word was they were gonna indict the whole crew, kingpin charges."

"And?"

"And we had a strategy meeting, the night your pops got back. He was on parole for the next ten years anyway."

"I know this. Keep going."

"So he says if he gets popped for smack again this time he's gonna do life, the judge told him."

"Like I said. Keep going."

Jackie didn't. He didn't say another word.

So Victor did. "You know what, fuck Joe, that fat piece of garbage. He's dead to me no matter what. He had to have approved all of this anyway so he's dead to me regardless. But Rebecca isn't. Not yet. So just envision which hole it is you want me to ram it in first."

"You motherfucker."

"No, Jackie. I'm a niece-fucker. But I don't have to be. Start fucking talking."

"And you leave Rebecca out of this? That's your word?"

"Start fucking talking."

After a moment, a moment filled with excruciating pain, he did so, begrudgingly: "Your father—he said he wasn't doin' life. He said he'd rather lam, go to Italy or some shit. He said there's no way he's goin' back."

"And that's why you did it? That's it?"

"I didn't do anything, nothing I wasn't supposed to."

"Yes you did. You piece of shit." Victor asked him, "You killed my father because he would've rather spent his days with me than with a bunch of inmates?"

Jackie just stared at him.

"I had to grow up without a father because of some scumbag like *you?* I had to live a lie because of *you?*"

"That wasn't it, Damian."

"Then what was it?"

"It was the boss. It was the life. It was an order, Damian, okay? Louie was captain back then, so he tells the number 3, asks him what to do we get indicted. He talks to Joe and Rusty and Rusty says before anything else to stick your father in a trunk."

"Why?"

"He had an intuition."

"He thought he was gonna rat?"

Jackie paused. "Nah." He shook his head. "He just didn't fucking like him."

Victor pointed the gun between Jackie's eyes. "Then why'd you kill Bobby's dad?"

Jackie smiled.

"Why the fuck did you kill him?"

"'Cause he was a fucking rat."

Victor smirked. He almost laughed. "You know, I gotta be honest with you, Jackie."

"What?"

"You know, it's funny."

"What Goddamnit?"

"When you're a kid. When you're a kid all you do is idolize people. You look up to them, and you wanna look up at them, your heroes, you do, and you listen to their speeches about on loyalty and family and every other fucking thing. But then when you grow up, when you grow up yourself, and when you get tall enough, when you're tall enough to look them in the eyes?"

"What?"

"You realize that they're just a fucking asshole like everybody else."

Boom.

Victor looked around as he walked out of Jackie's office: the assistant was gone, the Mexicans in the kitchen had cleared out, but still—Pepe remained. He was old school Sicilian so he had no choice but to stay behind.

Didn't matter though, he got Victor's gun pointed at him anyway.

But Pepe didn't even bother to put his hands up. "Whatever you gonna to do, you gotta to do," he said, with his immigrant dialect.

Victor stared at him.

"You're gonna to do it, fucking to do it. I never like that piece a shit anyway."

Victor smiled. He lowered his pistol. He put it in his waistband, behind him. "I gotta say, you're alright, Pepe. Always were."

Pepe was surprised. "So we cool?"

"Yeah, we cool."

With a world-weary look in his eye, Pepe extended his 75-year-old hand over the counter.

Victor shook it.

"I doubt you're gonna see me again, Pepe, but do me a favor."

"What? If I can a to do it I'm a gonna to do it."

Still gripping their hands together, Victor told him, "My son. When you see him, you tell him—"

"Five poppin'," a nearby voice said.

Victor let go of Pepe's hand and turned towards the door. He stared at them.

Two black guys, Pramal's guys, gangbangers from the Bloods who stared right back at him.

"Two droppin'," the shorter one said.

But Victor didn't even hear it.

He just stared at the sawed off shotguns that were in their hands.

For Blood And Loyalty.

NINE MONTHS LATER

Lauren walked down the steps that led to the back door, behind the gym. There were 20 steps that led down to the bottom, and she held her head high, her chin up, as she went down each one. She wasn't happy going where she was going, but she had to be strong.

If not for her, for her son.

So she got into her car that was parked there in the small lot, and she checked her make up in the mirror. She looked into it. But what she really did was look herself in the eyes. These days she found it more and more necessary to give herself pep talks.

Once she did though, she put her right hand on the back of the passenger seat and looked behind her as she drove in reverse to turn her car around.

And after she did, she looked around. The parking lot was empty. The lights that used to emanate through the back door of the gym were turned off. And across from it, there was a dumpster, filled with shit.

The place was sold and today was the last time she would ever have a reason to be there. So she reflected for a moment, and then, slowly, she drove down the alleyway that led to Francis Lewis Boulevard. Even though it was early that morning, and nice out, it wasn't to her. To her it was just cold out. It was sunny but there was no sunshine anywhere near her face.

She brought her car to the end of the alleyway, and then put her foot on the brake. This was the part where she'd usually stop to look to her left to make sure it was okay, to make sure there wasn't a car coming in her direction.

Instead she just put her car into park.

Then, she put her head down.

The corrections officer walked the gloomy hallway inside Rikers Island. He passed through a loud, metal door, and walked down a quiet corridor, passed locked cell door after locked cell door. They didn't have bars on them, they were just solid metal. And when he got to Bobby's, he looked inside, through the small window.

Bobby was lying down on his bed, in his single room. He was staring at the ceiling, surrounded by nothing. There were a few books around, a pad of paper and some pencils, but he was alone. He was just staring at the ceiling. He was in solitary.

Then the guard called him by his last name. "Wake up."

Bobby moved his eyes from the cracked roof above him, to the metal door in front of him. As it opened his eyes locked with the officer's.

Bobby inhaled, and exhaled.

Lauren hated being there. Seated in an empty room, in a small booth, with nothing but a phone hanging next to her and a glass screen in front of her, she hated it. Especially the guard who would always stand on the other side of the glass, against the wall behind it, behind where the prisoner would sit. He was white, middle aged and tried his best to let her know via eye contact that he would give it to her in ways that Bobby no longer could.

Lauren though, she just looked at the phone hanging next to her. All these trips did, when she was even able to make them, was humiliate her.

But even though the cops didn't, the prosecutors wanted Bobby alive, so they met in the protective custody section of the jail. They met alone, where no other inmates could get anywhere near them.

Then she heard the buzzing. The buzz of the strong metal door at the end of the room, the sound it made right before it opened, the sound it made right before a prisoner walked through it escorted by a guard.

Then it did open, and Bobby stopped right after he walked inside. He locked eyes with Lauren's as the guards patted him down yet again, and un-cuffed his hands and his feet.

When the door closed behind him, he was allowed to walk to the booth. He was allowed to sit down. The guard that brought him there remained outside the door after it closed and the one who was inside before it opened stayed there, behind Bobby, with his eyes still on Lauren as she tried to imagine they weren't.

It was degrading.

To Bobby, too. He was sorry for everything Lauren had to go through in order to see him. He knew she hated it. She wasn't smiling or happy. She was just looking at him. Looking at him through glass, she was cold, aloof, and he had no idea what to say. He was even madder at himself than she was. But he had to say something, anything. They couldn't sit in silence forever. They couldn't sit there thinking about the obnoxious guard behind them, standing there against the wall with one foot on it, relaxed, with arms crossed chewing gum loudly with a smirk on his face, forever. So Bobby just told her the only thing he could think of. He picked up the phone, and he asked her, "How are you?"

"How do you think?" she replied.

Bobby didn't have to speak to answer. He knew the guards looked forward to humiliating her every chance they got.

"They strip-searched me again. Again, Bobby."

The asshole behind him smiled.

"I don't know how many times I can keep coming here," she said into the phone.

"I already told you, Lauren. If it upsets you—whatever you gotta do to be happy, just do it. This is my mess, not yours."

She didn't say anything. She just looked at him.

"I'm sorry, Lauren. I'm sorry."

She paused before responding. She couldn't help but just stare at him and Bobby couldn't tell if she was staring at him more out of pity or disgust.

All she did was keep her eyes on him. And he looked at her eyes, looking back at his, at his face. At his olive skin that was looking lighter than usual. That's what happens when you've been stuck in a cell in 23 hour a day lock down for almost nine months straight.

That's what happens when there's a price on your head, one confirmed by the set of knife scars across his right cheek and down the side of his skull. Bobby's nose was even a little to the left. They tried to kill him in there the first chance they got. But they tried to kill him slowly, painfully.

His hand holding the phone against his ear, Lauren couldn't help but look at the spot where that gash was, just after his knuckles, that place where the blade struck when he tried to defend himself. He had some knife wounds on his body, too, from where he was stabbed, shanked, and had a slight limp in his step to go along with it.

But Lauren wasn't as strong as everyone else. While she didn't know what to make of all this anymore, all she did know was that she couldn't take any of this anymore. "I'm done, Bobby."

"*Lauren.*"

"I'm done. I can't take this anymore. I can't deal with coming down here anymore."

Bobby inhaled, and exhaled. He paused. "Look, sentencing's coming up. They're gonna move me within the next few months, maybe even right after it's over."

"To Brooklyn?"

"So says Peters."

Lauren thought about it. "Then don't expect to see me there either. I can't do this anymore, Bobby. I love you, I'll always love you, but where you're going, I can't do this anymore. I can't be with you, I can't follow you. I'm sorry, I'm just—I'm done with it."

He just looked at her. He didn't know what to say. But he had to be honest: "I'd be done with me, too."

"I'm taking Michael to Florence."

"What? When?"

"I'm buying the tickets after your court date."

Bobby paused. "If that's what makes you happy."

"We need our space, from all of this."

"I know."

"Good. You need to sign some papers. I'm giving them to the lawyer to bring over. I need your signature."

"Signature?"

"To take Michael with me."

"To take him with you? How long are you taking him for? How long are you planning for?"

"I don't know. We just need a fresh start, Bobby, that's all."

"Look, I realize you don't want to raise him around here, Lauren. I get that, I do. But you're gonna raise him in Italy now?"

"We just need to get away for a while, Bobby. Summer's around the corner."

"So you'll be back then?"

"Maybe. Maybe not. I don't know yet."

"I want to be a part of his life, Lauren. It's what Victor would have wanted. And besides, it's what I want. It's what Michael wants. It's what's best."

"From behind bars, you're going to be a part of his life?"

"The lawyer said I should only be looking at 5 years on this, max. I could be home in less than that. Look I got nearly one down off of that already anyway."

She looked at him cynically: "Fed time included?"

"Honestly—honestly, I don't know. I hope so."

"So really what you're saying is that you could be looking at 20?"

"It depends on the judge."

"2 cops got killed at that shootout at the pizzeria, Bobby. From what I understand it depends a lot more on how many other cops show up at the courthouse."

"That's not the point. You're missing the point."

She seemed distant. Ever since she had gotten there she seemed distant. "So what's the point, then?"

"Stay with me, Lauren. Don't go."

"I can't."

"Lauren. I need you, Lauren."

"I'm sorry. I can't, I can't be involved with you, and this, and all of this, anymore. And I'm not letting Michael be a part of it, either."

"Yeah well he's my son too. At least that's what the law says. Eyes of the law, he's my son too, and I need to see him. He needs to see me."

"Not through glass he doesn't."

"He needs a male figure in his life."

"Not one in prison he doesn't. I don't care what the law says; I'm not bringing him into a jail."

"You have to."

"Why? So they can strip-search him just like they strip-search me? Every time I come here I'm humiliated, don't you get that? Every time I see my friends, or my neighbors or my family, I'm humiliated. I'm embarrassed, Bobby. Why don't you get that? I hate this. I hate all of it."

"I know, Lauren. But I still love him. And I'll always love *you*."

"Bobby."

"I'm being serious. I love the both of you. How could I not?"

"Bobby."

"What?"

She paused. "Bobby."

"What?"

"Bobby—I met someone."

He didn't know what to say.

So he leaned back in his chair.

But he still didn't know what to say.

Neither did she.

The guard smiled.

"Who?" Bobby asked.

"Just, someone," she said.

"And you have him around the kid?"

"Excuse me?"

"I asked you a question."

"Bobby, look—"

"No, Lauren, you look. I mean, what the fuck, right? What the hell am I gonna do for you; rotting here in jail the next 4 or 5 years, at a minimum, anyway. But we made an agreement that you were gonna be careful."

"And how do you know that I'm not?"

"I know because you didn't tell me first. After everything that went on? He can't be around strangers. We made an agreement you were gonna tell me before you brought people around him."

"And you made an agreement you weren't gonna go to jail again."

"Lauren, look—"

"No, you look. I'm done, Bobby, I'm done with all of this."

Bobby paused. "What does that mean?"

"It means we're leaving, and you're going to help us leave. You're going to sign the papers."

"And if I don't?"

"Then you're selfish, and you're a hypocrite."

"I've never been a hypocrite in my life."

"Oh, yeah? You're talking all this stuff about protecting this kid and watching out for his best interests and keeping him out of harm's way, yet you still want me to raise him around here, right in the middle of harm's way. This is our chance to get out, Bobby, me and Michael. The kid's got no one."

"But us."

"But me, at least for now. We need to leave, Bobby, and you have to let us."

Bobby knew she was right. But he still loved her. "So I'm supposed to let some stranger I never even met raise this kid in some foreign country I've never even been to?"

"You could've gone. You had the chance."

"Please, remind me."

"Look, another 4 years, it's not that long. You've done it before, you can do it again. Even if it's longer than that, you can do it. I know you can."

"The whole time thinking about you and whatever schmuck it is you're running around with. Great."

"What did you expect?"

"For you to be with me, no matter what."

"Yeah, well." She shrugged her shoulders. "Maybe when you get out."

"Maybe? Maybe? Let me ask you, Lauren, you like this guy?"

Lauren didn't want to talk about it.

"I mean, you must, if you told me about him."

"Like I said, I don't want to get into it. I was just telling you out of respect."

"After the fact, of course."

"What, I'm supposed to ask your permission, to see somebody?"

"I mean, I know I haven't been around lately, but—"

"But what? I'm your woman?"

Bobby breathed. "I don't want to lose you, Lauren. Not again. No matter what, I really don't, Lauren." Bobby looked around the room. Then he looked back at her: "Even if I already have."

"So then do your time and get out. Then we'll see what's what."

"And what happens you end up with this guy? Or some other guy? It's not gonna be the same."

"Of course it's not gonna be the same. Another four, five, maybe even up to the next 20 years in prison, of course it's not gonna be the same. What did you expect?"

"Lauren—"

"I told you, I can't deal with you, with this, again. I told you not to get back involved, I told you, Bobby. But here we are."

"Here we are."

"Yeah."

"Yup."

"I told you, Bobby. And you lied to me."

"What do you want me to say? What do you want me to say, Lauren? Go run off with some guy? Go run off to Europe with Victor's son? What do you want me to say, go do it I guess, then. What do you want me to say? Personally, I wish you never even told me to begin with. I gotta think about this shit now. I've been in total isolation for months, against my own fucking will, sometimes I think I'd rather take my chances on the tier. But they won't even let me on the tier. They're keeping me here against my own will."

"You should've just cooperated then."

"Cooperate against who? Everyone's dead or cooperating themselves."

"There's gotta be somebody you could have given up. You'd probably be on your way home by now."

Bobby just looked at her. "I can't do that, Lauren. You know I can't do that. I can't."

"The same way I can't bring Michael into a jail to get strip searched."

"Lauren, I just want to see him."

"Because you're going stir crazy. Not because you miss him."

"Lauren."

"I'll send you some more pictures."

"Marvelous."

"Look, Bobby. I gotta go, Michael and I, we've gotta go. It's for the best."

"And your friend over there. He's gonna raise Victor's kid? What, you gonna run off, I'm guessing sooner or later you're gonna end up pregnant, too. Somebody else's kid, not mine. I know I fucked up, Lauren, believe me, the fucking shame I face I look in the mirror. I wish I could do it all over again, believe me, I do. But what the fuck, right? I love you, Lauren. But I can't love you. Not from here at least."

"Just give me your blessing. That's enough."

"Yeah, you and some guy. You want my blessing? Great. Great, here's my blessing, go start a fucking family. Go get some more dogs and make some more kids. Great, fucking great. I'll be here rotting here in case you change your mind."

Lauren paused.

"What?" Bobby asked.

"Bobby."

"What, Lauren?"

"We're not having kids."

"How do you know?"

"Because I can't have kids."

"How do you know? You think kids happen on purpose? Kids happen by accident."

"I wish."

"I'm sure you wish."

"I do wish, Bobby."

"Why? Why the fuck would you wish to get pregnant, by accident?"

"Because once upon a time, Bobby. Once upon a time, a long, long time ago—once upon time, Bobby, I had an abortion. An abortion that ever since, having kids hasn't even been possible."

"What?"

"You think you're the only one with secrets?"

"What? What secrets? What are you saying?"

Lauren just looked at him: "What do you think I'm saying?"

"I don't even know, Lauren."

"I can't have kids, Bobby. You think you're damaged goods? I'm damaged goods. I've been damaged goods." She was getting upset. "For years, now."

"Lauren—" He wasn't sure what to say. "Lauren—how could you not tell me that?" He reached for her hand.

But all he could do was put his palm up against the glass window.

"No touching the glass," the guard said.

They both stared at him. He stared right back.

Regardless of whatever, of anything that might have happened between them, Bobby and Lauren still had a mutual hatred for the asshole watching over their shoulders.

"Lauren," Bobby said. "Lauren, how could you not tell me that?"

"Because I was ashamed, alright, Bobby? Because I'm still ashamed. It makes me feel like half a woman. But Michael? Michael makes me feel alive, Bobby. He's my son, and the only son I'm gonna have. My only chance at a kid is Victor's kid, Bobby. Michael's my kid. Michael's our kid. But this guy I met? He's not coming to Italy. He's just someone here to pass the time. Because I've got needs, Bobby. I get lonely. I'm so lonely. But once you find out how long you're gonna be gone for? When you get settled? I'm taking Michael away from all of this. And frankly, you should be happy I'm waiting till you get settled. And more importantly, you stop being so Goddamned selfish and be happy that I'm giving this kid a shot. That I'm raising our kid where he'll have a shot."

"Lauren—"

"Bobby. Sign the papers. Sign the fucking papers, Bobby."

FOR BLOOD
AND LOYALTY

ABOUT THE AUTHOR

Chris Kasparoza grew up in Bayside, Queens, New York City. This is his first novel. Connect with him at:

www.Kasparoza.com

Twitter.com/Kasparoza
Facebook.com/Kasparoza
Instagram.com/Kasparoza

PS: If you liked this novel please Tweet it, Share it, email it and leave an honest review on Amazon, Goodreads and anywhere else that will have you. Ratings, reviews and word of mouth have a direct impact on sales, rankings and visibility, especially for the self-published.

To get on the beta-reading list for the next Kasparoza novel, just ask.

Thank You for Your Support.
--Chris Kasparoza

Also by Chris Kasparoza

The Chapter

www.TheChapter.tv

Printed in Great Britain
by Amazon